EPOCH

Kat Elle

CENTRAL PARK SOUTH PUBLISHING

Published by Central Park South Publishing 2023
www.centralparksouthpublishing.com

Copyright © Kat Elle, 2023

Typesetting and e-book formatting services by Victor Marcos

ISBN:
978-1-956452-43-3 (pbk)
978-1-956452-44-0 (hbk)
978-1-956452-45-7 (ebk)

This book is dedicated to my dad, Brian.
You are the inspiration behind the inspiration.

CHAPTER 1

When you reach the end of your rope,
tie a knot in it and hang on.
—Franklin D. Roosevelt

D*amn, it's hot.*

Blanca's eyes ticked over the large group of people waiting nearby. Most of them were disgruntled parents waiting on their kids, the moms in heavy costume jewelry and the dads in caps and sandals. Some of the women looked like they were trying to pass for college students, wearing too-tight blouses or heavy makeup that was already starting to melt and clump in the stifling Texas heat. Blanca watched disinterestedly, fingers twitching without something to do. She pulled out a large pocketknife and began toying with it.

One of the women standing nearby watched her for a few seconds, features twisted. "Knives aren't allowed on campus."

Blanca paused, knife blade on her fingertip. She clicked her tongue, but didn't say anything.

The woman—who almost certainly spent her days arguing with helpless cashiers over expired coupons—huffed and shifted closer, as if the new and improved proximity might make her point clearer. "The orientation leaders explicitly stated—"

"Are you security?" interrupted Blanca.

"Well, no—"

"Then mind your own damn business."

The woman bristled, but at that moment, the doors to the building opened and the newly minted college freshmen poured out in droves, separating the group of tired and cranky parents into tired and cranky families. With a huff, the woman left, and Blanca stretched up on her tiptoes to look into the crowd so she could watch for her brother.

Soon enough, a gangly eighteen-year-old shuffled over wearing the same unenthusiastic grimace he'd had all morning. Mateo was taller than his sister, able to see over the hordes of people, but stick-thin and with a floppy mess of black hair he refused to cut. A thick strand of it was stuck to his forehead with perspiration. He nudged it with his shoulder and scowled. "It's ho-o-o-t," he complained.

"Suck it up." Blanca pulled out a paper map and studied it. "Damn, I didn't know college campuses were this big. Okay, so if A Building is there, and the library is here, then – "

"Blanca," Mateo groaned, "let's just go, we've seen enough—"

"No, we're supposed to figure out where all your classes are!"

"I can find them *later*—"

"So logically, B Building should be…at least nearby, right? Wait, here it is. What the hell, it's on the other side of campus!"

"Can I just go buy my textbooks now?" Mateo cut in irritably. Blanca rolled her eyes and dropped the map.

"Yeah, sure, let's go and we can—"

"I can go by myself, god." He turned swiftly and marched off.

Blanca rolled her eyes. *Teenagers.* At twenty-three, Blanca wasn't far from her own adolescent years, but Mateo still seemed particularly young and immature for his age. Blanca worried for him constantly.

He'd fallen in with a bad crowd during school. It hadn't seemed too serious at first; there were a few detention visits, some skipped classes. Then it turned into smoking weed behind the cafeteria and mouthing off to teachers. When Mateo got arrested for stealing from a convenience store, Blanca finally had enough. She'd talked to his foster parents, and he'd finished his senior year online.

A few minutes later, Mateo reappeared, looking no less sullen than before. "These are heavy," he groaned.

"Did you get 'em all?" Blanca peeked in his hefty backpack.

"Just the English, Algebra, and History. All the others are back ordered," he explained wearily. "Can we go now?"

"One more building." Blanca pulled out the map again. "Your first class is in the…uh, let's see…science lab. You're taking Biology, so—shut up, stop complaining—let's go in with those people there."

The duo quickly joined a large group being led by a student worker. The poor guy was drenched in sweat and looked like he'd rather be anywhere else on the planet. *Mateo will fit right in around here*, Blanca thought wryly.

Moving along in a shuffling herd, the families followed the guide down a hallway and into the various labs. Most of the soon-to-be college students were on their cell phones, tapping away, but Mateo was staring dully out a window, a blank look on his face.

Blanca noticed some movement in the hallway. A small group of men in lab coats hurried by, and barely a minute later, two more followed, looking anxious.

Curious, Blanca shifted away from the group and peered out. Another cluster of people appeared, looking no less jittery than the first. They quickly vanished behind a set of double doors locked with a key card. Blanca narrowed her eyes. She didn't like people bustling around, looking nervous.

The last person to appear was a freckled man in his thirties with sandy-colored hair and a blue button-up shirt. Blanca caught a quick look at his face before he, too, vanished down a set of stairs. Unnerved, she rejoined the group just as the student worker finished up his toneless monologue.

"Where were you?" Mateo whispered.

She shrugged. "Just scoping some things out."

"Relax. Everything is fine."

The group moved to leave, but their progress was halted by a loud mechanical *hiss*. Blanca and Mateo—now at the front of the retreating group—paused. The group leader urged them to keep moving, but the hissing rang out again, this time followed by a loud *POP* and *CLANK*.

The building shuddered, and the lights flickered before they turned off completely. Blanca's eyes shot up to the ceiling, where the light fixtures rattled and swayed.

"Uh, let's just go outside," the student worker said uncertainly. "There must be a short—a lot of these buildings are old—"

Just then, the building trembled violently. Beakers and tubes fell from the shelves and crashed to the floor, creating a carpet of broken glass. Blanca snatched the corner of a table and gripped Mateo as people shrieked behind them.

"Earthquake!" someone shouted, but that didn't make any sense, *not in Texas*—

A loud metal *crack* sounded, and Blanca's heart stopped as she looked down to see the linoleum floor splitting beneath their feet. In the growing crevice, there was a heated glow, followed by a humming noise, loud and mechanical. It sent shockwaves up their legs and locked their knees. Then the floor began to rise and fall with a throbbing pulse.

"Get out!" Blanca shouted, snatching Mateo's shirtsleeve and shoving him toward the door. The walls cracked and crumbled, and the ceiling fractured under the strain of the vibrations below. Debris fell around their heads, crashing to the floor in huge chunks of stone and metal. The floor groaned and split apart completely, and screams rang out as people fell into the glowing light, which had swollen into an angry red fissure.

In the distance, sirens blared in a sudden, keening wail.

The sound hit Blanca like a punch to the gut, and she froze. Mateo was yelling at her, but she could only see the movement of his mouth. She was, in that moment, deaf to everything except the sirens. They invaded her senses like a poison.

Mateo leaped forward to grab for the door, but the floor heaved as if taking a deep breath, and the last thing Blanca saw right before it exploded was Mateo's face, stricken with fear, as the entire building burst around them in a hellish blaze of energy.

"MATEO!" she screamed, jaw finally unlocking in a last moment of panic. Heat blasted her stomach, and the world around her became a pitch-black void. The air was ripped from her lungs, and her body lurched painfully as she tumbled out of control. In the very next moment, the world snapped back into place, and a flood of light engulfed her.

Then came a single, blinding moment in which she was flying.

She hit the ground and skipped like a stone on water, bouncing once, twice, and then a third time before colliding with a thin tree, which snapped under her weight. The ground rushed up to meet her, and Blanca crashed into the dirt under a storm of wooden shards. For a few agonizing seconds, she didn't have the strength to open her eyes. When she finally managed to inhale, regret quickly followed.

"Argh, damnit," she groaned, rolling over and clutching her side.

With a tight swallow, she pulled up her t-shirt and investigated a long, deep scrape that stretched across her ribs. Blood mingled unpleasantly with dark dirt and a few stray pine needles.

"What in the hell…" She dropped her shirt and forced her elbows into the dirt so she could push herself up. The scene around her slowly came into focus. She was outside. Blanca's eyes widened.

Mateo.

She struggled to a stand and looked around wildly. Distantly, she registered people moving around her. Some looked as haggard as Blanca did; others looked far worse. A few feet away, a young girl cried hysterically as she tried to stir her motionless dad. Blanca looked away. She couldn't worry about them just yet.

"MATEO!" she called out as she fumbled forward, hair stuck to her face and a smear of dirt on her cheek from the fall. "MATEO!" She stumbled into a tree and used it to hold herself up. "MAT—"

"Blanca!"

Blanca turned sharply and let out a cry of relief as Mateo appeared from behind a group of hysterical teens. He quickly jumped into her arms. "Oh my god, Blanca! What—What's going on, what happened..."

Slowly, the pair turned in a circle, mouths gaping as they took in their surroundings. The campus they'd been on moments before was gone; now they were surrounded by a dark forest crowded with towering trees and damp undergrowth. Between the heavy branches, they could see glimpses of a dark-gray sky. The air, Blanca noticed at last, was quite cold. The sweat on her back from the sweltering July heat now felt ice-cold as it trickled down her spine. A lump formed in her throat.

"Your – your phone, Mateo."

Mateo snatched his phone out of his pocket, but his trembling hands quickly froze. "It's not working. There's no signal."

Around them, others were discovering the same thing.

"Call 9-1-1!" shouted a desperate mother whose son was sobbing and holding his ribs. Blanca gripped her head in frustration before forcing herself to take a deep breath.

"Okay," she managed after a moment, "Mateo, keep trying to find a way to call for help. I'm going to see what I can do." Blanca wiped at her face before dropping to her knees next to the boy with the broken ribs. "Okay, we need to get him here... I need something to wrap him with. Take this..."

One by one, Blanca moved between those with serious injuries, doing what she could. After nearly twenty minutes, nothing else had happened and all anyone had done was suffer.

Blanca wiped her bloody hands on her jeans and scanned the treetops listlessly. In that moment of pause, a terrible realization hit her: she couldn't hear anything except the people from their group. There was no clatter of traffic, no far-off hum of civilization. Only the occasional distant chirp of a bird or shifting tree limb stirred around them. Everything else was unnaturally quiet.

Unnerved, she jogged away from the bleeding teenager and found Mateo. "Anything?" she asked quietly.

"No one can get any calls out, and no one's gotten any messages either," he reported grimly. "Where the hell are we, Blanca…"

Blanca put her hands on her hips and looked around. "No freakin' idea," she admitted at last, rubbing at her face with a dirty hand. "Do you think this is everyone who was with us in the lab?"

Mateo scanned the frightened group. "Most of them, I think."

Blanca nodded. "Okay, stay here with the others. I'm going to go look around, see if I can figure out where we are."

Mateo frowned. "Don't go far."

"I won't," she promised. Seeing Mateo's worried look, she smiled and placed a hand on the back of his head, lightly ruffling his hair. "No worries, kid. We're good."

Mateo relaxed a little. "Okay," he said softly.

She managed a tiny smile in return, then walked off and left the group behind, careful to note where the sun's rays pushed through the misty clouds overhead. As she walked, pine needles and twigs crunched underfoot. A breeze stirred, and as she turned her head up at the sky to check her direction again, unease settled deep within her chest. No matter how she strained to listen, there were no sounds of civilization nearby.

The further she went, the heavier the pit of dread in her stomach became. *Where are we? What the hell brought us here?*

At last, she saw a break in the tree line. There didn't seem to be any movement beyond the forest, but she reached for her knife anyway and flicked it open with a jerk of her thumb. After taking a deep breath, she edged away from the cover of the foliage and peeked out into the clearing.

In front of her was a dirt road, wide enough for just one vehicle and with recent tire marks near its edges. Anxiety swelled in her chest. They'd been in the city just minutes before. What could have brought them to such an isolated area? Texas had its fair share of dirt roads, but for whatever reason, Blanca didn't find much comfort in that. This didn't feel like home.

Unsettled, she looked around slowly, brows furrowed and knife in hand. She peered in one direction and saw where the road twisted and went further into the forest. Shifting on the loose gravel, she looked in the other direction and spotted what appeared to be the tail end of an overturned truck.

Blanca's jaw locked, and her dark eyes darted around as she remained stock-still in her spot, unwilling to move. Distantly, she registered the flapping of fabric in the breeze.

The truck had the look of a military vehicle. Blanca's eyes flickered up to the top, wondering what emblem was on the side that she couldn't see. She moved a little closer, careful to watch for any signs of movement. There didn't seem to be anyone around, but as Blanca approached the truck, she saw something that made her freeze once more.

This was a military barricade.

Heavy splatters of blood, partially obscured by debris and loose paper, came into view. More blood, faded to the color of rust, decorated the barricade itself. Some of the temporary panels were riddled with bullets. The gate, smashed to the ground, bore track marks from heavy truck wheels.

Blanca turned in a slow circle and looked for bodies, but she didn't see any.

The wind picked up once more, and the flapping sound returned. Blanca's eyes snapped to the canvas-covered truck bed, but that wasn't the source of the noise. Finally, she caught sight of a metal pole next to the barricade railing.

Her eyes traveled up, up to the top, where a flag billowed in the wind.

Blanca stepped closer and squinted to see the flag in the dying afternoon light. This should, at the very least, tell her what kind of military detail was nearby. This could be their chance to get help.

But as the wind gripped the flag and unfurled it to its full length, stark and bright against the colorless sky, Blanca felt her heart sink. For a moment, her mind refused to register what she was seeing. And then it hit her all at once.

The waving banner above her was the flag of Nazi Germany.

This is impossible.

Blanca took a step back and reached up to grip her hair and look around, as if someone else might appear to tell her this was all some sick joke. Her throat felt dry, and she tried to swallow, but the effort only left a painful bubble in her chest. She looked back at the dark forest. *No*, she thought with conviction. *There has to be some kind of mistake. There's a reason for all this.*

Trembling, but staunchly refusing to give in to panic, Blanca reached for the long beads wrapped around her wrist and said a quick prayer. This gave her a small bit of peace, and her breathing steadied. After tucking the charm back into the beads, Blanca turned to the truck with renewed purpose and yanked the canvas back so she could peer inside.

There had to be a clue, a sign—anything to tell her where they were or what was going on.

Blanca stepped inside unsteadily and looked around. The truck was mostly empty. A few bare crates lay in various states of brokenness and decay. A glass bottle with no label sat motionless in the center.

Just then, she spotted a piece of paper jammed in the passenger-side door. Hopping up, she pulled on the crooked door until the paper came out in her hand. It looked like a newspaper.

Der Stürmer it read on the top, and below that, a blaring tagline in German: *Die Juden sind unser Unglück!*

After that was a grotesque cartoon featuring Jewish priests committing a god-awful ritual sacrifice. Blanca flinched. She didn't need to know the language to feel disgusted; the intention of the publication was brutally clear. Her eyes drifted to the top of the page.

2 Dezember
1943

Blanca's fingers tightened on the page. Panic overwhelmed her, hitting her right in the joints and making them feel weak. She sucked in a deep breath and folded the paper with unsteady hands.

This is wrong, this is wrong—you're wrong, Blanca! Don't be stupid! This can't be real!

She shoved the paper into the back pocket of her jeans and turned to head back to the others. A humming noise in the distance drew her attention, and she stopped. The hair on her arms stood up. Like the sirens, this noise was painfully familiar to her. Blanca shifted fearfully to look up at the dim gray sky.

A regiment of fighter planes, uniform as a flock of birds, sped through the northwest corner of the sky. Whipping her head around, she saw another group of planes flying right at them from the opposite direction. Her blood ran cold.

Blanca couldn't see their insignias, but it didn't matter. The two squadrons were about to meet right over the group of people she'd left behind.

"*Shit*," she whispered shrilly, before turning on her heel and sprinting into the woods.

Back at the clearing, Mateo struggled to comfort an elderly woman who was bleeding from her head. "Don't worry," he reassured the woman with a shaky smile. "My sister will be back soon. She'll find help for us." That was when he heard the smashing of twigs and branches underfoot, and Blanca's voice yelling out.

"Blanca!" Mateo turned to face her. "What's going on—"

Blanca flew into the clearing and started yanking people to their feet. "Come on, we've got to find cover, come on!"

The others protested.

"We can't!"

"I still haven't found my daughter!"

"Where are we supposed to go?"

Blanca waved her arms frantically. "DAMN IT, PEOPLE! JUST MOVE—"

The ground next to her exploded.

People screamed and ducked, and suddenly the air was filled with deafening gunfire from above. A whistling sound pierced the sky, and Blanca scrambled forward, shoving Mateo ahead of her as a great fiery plume burst near them and set the trees ablaze.

In seconds, the forest around them was burning, and crackling heat battered them from every side.

"GO, GO!" Blanca shouted as the earth erupted right in front of them. People jumped to their feet, running frantically in all directions as the warring squadrons above their heads met in a furious violent clash.

The group split, some people ducking behind trees and disappearing in bursts of glaring flame. A massive *boom* sounded from above, and Blanca looked up to see a fighter plane spinning wildly in the sky, cutting several trees at their tops before crashing to the forest floor in an enormous blaze. Heat blasted the group, knocking several people off their feet.

"NO!" screamed someone she couldn't see. "DAD!"

Overhead, gunfire shattered foliage and pine needles and branches rained down on them. Trees cracked and fell, and the air filled with thick clouds of black smoke that stole what little oxygen they had. Blanca stumbled once but regained her footing just as a blood-splattered cockpit smashed into the earth to her left. The impact sent shockwaves up her legs.

A group of teens ran next to Mateo. In a split second, they were lost to a falling oak tree fully engulfed in flames. Mateo stared in horror and fell, hands waving wildly before he caught himself on the dirt. Blanca snatched him up.

"Blanca, those people!"

"JUST RUN!"

"WHERE ARE WE GOING?" someone shouted, but no one knew, so they kept running, running until their bodies, already aching, began to slow down.

Blanca and the others burst out of the forest and into a clearing just as two planes raced at each other over their heads, diving in opposite directions at the last second and nearly touching wing to wing.

Blanca slid to a stop. "We—we have to stay out of the open," she rasped, but a young couple nearby didn't listen and tried to sprint across the field. A dive-bombing plane failed to pull up in time and crashed into the open meadow. The broken wings shattered, and the propeller went spinning, catching the young couple and killing them in a flash of steel and blood.

"Oh my god!" cried a young girl next to them.

Blanca tugged on the girl's hand. "GET MOVING!" she shouted before shoving her forward. They ran back into the trees, but the aerial battle above raged on, and more gunfire broke through the thin protection of the branches and dogged their every step.

A boy running next to them caught a shot in the leg and went down. His brother went back for him and was killed just as Blanca looked over her shoulder.

"Blanca!" Mateo shouted. "Look!"

Another explosion burst overhead as the group hurled themselves through the doors of a forgotten barn and dove into an open crawlspace. Blanca didn't see their faces, didn't register their voices. All she knew was *Safety, safety, get everyone to safety*.

"GET IN!" she screamed, pushing them forward. After the last person fell in, she grabbed the rickety wooden door closed, and darkness fell around them.

Outside, explosions hammered the ground and rattled the hinges of the door. Their fragile shelter trembled under each blast, but hours later, it remained intact. Blanca held tight to Mateo's hand, so much bigger than she remembered, and with the other hand she grasped for the beads on her wrist.

Please, God, she thought, letting a few tears escape under the cover of darkness. *Help me. I can't be here again.*

Texas, USA
2008

Blanca did not like the Morrisons.

At first, she didn't like the Morrisons because of their house. It was large and square, with windows all along the front and a strange plastic-looking door. Blanca didn't like it because it looked like a dollhouse. Dollhouses were fake.

And the people there—the Morrisons—they were fake, too.

Mateo loved them, though. He was too young to understand the duplicity of people, but at the tender age of eleven, Blanca knew it well. She could spot the artificial smiles and empty eyes. She could feel the strain in the hugs and the hesitation in the praise. She had seen it in countless foster homes before this one.

One day, Blanca realized seven-year-old Mateo was not on the school bus home. When she arrived at the Morrison house, she found Mr. Morrison seated in a chair and holding Mateo in his lap. He was stroking Mateo's hair, petting it lovingly, and then he patted and stroked lower and lower until his hand was on the inside of Mateo's thigh.

When he reached in even further, Blanca knocked over a pile of books.

Mr. Morrison quickly ushered Mateo out of his lap. "Oh, Blanca. I didn't know you were home."

"Why wasn't Mateo at school?" she asked suspiciously.

"He wasn't feeling well," Mr. Morrison said. "So, I went to pick him up. Isn't that right, Mateo?"

"My tummy hurt," Mateo explained, but he had a funny look on his face. Blanca watched him for a split second, then looked back at Mr. Morrison.

"Okay." She took Mateo's hand and led him out of the office. They played together the rest of the afternoon, and once Mateo was in bed, Blanca sat next to him all night without moving. The next morning, they left for school together, and Blanca waved good-bye like she always did. In her own classroom, she sat at her desk and thought very hard.

Recess came. Blanca went out to the playground, and as soon as the teachers weren't looking, she ducked under an opening in the chain-link fence and hurried back to the Morrison house, which was only a few blocks away. Mr. Morrison worked from home, but Mrs. Morrison would be out.

Quietly, Blanca slipped in through a window and went to the door leading down to the basement. She opened it and peered into the inky blackness. Without turning on the light, she walked down each step, listening for the sounds they made. When she was satisfied, she went down deeper into the basement and found the metal baseball bat she'd seen Mateo play with. She placed it next to the cellar door, then climbed up on the railing and untwisted the lightbulb from its socket. Once she was done, she went back upstairs and peeked down the hallway in the direction of Mr. Morrison's office.

"HEY!" she shouted at the top of her lungs, loud and sudden.

"Wha—Who's there?" Mr. Morrison rushed out into the hallway. When he spotted her, he relaxed and let out a huff. "What're you doing home, Blanca?"

He began to march in her direction. Blanca turned and hurried back to the basement, little feet quickly scampering down the wooden steps. Before she reached the bottom step, she ducked under the railing and crawled back up, so she was hidden near the basement door.

Mr. Morrison appeared at the top of the steps, and he hesitated. Tentatively, he reached out for the string near the empty light socket. A tug, and nothing happened. He took one step farther into the darkness. "Blanca?" he called, straining to sound kind. Blanca could hear the tremor in his voice. "Where did you go, little one?"

Blanca narrowed her eyes, fingers gripping the railing.

Mr. Morrison stepped down further. "Blanca?"

Lips set in a tight line, Blanca pulled herself up and over the railing. Now behind him, she put her hands on the baseball bat.

Mr. Morrison saw her shadow fall over him, and he turned.

THWACK!

Blanca smashed the bat across his face with all her might. The blow landed squarely on his jaw, and though delivered with only a fraction of a grown person's power, it was enough to send Mr. Morrison flying down the stairs.

He tumbled blindly, limbs flailing as he fought to catch himself. When the concrete floor rushed up to meet him, it was his head that hit first.

Blanca could not see the fall, but she heard it—a thick, wet *crack*.

"Mr. Morrison?" she called, bat still in hand.

When she heard nothing, she hopped down the stairs, found a flashlight, and pointed the beam of light at Mr. Morrison's lifeless body. Her pink shoe was near a growing pool of blood, and she carefully stepped back to avoid making tracks.

Blanca looked at him for a few seconds. Then she turned and went back up the stairs, leaving the basement door open, as she exited through the unlocked window. She kept the bat in her hand, pausing only to wipe off the small crimson streak on a sheet hanging on a clothesline in someone's backyard.

Walking in no real rush, she made her way back to the school, stopping only to toss the baseball bat into a dumpster. Then she stepped back to watch as the garbage truck came by, picked up the dumpster, and crushed all the contents inside.

The garbageman waved at her. Blanca waved back.

She made her return to school just as recess was ending, and she climbed under the fence so she could go in with the others. At the end of that day, Blanca and Mateo returned to the Morrison house. The police were already there, as was the social worker.

Initially, the officers were very concerned about Mr. Morrison's death. However, after looking through his office in search of evidence and, in the process, uncovering some hidden folders and encrypted files, they became much less enthusiastic about tracking down his killer.

CHAPTER 2

In war, there are no unwounded soldiers.
—Jose Narosky

Gradually, the noise of the airplanes faded away, and the trembling eased until it vanished entirely. Blanca turned her head up to the low ceiling of the barn's freezing cellar. Outside, there seemed to be only darkness. After a while, Mateo moved through the shadows and pushed open the entrance so he could peer out.

"Oh my god," he exhaled, looking all around.

Blanca came up next to him, and shock stole the air from her lungs. The barn they'd used for refuge had been utterly destroyed. Fire burned brightly in the distance, creating pockets of pulsing light deep in the forest. Smoke drifted through the air and curled into the night sky, blotting out the stars. The world felt unnaturally still and overly large.

Chest tight, Blanca pulled herself from the cellar and stood up. Behind her, Mateo emerged cautiously. Behind him came a trembling young Indian girl.

An unfamiliar man appeared last, someone Blanca hadn't noticed before. His eyes, wide with disbelief, surveyed the brutalized landscape before landing on Blanca. He had barely a split second to react before she snatched his shirt and rocked him backward.

"*You!*" she snarled. "You were with those other scientists back at the college!"

The man glanced at the others nervously.

"You weren't part of the orientation group," she growled, twisting the fabric of his shirt roughly. "You and the others knew something was wrong—"

"I… Please, I don't know much…" His heavy Irish accent grew thicker in his discomfort.

Blanca released him with a jerk. "Don't lie! I saw all you lab coats running downstairs just before this happened! Now tell me what the hell is going on!"

"I don't know!" the man protested. "Look, there were…lots of things going on in the lab, and I…I didn't…I mean, no one really listens to me down there—"

"Are you really trying to tell me you don't know?"

"I don't!"

Blanca yanked out the racist newspaper she'd found and slapped it against his chest. "I found this," she managed to say, "right next to a Nazi military checkpoint."

"A Nazi…what?" Mateo asked. "You don't mean real Nazis, right?"

"Yeah," Blanca confirmed without taking her eyes off the scientist. "Plus, a military barricade and a lot of blood."

"Maybe we're in the middle of some kind of like, war reenactment or something," the Indian girl spoke up fearfully. "My dad used to go to those."

"Tell me," Blanca commanded. "What the hell were you people doing in that school?"

The man met her gaze reluctantly. "I…" He looked around at their expectant faces, and at last his resolve seemed to break. "It was an attempt to recreate a project started years ago by the American government, something highly… unstable."

"What kind of project?" prompted Blanca impatiently. "What were they trying to do?"

"The Philadelphia Experiment." He dropped his defensive posture, eyes growing soft and scared. "We were trying to use unified field theory to create isolated time jumps."

"*Time* jumps?" Mateo repeated incredulously.

Blanca stared hard. "So you mean what I saw was real? We actually went through time?" *This is ridiculous,* she thought with a sudden burst of venom.

"It was highly unlikely to happen," the Irishman went on vehemently. "And the original experiment wasn't even meant to produce time travel, it was supposed to be for evading surveillance, but this is all—theoretical, it's nearly impossible to predict—"

"Where are we?" Blanca interrupted roughly. "Where have you sent us?"

"I don't *know*," the man insisted. "We weren't trying to send anyone anywhere, we were just testing the generators and something went wrong!" He tossed up his arms. "I told Dr. Sorenson the machine was overcharged, that we needed to switch out the circuits—"

"Where do you think we are?"

"No idea," he whispered.

"This is freaking impossible!" The young Indian girl sobbed, tears pouring down her cheeks. "What happened before—all those planes and stuff—this has to be some kind of joke!"

Mateo hesitated before touching her shoulder and drawing the hysterical girl into his arms. She immediately melted into his embrace, and her crying became muffled in his shirt.

"What's your name?" Mateo asked the Irishman, who was watching the two teens.

"Iain," he murmured without looking away from them. "Iain Claflin."

"I'm Mateo," he said in a surprisingly steady voice.

The young girl pulled herself away from Mateo and folded her arms fearfully over her stomach. "Priya Simmons," she murmured, eyes low.

Iain and the others looked expectantly to Blanca. She narrowed her eyes at Iain and brushed past him without a word. She didn't go far, but she kept her back to the others.

"Her name is Blanca," Mateo volunteered quietly.

"Look, I..." Iain paused again before taking a deep breath. "I might be able to rebuild the machine and get us home, but I would need a *whole team* of physicists and engineers to help me. I would also need access to a laboratory and tools, and if this really is the era I think it is, then the only people with technology like that... are the Nazis." He flapped his arms helplessly.

Blanca clicked her tongue and said nothing. A heavy silence fell over the group.

In the distance, clouds gathered in anticipation of a storm, and thunder rumbled ominously, filling the air with an electric unease. Blanca closed her eyes against the cool, damp wind and did her best not to think about the twenty some-odd bodies that no doubt littered the area they'd fled.

Mateo stepped up cautiously. "What do we do, Blanca?"

"We stay here tonight," she said, shifting jerkily. "Tomorrow, we go back to where we landed. See if anyone else survived, get whatever we can."

Dawn arrived, unconcerned about the devastation it loomed over.

Once the sun was up and buried again behind the ashen sky, Blanca led the group out of the cellar and away from the barn, with Mateo and Priya trailing behind her and Iain at the rear. They re-traced their steps to the pocket of forest they'd come from. Their walk led them by the scattered remains of people and planes alike.

Blanca snapped at Mateo more than once to keep his gaze ahead, but she still caught him looking, eyes large and glassy, each time they encountered a battered body. Unanchored limbs tripped them up like tree roots, and the smell of blood was thick in the air. Priya stopped more than once and vomited, but after a while, she simply turned her head up at the sky and refused to look around her.

Finally, they came to the spot where they'd first landed. They hadn't encountered anyone alive, and when they paused to listen, the area was eerily silent. It didn't look like anyone had camped there, either.

Blanca climbed over fallen trees and bypassed deep craters to find the bag she had dropped in her haste to escape. She picked it up and threw the long strap over her torso. The bag didn't have much in it, and none of it would really help them, but buried in her wallet were two items of the utmost importance: an aged photo of Blanca, Mateo, and their mother and a set of identification tags on a silver chain.

With a hard swallow, Blanca tugged out the chain and studied the tags in her hand:

HERNANDEZ, BLANCA
221-34-1882
A NEG
CATHOLIC

She snapped her fingers closed and pulled the chain over
her neck so she could tuck the tags into her t-shirt. The metal
felt cold against her skin, and a chill raced down her spine.

"Blanca?"

She turned to see Iain hovering nearby. He didn't
have anything to collect, and he looked stupid and useless
with his hands empty. "Do you…need any help?" he asked
uncertainly. Blanca shoved her wallet into the bag and
moved past him.

"No. Get out of my face."

Iain watched her go.

Mateo appeared a moment later. "I found my
backpack," he told Blanca. "Some of the books got
destroyed, but…" He held up the American History
textbook he'd bought at the campus store. "I thought we
might want to keep this. Just in case."

Blanca's expression softened. "Yeah, good thinking.
Let me carry it, though. I don't want you caught with it."

Mateo's brows furrowed. "What would happen if I was?"

"I don't know," she admitted, tucking the book into her
bag. "But I'm not taking any chances. Keep the backpack,
though. We'll probably need it."

Priya approached. "I can't find my purse. All I have is
my phone and ID." She waved her cell phone, which had
a card slot stuck to the back of it.

"Blanca, what are we going to eat?" Mateo asked,
touching his stomach with a frown.

She scanned the forest. "We'll find something soon."

Iain got their attention and nodded his head to the south. "There's smoke in that direction. I bet that's one of the planes that went down. Maybe we could find something useful."

"Like what?" Mateo asked. They started off in the direction of the smoke. Blanca shrugged.

"A map, maybe a gun. Pilots usually carry pistols," she told him. "If we can find a body that wasn't burned to hell and back, maybe we'll get lucky."

"How do you know that?" Priya asked, stumbling alongside them. "About pilots?"

Blanca kept her gaze straight ahead and said nothing. Priya twisted her fingers anxiously, eyes darting around and then dropping when no one answered her. Together, the group stepped out of the woods and crossed the open field. There were no cities in sight; instead, there were only rolling hills and low valleys, the latter of which was choked with thick, dense foliage. Getting lost there, Blanca realized, would mean certain death.

"Maybe we should go see if that truck Blanca found works," Priya suggested.

"I can hotwire a car," Mateo volunteered, and Blanca scowled.

"Yeah, I bet you learned that from those dumbass thugs you were hanging out with at school."

"They weren't thugs," he argued crossly. "They were actually really smart. They just didn't like school."

"Go figure."

"You wouldn't even try to get to know them—"

"Because they were trouble, Mateo!"

"No, they weren't!"

"Look!" Priya interrupted, pointing.

The group turned and spotted a smoldering pile of wreckage in the distance. Iain stepped up. "That's the smoke I saw." He moved ahead of the group with Blanca. Together, they approached the plane at a cautious pace, careful to listen for any movement. The plane, it seemed, was mostly intact. The front end was smashed, but the cockpit was in one piece, with a shattered canopy. There were no body parts or blood to be seen. One of the plane's gray wings was several feet away, half-embedded in the grass, while the other was still attached, bent and tilted high. The cockpit was empty.

Blanca paused as she came to the broad side of the plane. Painted on the charred metal was a black Iron Cross, and further than that, at the plane's tail end, was the swastika. Blanca sneered at the symbol and ducked around it, expression grim.

"Looks like he got out," Iain observed, climbing up and peering inside the cockpit. He dug around for a few seconds before emerging with a small bag. "Hey, look."

"A first aid kit," Blanca confirmed with relief. She tucked it into her bag. "Anything else?"

"Flares." He tossed them to Blanca, before rummaging around more. "Hey, there's a map!" He hopped down and showed it to Blanca. They peered at it together. "Bloody hell," Iain whispered. "We're in Poland."

The two met gazes, eyes wide.

Suddenly, a voice attracted their attention.

"*Scheiße!*" the voice snarled furiously, and then more clattering and grunting sounded, followed quickly by, "*der Scheißkerl!*"

Blanca didn't recognize the words, but she knew swearing when she heard it, being something of an expert on the matter. She and Iain exchanged quick looks before jogging around the plane.

That was when they saw, not too far away, a struggling man in a tree.

The stranger was tangled in a parachute, with one of his arms pinned by cords and the other grasping fruitlessly at his belt. A generous amount of blood coated his right arm and splashed up his neck.

"Jesus Christ," Blanca muttered in disbelief.

It was then that the man looked up at them, eyes wide with shock.

If anyone had ever asked Blanca to imagine what a Nazi fighter pilot might look like—as strange a request as that would have been—she probably would have conjured up an image of this exact man. He was young, older than Blanca but not by much, and he had light skin, blue eyes, and hair so blonde it was almost white. His helmet was on the ground a few feet away, but he still wore his leather jacket and tan flight suit, as well as a pair of heavy fur-lined boots.

As soon as he spotted Blanca and the others, he froze. For a few seconds, no one moved. Then, in a flash of movement, he reached to his side and snatched out a gun.

Everyone jumped out of the way, including Blanca, who threw her arms out in front of Mateo and Priya. Iain ducked behind a nearby tree. The man couldn't do much from his tangled position, so Blanca rushed forward and grappled with him for a moment before snatching the pistol from his belt. The German snarled, and Blanca scrambled back just before the cords finally loosened and he fell awkwardly to the ground. He groaned and slowly pushed himself up, only to find his own pistol pointed directly at his face. He narrowed his eyes deeply but said nothing.

"By God," Iain said incredulously. "This man is really—"

"Shut up," Blanca snapped, before turning her eyes back to the German. She held the gun steady. "You speak English?"

The German paused before answering. "*Nein*," he grunted.

"We should let him go," Iain said very quietly. "He's injured. He isn't going to do anything."

Blanca cocked her head to the side, her gaze never leaving the pilot. "I don't know. I'm willing to bet he knows something useful."

"He doesn't speak English. What's he going to tell us?"

Blanca paused and let her eyes shift over the German. He was clearly in pain, but he kept his spine straight and his jaw tight. Blood, dirt, and grime coated his face, and the burns on his shoulder seemed to simmer with residual heat. A large piece of glass was embedded in his shoulder, and if she removed it without treating him, he'd likely bleed out.

Blanca glanced around before picking up a piece of metal debris from the plane and handing it to Iain. "Stick this over the flame," she ordered. "Get the tip hot."

Iain hesitantly took the metal and did as he was told. Blanca looked at Mateo and Priya. "You two go on the other side of the plane."

Mateo balked. "Why?"

"Just do as I say," Blanca ordered, eyes flashing as she turned to look at him. Mateo quickly took Priya's hand and hurried away with her. Blanca shifted to look at the captive German again.

"We could use him as collateral," she mused aloud, and Iain frowned. "Doubt he's important enough to matter, though."

The German's eyes narrowed minutely. Blanca noticed, but Iain didn't.

She kneeled in front of the German, and he matched her steely expression with a hate-filled glare of his own. Blanca didn't flinch; plenty of things in life had hurt her, but a look was never one of them. "What do you think, German?" she asked, raising her eyebrows suggestively. "Can you be any use to us?"

The German said nothing. Blanca reached out and shoved her hand beneath the collar of his flight suit. Her fingers quickly brushed a cold steel chain, and she yanked it out so she could inspect the oval-shaped tag on the end. "You *sure* you don't have anything to say…Otto Zimmler?"

The German—Otto—clenched his jaw and remained silent.

Blanca ripped the ID from his neck and shoved it in her pocket. "Listen here, you smug son of a bitch," she growled before reaching forward and grabbing the piece of glass embedded in his arm. Otto swallowed hard and sweat beaded at his temple.

"You have two options," she went on in a low, dangerous whisper. "Either you speak up and agree to help us with what we need…or I yank this piece of glass out and let you bleed to death right next to your heap of shit plane."

Otto's eyes narrowed deeply, but the anguish was evident in his face. Blanca jerked on the glass, and he let out a choked noise. "I don't have time to play with you," she snarled. "I've got people to take care of."

Ian stepped forward. "Blanca, he doesn't understand—"

"Shut up."

Iain fell silent.

"I'll give you until the count of three," she murmured.

The German's eyes grew wide.

"One..."

He swallowed tightly.

"Two..."

Blanca twisted the glass further and Otto's knees buckled.

"Three—"

"Stop!" the German shouted, and Blanca stopped. "I speak English," he gasped in a crisp, clear accent.

"Good." She yanked out the glass.

Otto let out an agonized yell and fell to his knees, all the color draining from his face. Blanca tossed aside the bloody piece of glass, then gestured to Iain, who quickly brought her the scrap of red-hot metal.

Dropping to one knee, Blanca snatched the German's shoulder and shoved the hot metal over his open wound.

"AGH!" The German man screamed in distress, startling a flock of birds from a nearby tree. The acrid smell of burning flesh filled the air and Iain scrambled back with his shirt over his mouth and nose.

Otto's cries went on for a few seconds before ending abruptly. Blanca glanced at his face.

"Passed out," she announced mildly, still holding the hot metal to his wound. Iain made a gagging noise and acknowledged this information with a shaky wave.

"Can we come out now?" Mateo called.

Blanca glanced up. "Yeah, sure," she said, and the two teens reappeared next to them. Mateo peered at the man's body.

"Jesus, Blanca. Did you kill him?"

"Nah, he's fine." Blanca pointed at them. "And when he wakes up, he's going to help us get somewhere safe, but he can't know the truth about where we came from, alright? We don't need to screw anything up by running our mouths and messing up history. Got it?"

Priya poked the man's unconscious body with a stick. "I bet an iPhone would blow his mind."

"No—damn—cell phones!" Blanca growled, and Priya held up her hands defensively before darting behind Mateo. "Now help me get him up—we need to find somewhere to put him until he wakes up."

⚬≈≈⚬

Unbeknownst to Blanca and the others, a gathering was taking place nearby.

Back at the pockmarked field of trees and bodies, soldiers spilled out of a cluster of German military vehicles. Officers looked curiously over the impromptu graveyard, and men in uniform poked through the pockets and bags of the deceased. Among the fallen, they found devices they'd never seen before, as well as identification that belied logic.

"What do you think happened here, sir?" an enlisted man asked. "Where did these people come from?"

The commanding officer, Wagner, frowned deeply. "Start loading them up," he ordered as he scanned the wreckage. The shattered body of a teenage boy sat next to his boot, arms outstretched. "Get as many as you can. Himmler will want to see this."

"Yes, sir," said the soldier, though his gaze remained curious. Wagner turned away from the men and clasped his hands behind his back. As he looked out, he spotted footprints leading away from the site. His eyes focused on the tracks, and then he turned and walked back to his truck.

Blanca and the others traveled for hours with little luck. They had no more understanding of where they were than they had before, and the darkening sky and dropping temperatures made optimism difficult. "This'll work for tonight," Blanca announced at last, and the group came to an exhausted halt near a small formation of rock with a low overhang. It wasn't much, but she figured it was their best bet at sheltering themselves from the winds.

"Thank god," Mateo muttered, dropping his side of Otto's weak body so the other man's weight fell on Iain. The German slipped through Iain's grip and hit the ground with a *thud*. Iain flapped his arms. "See what you did?"

Mateo shrugged. With a sigh, Iain hoisted Otto into his arms and dragged him to a tree so he wasn't facedown in the dirt.

Priya frowned and sat down heavily on a rock. "I hope we find food soon," she grumbled. "I'm starving."

Blanca stepped away and turned her head up to peer at the darkening sky. Iain approached her from behind.

"Blanca?"

She glanced over her shoulder and said nothing. Iain shifted uncomfortably. "I just—please know, I am…so very sorry. We never meant to endanger anyone."

"Yeah?" Blanca scanned the woods speculatively. "Tell that to the two dozen dead people back where we landed."

Iain's expression dropped miserably, and Blanca frowned. The desire to be sympathetic flickered in her chest, but it was quickly smothered by anger. "You don't get it. You don't understand what you've done."

"I'm sorry—"

"You put us in a *war*, Iain," she hissed. "And I can't do it. I can't be here again."

"Again? When is the last time you were in Nazi-occupied Poland?"

There was a pause.

"Forget it," she said flatly. Before he could say anything else, she bypassed him and returned to the others. The teens sat huddled together, talking quietly. Blanca said nothing until Iain showed up a half-hour later, a smile on his freckled face.

"Look what I found! Apples!" He showed the fruits gathered in his shirt.

"Oh!" Mateo said excitedly, jumping to his feet and accepting his share. Blanca took one and crammed it in her mouth gracelessly.

"They're freakin' delicious," Priya said over a mouthful of food. She took a seat on a rock and munched happily.

They had three spares, so Iain put them in Blanca's bag and settled down with the others to eat. After a while, Mateo and Priya fell asleep—not quite full, but no longer whining about hungry bellies—and Blanca set up a watch schedule with Iain.

"What about him?" Iain asked, looking at Otto, who lingered in a semi-conscious state. "Do you think he'll live?"

Blanca finished the last of her apple and tossed away the core. "Guess we'll see in the morning. Keep an eye on him."

———❦———

Iain took first shift, and the others settled into an uneasy sleep. Unfortunately, they had nothing to sleep on, and the ground was cold and unforgiving beneath their aching bodies. Strange sounds echoed from every direction, invading their dreams, and the frigid air made the dreary nighttime hours crawl by at a glacial pace. More than once, Priya woke up, cried, and went back to sleep.

After what felt like an eternity, dawn grew in the eastern sky. Blanca stood up and stretched, trying to roll the pain out of her stiff shoulder.

A noise drew her attention, and she looked over to see the German man, Otto, stirring against the tree. He appeared to be regaining consciousness, so she waved away the others and moved to crouch in front of him. When he took too long to wake up fully, she pulled a hair tie off her wrist and used it to pop him on his burned arm.

"ARGH!" He lurched forward.

"Rise and shine, Q-Tip."

Otto grunted hoarsely and muttered another swear word in German. Blanca assumed it was aimed at her. "How ya' feeling?" she asked not very nicely.

"Disfigured."

"Be grateful you're in one piece. You could be looking just like your busted-up plane right now." Blanca cocked her head at him and pointed with the hand that held the apple. "I knew you spoke English, you lying bastard. I saw you look at me when I was talking about how worthless you are."

The man sighed deeply. "Yes, you are very clever."

Blanca's brows furrowed. Otto certainly sounded German, but he didn't just speak English; he was clearly fluent. For whatever reason, that surprised her. "Listen to me," she said, and the German shifted to give her a condescending look. "We need to get out of this country."

Otto chuckled darkly. "That is an understatement."

"We found this map in your plane." Blanca held it up. "Show me where we are."

Otto made a tired noise and let his head fall back against the tree. "Why should I help you? Who are you people?"

"We're not here to fight."

Otto snorted. "Obviously... but you sound American, which makes me wonder. Why are you here?"

"Don't worry about it." Blanca held up the map again. "All I need you to do right now is tell us where we are so we can get out. We're not trying to cause trouble. We just want to leave."

"You are in German territory," Otto informed her snidely. "You will never be able to travel without attracting notice." He leaned forward. "And just so you know, I am certainly important enough to warrant a search, so if you value your lives, you will let me leave and escape on your own. I will only draw more attention to you."

Blanca shook her head. "You don't understand, we have to have someone from this—" she paused before going on more slowly and carefully, "someone who's familiar with the area."

"Are you blind?" he asked with a sneer. "I am no Pole. Besides, I was in a *plane*. I do not know this area any more than you do."

Blanca growled. "You know where you were flying, jackass! Just tell me where we are!"

"And what will you give me if I do?"

Blanca grabbed the pistol and pointed it directly at his face. "How about I tell you what I'll give you if you don't?"

Apprehension finally leaked into Otto's features, and he pulled back a little, eyes on the gun. "I need my hands," he said after a moment.

Standing, Blanca lifted him on his good side and Otto slipped his bound hands forward with a gasp of pain. He muttered something that could have only been another swear word and then looked at his burned arm before glaring at Blanca.

"*Map*," she said flatly, shoving it at his face. "I'm not worried about how pretty your damn arm is."

Scowling, Otto jabbed a finger at the paper. "There. We are just west of Kraków, near the Vistula."

"Vistula?"

"The *river*," he said, as if she were very stupid. "You can follow it north all the way to the coast, where you will find the Baltic Sea, or you can cross it and go east, into Slovakia." He gave her a cynical smile. "East is the shortest route by far. If you follow the river north, you will be forced to travel through Warsaw."

Blanca looked at him suspiciously. "So?"

"So?" He laughed mockingly. "Warsaw is firmly in our control. We have soldiers and Gestapo everywhere. You would be arrested before you even saw the city walls."

Blanca folded up the map. "Let us worry about that."

She stood and marched away. Otto opened his mouth to protest, but Blanca turned and hurled the apple at him, hitting him in the gut. He turned the apple in his hands before taking a massive bite and falling quiet.

A few feet away, Mateo and Priya eyed Otto from a safe distance. Once Blanca was occupied, Mateo edged closer. "So you're a fighter pilot?" he asked Otto, who was finishing his apple. Otto tossed the stripped apple core aside and gave them a cocky look.

"Not just any fighter pilot," he gloated. "An officer of the great *Luftwaffe*, finest air force in all the world and pride of the Third Reich."

"So, I've always wondered, why is it called the *Third* Reich?" Priya asked.

"It is pronounced *Reich*, not *Rike*," Otto snapped.

Priya fluttered her fingers mockingly. "Ooh, so sorry. So why is it the Third *Rei-chhh?*" she asked, greatly exaggerating Otto's accent and making Mateo snicker.

"Yeah," Mateo piped up. "What happened to the first two? They get shot down like you did?"

Priya and Mateo burst into laughter, and Otto scowled. "*Reich* means empire, you stupid brats. And I will have you know, I shot down three Russians before even one of them touched me."

"Whatever you say, dude."

"Mateo!" Blanca snapped. "Stop talking to the damn Nazi!"

Mateo groaned. "You were talking to him!"

Otto pursed his lips. "As if I want to be here with a bunch of low-class American delinquents anyway."

"Who says we're delinquents?" Mateo asked.

"I am just assuming," Otto said, looking over Mateo's dark complexion and black hair suggestively. Mateo huffed and flipped him off before turning back to Priya. Otto settled against the tree again. After a few minutes in which everyone ignored him, he closed his eyes and fell asleep.

Iain, who had watched the exchange silently, stood and crossed their makeshift campsite to Blanca. They studied the map together. "Like he said, east is the shorter route, but I don't know anything about Slovakia. Do you?"

"No," Blanca admitted. She glanced back over at Otto's lax form. "He seemed like he wanted us to go that way, but…"

"There's something about Kraków—something I can't remember." He scratched his head. "I guess we should check out the river, see if we can tell what's going on from there. At least we'll know if he was telling the truth about where we're at." He sighed. "This is going to be rough no matter what direction we go."

Blanca was forced to agree. A few minutes later, they gathered their things and headed out. At the back of the group, Otto struggled to keep up. He looked sicker than he had that morning, and he was covered in a cold sweat despite the chilly air. When Blanca slapped a hand over his head, it felt hot and feverish.

"Damn it," she hissed. "I think he's got an infection." Otto staggered to a rock and sat down, his head between his legs. Iain frowned.

"Maybe we should leave him near a hospital," he suggested.

"We're not leaving him anywhere," Blanca said gruffly. "He already knows too much. All he's got to do is point in our direction and we'll have Nazis all over us."

"He is still a person!" Iain argued firmly. He glanced at Otto, who was in a stupefied, fever-induced haze and not listening. "Besides, he's part of a totally different era. He doesn't have any idea how his government will be remembered in history."

"So, you think he doesn't know what's going on in those concentration camps right now?"

"I'm not making excuses for him!" Iain insisted vehemently. "All I'm saying is, show the man a little human decency!" He gestured to Otto's slumped form. "Never mind the fact that killing him will almost certainly alter something in history."

"We've already altered things," Blanca pointed out quietly. "It isn't our fault."

She didn't say whose fault it was, but Iain frowned and shifted away guiltily. "I'm just saying. The man is a prisoner of war. That's bad enough. Let's not torture him."

"Uh, guys?"

The pair looked over to Mateo peering down at Otto, who had fallen face first into the grass and was likely dying as they spoke.

Mateo pointed. "I think he needs some help."

Priya nudged Otto with her foot and then shrugged as if to say she'd done all she could.

With a sigh, Blanca hurried over with Iain and hauled Otto to a stand so they could move on. Within an hour, they emerged from the forest. The Vistula River stretched out in front of them, wide and blue under the twinkling lights of a bright afternoon. The sun had at last managed to break through the clouds, and it lit up the water in a dazzling rush of crystalline shimmers. The grass along the river was lush and green, and as Blanca stepped forward and peered downriver, she saw it ran for miles into the distant countryside, growing narrow in some places and too wide to cross in others.

More trees dotted the bank on the other side, sparse at first and then growing thicker so the hills beyond them were eclipsed. Somewhere above the pointed tips of evergreens, a bell tower jutted into the eastern sky. Further down the opposite bank to their left, a fishing shack sat with an open front and overturned buckets, unused for what looked like a very long time.

The river here was wide but languid, moving unhurriedly over visible stones and darting silver fish. Blanca wondered if they could cross it safely. She wasn't a strong swimmer, and neither was Mateo. Best not to risk it unless they absolutely had to.

"Do you think that's Kraków?" Iain asked, nodding to the bell tower in the distance.

"Yeah, probably." She wrinkled her nose. "What the hell is that smell?"

"I don't know. I smell it, too. It's almost like…sulfur."

Blanca's eyes ticked over the horizon, and beyond the distant bell tower, she spotted thick plumes of black smoke pouring from tall brick chimneys. It looked like some sort of factory. Blanca's stomach turned, though she couldn't say why.

"I don't like the look of this." She glanced quickly at the map and tried to find their position. "Okay, so if we're at…this bend in the river, here…" She traced a path on the map over the river, and her insides ran cold as she realized that the structure ahead of them wasn't a factory at all.

It was Auschwitz-Birkenau, the infamous concentration camp.

"Jesus," she murmured in horror.

"Blanca!" called out Mateo. "I think I hear something—"

"Bollocks!"

Blanca jerked at the sound of Iain's cry, only to see Otto Zimmler on his feet, sprinting along the bank of the river, rasping for air. Iain darted after him, as did Blanca and the others, but Otto reached his destination: a dirt road leading to a small bridge over the river.

A military truck rolled toward them, and Otto raised his bound hands, waving wildly.

"*HALT!*" he shouted hoarsely to the truck. "*HELFEN SIE MIR!*"

Iain tackled him into the dirt.

Blanca came running up from behind, but the truck had stopped and two German soldiers jumped out, guns raised. Blanca wobbled and fell still. Iain hauled Otto up in front of him, but his expression was panicked. The Germans shouted and advanced with their rifles held high.

"Blanca, what do we do?" Mateo exclaimed.

"Don't move!" she told them, hands up as her eyes darted all around the dirt road. Iain kept a hold on Otto, who was too weak and winded from his run to fight back.

The Germans advanced on them, one saying something swiftly to Otto, who started to answer. The reply turned into a shriek instead when Blanca snatched out Otto's pistol and fired wildly. The Germans scrambled back, surprised. Blanca ran at the nearest soldier and tackled him.

Priya screamed shrilly and Mateo yanked her back into the woods while Iain tossed Otto roughly to the ground and then ran to Blanca, who was struggling with a German soldier for control of his gun. He overpowered her and kicked her away, but Iain sprang forward, grabbing the German around his neck.

Blanca brought out her knife, flicked open the blade, and jabbed it into the German's side. Blood coated her hand as she snatched the knife away. Another series of gunshots rang out, brief and explosive, and Blanca shifted her head to the side to see Mateo barely dodge a barrage of gunfire.

"Protect the kids!" she ordered Iain, and then she did something she had promised herself she would never do again.

With a bitter noise in her throat, Blanca picked up the German rifle, seated it against her shoulder, and opened fire on the soldier.

The effect was instantaneous. The jolt of the gun rocked her body, jump-starting a poisonous tremor that shot down her spine and filled her with dread. The gun felt hot in her hands, too hot, burning her skin, and everything was suddenly so loud, so deafening. In that moment, Blanca's chest seemed to collapse in on itself. Terror locked her joints and electrified her nerves.

But the shots landed. The last German twisted violently and fell against the truck, helmeted head slapping against the steel hood before he fell over, dead.

Fingers trembling, Blanca lowered the gun. She rubbed at her face with her shoulder, expression hollow. Vaguely, she wondered what the mess hall was serving today.

"...Blanca?"

Still trapped in her stupor, Blanca took a moment to recognize Iain's anxious face.

"Are you alright?" he asked. Within a few seconds, everything came back: the sounds, the wind, the steady hum of a truck engine still running quietly nearby.

Blanca nodded vaguely before her focus narrowed and she pulled away. "Mateo!" she called out quickly, suddenly panicked. "Mateo!"

"I'm here!" he answered, emerging from the trees with Priya. He was trembling too.

All eyes turned to look at Otto Zimmler, who was on his knees, wheezing, close to the ground. Blanca approached and stood over him, hand clenched.

Otto Zimmler looked up at her. His eyes were pained and angry, jumping constantly between Blanca and the dead German soldiers. His skin was slick with fever sweat. His breathing was labored, and each blink of his cold blue eyes seemed to take monumental effort. He opened his mouth to say something, probably to insult her, but what came out was a bone-rattling gasp.

Blanca considered killing him. By god, she wanted to. Her hand tightened on the gun. In the end, her rage cleared—just enough—to remind her of the daunting task that lay ahead. She had to get Mateo home.

And so, she raised the butt of the rifle and smashed it across Otto's face.

Bavaria, Germany
1923

"Come on, come on!"

"Wait for me!"

For two little boys, getting to the street was imperative when something so exciting was going on, and they pressed on with reckless abandon, pushing their way past anxious bodies and whispered conversations.

"… really going to do this?"

"Do you think it will work?"

"He's going after Kahr!"

"Look how many men he has with him!"

Breathless with excitement, Otto shoved his way to the front of the crowd with his friend Jacob at his side. Together, they turned their eyes to the parade with rapturous awe.

A group of some six hundred men marched in perfect lines with their hands and heads held high. They moved together in a fearsome stomp, tall and firm, and Otto's mouth gaped open as he watched. He had never seen soldiers look so strong; all the soldiers he knew had come from the Great War, and they all bore the same limp, the same sad faces, the same look of defeat. They were dead men with beating hearts, and Otto pitied them.

More people joined the growing crowds, so Otto and Jacob climbed on top of some newspaper boxes to see better. All around them, spectators shouted their support to the marchers.

Someone called his name, and the small boy nearly tumbled off the box, startled. With a quick glance at his friend, Otto jumped down from the news box and hurried over.

"Yes, Father?"

"Look," his father commanded, and Otto did.

At the front of the parade was a military truck armed with a machine gun, and in front of that, a row of important-looking men in uniform. On each end of the row, a soldier proudly brandished a red flag with a twisted black symbol in the middle. Otto was too young to know what it was, but it impressed him as much as anything had impressed him in his life.

And then Otto's eyes were drawn to the man in the center of the line.

His eyes and hair were dark, and his posture was strong. When he extended his hand, jutting it into the air with such strength and finesse, Otto was not the only member of the crowd who strained to get closer.

"Who is he, Father?" Otto asked.

Otto's father touched his shoulder, a rare show of physical affection. The tender effect was brief, though; within seconds, the grip was painfully tight. "That," said his father, "is the man who will save Germany."

The men continued to march, pushing down the crowded streets with certainty and purpose, but it was not long before the Munich police arrived, and as Otto watched in horror, gunfire filled the air and the streets became a den of chaos.

"Father!" Otto exclaimed, but he lost him in the crowd. The frightened boy let out a cry and tossed his arms over his head as people rushed around him like water breaking over a rock. Panicked, he turned and ran as fast as he could, only to slip and fall to the pavement.

When he looked down, he realized he had tripped over the lifeless body of his friend Jacob, who had been hit by a stray bullet.

Chapter 3

*There were only a handful of Americans
there, but they fought like wildmen.*
—Private Antone Furhmann

Blanca and the others dragged the dead soldiers off
the road, shoved Otto's unconscious body gracelessly
into the truck, and left. They only drove for a short while
before coming to a stop. No one spoke. They didn't know
where to go.

With a sigh, Iain squinted past the fading afternoon
light to peer at an old iron sign. It read *Oświęcim* and
urged travelers onward with a cheerful illustration. The
bullet holes in the sign detracted from the invitation's
friendliness quite a bit.

"We don't need to get spotted. What should we do?"
Iain asked, hands tight on the steering wheel.

Blanca looked around cautiously. The stench of
burning human flesh from the nearby camp was even more
abrasive at this distance. They couldn't go any farther in
that direction without attracting attention, and if that
happened, they were as good as dead.

"Even if we got into Slovakia, they have no reason to
shelter Americans." Blanca looked back at the map. "I don't
think we have any choice but to go north. If we can get

across water, we'll be safe." Her eyes shifted to Iain. "And
once we are there, you can get what you need to build us
a way back to our own time. Right?"

Iain hesitated. "I will do everything I can," he said at last.

Blanca's gaze hardened, but nothing more was said.
Iain reversed the truck and drove away from the camp,
eventually steering it off into the woods and enlisting
Mateo's help to cover their tracks off the road. They
drove as far as they could manage, stopping only when the
trees became too dense. Daylight slipped away, and they
resolved to stay near the truck for one more night. Despite
her exhaustion, Blanca slept in fits and starts.

The next morning, after everyone was awake, Blanca
dug around in the cab of the truck and eventually found
something useful: a hand radio. "Hell, yeah," she muttered,
tucking it away. She also found a small can with a piece
of metal and a rock. When she showed it to the others,
Iain perked up.

"Brilliant!" he declared, taking it from her. As Blanca
and the others watched, he gathered up a pile of brush and
surrounded it with stones. Then he kneeled in front of the
pit and struck the stone and metal together. After a few
clicks, a spark appeared.

"Oh, god! Finally!" Priya yelped, dropping next to the
growing fire with a happy little hum. "It is *bitchin'* cold
out here!"

Satisfied, Blanca left the group behind to go check
on the German.

Inside the truck, she opened Otto's suit and inspected
his wound. She *had* actually closed it, which left her sitting
back on her haunches, wondering what she'd missed. After
thinking for a moment, she cut open the white tank he

wore under the flight suit and scanned his bare torso. She'd
half-expected to see a swastika tattoo on his chest and was
a little disappointed to find only honey-colored chest hair.
Too bad, she thought. *Would've been fun to scrape it off his body
with a cheese grater.* The mental image made her chuckle.

She turned him on his side with a grunt. Otto was
bigger than she'd first thought; grimly, she realized he'd be
difficult to handle once he recovered...if, in fact, he did.

Otto stirred weakly, swatting at her hand and
muttering something incoherent in garbled German. "Shut
up," she commanded, shoving away his hand. "Show me
where you're having pain."

Otto gestured senselessly to his whole body, muttering
nonstop. Finally, he brushed his fingers over the lower
right corner of his torso, and Blanca yanked down his
flight suit far enough to see a nicely infected wound right
beside the "v" of his hips. She sighed heavily. The first aid
kit had some rubbing alcohol in it, but she really didn't
want to waste such a valuable resource on Otto.

As she shifted his flight suit back into place, her hands
brushed a pocket she hadn't noticed before. Reaching in
through the zipper, she pulled out a small drinking flask.
She unscrewed the cap and sniffed it. "Eugh. Whiskey."
She doused a bit of cloth in the flask's contents and stuck
it over his wound. "This'll have to work."

Otto jerked and whined pitifully, but he didn't have
the strength to move away.

"Be still," Blanca snapped. When she was satisfied,
she wrapped up the wound with a patch from the first aid
kit, then yanked his flight suit back up.

Otto jerked, then fell still again, and Blanca sat back
with a sigh. She was exhausted and hungry, and every joint

in her body ached with fatigue. None of these were new feelings though, so she dismissed them.

———◦◦◦———

The next morning dawned, cold and sunless.

As they ate their remaining apples around the dying campfire, a loud series of German swear words rang out from the truck. Ticking her head to the side, Blanca stood and approached Otto as he half-climbed, half-fell from the truck. "Oh, man. You look like shit," she observed, folding her arms.

Otto gave her his ugliest scowl. "Well, you look like a dirty Roma whore," he spat.

Blanca slapped a hand over her heart. "That cuts me deep, Zimmler." Before he could respond, she grabbed his collarbone, causing him to yelp, then shoved him down to the ground near the fire. Iain passed him a small portion of food, which Otto ate begrudgingly.

Blanca sat in front of him, and Otto stopped chewing long enough to channel the full force of his glare on her. Undaunted, she held up her newest discovery. "We found a radio."

"Congratulations. Too bad you do not speak German."

"We don't need to speak German. We have you."

Otto finished his small meal and wiped his bound hands off on the knees of his flight suit. "For now," he conceded. "But I am not translating for you. I will not help you cause harm to Germans."

"A little late for that, don't you think?"

Otto's smile slipped away, and his mouth twitched.

Blanca held up the radio again. "You are not allowed to touch this. I just want you to listen and tell us *accurately* what's being said and what we need to avoid."

"And if I do not? What then?"

Blanca leaned close. "I will beat your ass to death, that's what."

Otto didn't recoil, but his eyes flickered tellingly. He believed her. After a long moment, he shrugged. "Fine. Your time will come soon enough."

"Can't wait."

A few minutes later, the group got up and Blanca handed off the map to Iain. Mateo hovered near Otto, looking concerned, and Priya trailed them. They set their destination as a coastal city called Danzig. By Blanca's estimation, they had almost 380 miles to go.

"I hope all you dirty beggars starve to death out here."

Everyone rolled their eyes but didn't say anything. They'd been walking for hours without interruption, but the relative peace was often ruined with Otto's complaints. Blanca secretly wished she had never forced him to speak English; now she wasn't sure if he would ever shut up.

"And when this war is over," Otto continued, even though no one had responded to him, "and Germany has its empire, we will have every resource at our disposal, and you will have nothing."

Mateo whirled around. "Man, I got news for you—"

"Ah! Mattie!" warned Blanca, holding up a finger.

"But Blanca!"

"Nope, zip it."

Mateo groaned while Otto looked at them oddly.

"Killjoy," he muttered. Blanca shrugged, but didn't disagree with him.

Mateo slowed down so he could walk next to Otto. "Do Nazis really, like, believe only White people are good?" he asked curiously.

Otto shifted to raise a brow at him. "We believe in the superiority of the Aryan race," he answered. "There are places for all peoples across the world. However, Germany belongs only to true ethnic Germans, not imposters or immigrants."

"So, what happens if you make a mixed baby?"

"Mixed?"

Mateo nodded. "Yeah, you know, not White. Like, biracial. What if you had a baby with someone who wasn't German?"

Otto huffed in amusement. "I would not."

"But what if you did?"

Blanca looked over her shoulder. "They'd probably feed it to a bunch of crocodiles like in Ancient Egypt or something."

"I am afraid we are short on crocodiles in Germany," Otto informed her peevishly. He looked back at Mateo. "And it would not reach that point. Relations between Germans and non-Germans are now outlawed. Transgressors are punished with public beatings and executions. I have seen a few myself."

Blanca made a loud noise of disgust.

"Did you stop it?" Mateo asked, concerned. "The beating?"

"Stop it?" repeated Otto in surprise. Shifting to glare at Blanca, he said haughtily, "No. I shot the Polish bastard myself for daring to think he was good enough for a German woman."

Mateo's jaw dropped. "What? You actually—a *Polish* guy? Aren't they White?"

"They are Slavs."

Mateo squinted. "So, they're not the right *kind* of White?"

"Mateo!" Blanca said sharply, and Mateo frowned deeply before edging away from Otto.

"That is freaking crazy," he muttered to Priya, who linked her arm with his and turned up her lip at Otto.

Otto cut his eyes at them and fell silent.

———

The day ended without incident, and Blanca found a small clearing for them to rest in. Iain took care of the fire while Blanca examined her new German rifle. It wasn't exactly what she was used to, but the concept was simple enough. She made sure to keep it well out of Otto's reach. Each time she glanced in his direction, she found him staring right back at her. After a while, he shifted his attention to Iain.

"You're not American like the rest."

"Irish," Iain confirmed offhandedly. He grew annoyed when Otto started laughing. "What's so funny about that?"

"Oh," Otto said, catching his breath, "just that anyone would admit to being from a country with nothing but dirt farmers and sheep herders. I mean, really, what even is Ireland? A pathetic little country that hides behind England like a little boy hides behind his mother's skirts."

Iain sighed heavily.

"Your country has a *whole* standing army," Otto crowed in delight. "Full of what I assume are able-bodied men. And yet..." He gestured. "Where are they? Sitting back and doing nothing because they let England protect them." He wiggled a finger at Iain. "And you. Are you not healthy enough to serve? A bit past your prime, perhaps—"

"I'm thirty-two!"

"But surely able to put on a uniform and shoot a gun?"
Otto drummed his fingers on his knees. "Well anyway, I
am sure it is for the best. After all, what would the rest of
the world do if we lost the great nation of Ireland?" He
laughed again, terribly amused.

When Iain shifted away and refused to engage him
further, Otto turned his gaze to the others. "But then again,
I do not hate the Irish. They are not worth the effort. And
Americans?" he eyed Blanca disparagingly. "Greedy and
stupid, but ultimately unimportant."

Blanca put her chin in her hand. "Gee, Zimmler. That
hits me right in the heart."

"Mmm," was Otto's response as he sighed and looked
around. "America is a silly child trying to keep up with
the big boys. It will learn its lesson soon enough. And
England? Far past its glory. Italy? Weak. France? Pathetic.
And Japan?" He looked to the group sardonically. "Have
you ever *seen* the Japanese? They are savages." He held up
a finger. "But Russians!" His eyes glittered with malice.
"Russians are the lowest of dogs who have never given a
word they did not take back, and if I had control of two
massive bombs, one meant for the demons of hell and the
other for Satan himself, I would bomb Moscow twice."

Everyone stared.

"Damn, dude," Mateo said.

Otto shrugged.

Blanca massaged her temples, said a quick prayer, and
stood up. "Come on, let's bed down for the night."

The group settled in, with Mateo and Priya sleeping
on a tarp they'd gotten from the German truck. They didn't
have proper sleeping bags—apparently the Germans had

not been going far enough to warrant any—but the tarp was better than nothing. The others slept in shifts, and Blanca took last watch.

The hours ticked by. Blanca hovered in a state between sleep and wakefulness, never able to fully commit to either. When Iain tapped her on the shoulder for her shift, she was relieved.

As morning shifted into the early shades of twilight, Blanca sat with her rifle in her lap, knees pulled up and head tilted back. Wind stirred the few stubborn leaves remaining on branches, and as she watched, the last of one tree's leafy foliage twisted off its branch and floated down in front of her. The air was bitterly cold, and when she reached out to touch the fallen leaf, it crumbled instantly. With nothing but quiet surrounding her, Blanca's thoughts drifted.

They did not exist here.

Even if they got back to the United States, there would be no record of them. No piece of paper signed, no fingerprint recorded. They were ghosts, nationless and without identity. Their own countries would not recognize or acknowledge them.

In fact, it was very possible they would make it all the way to the United States only to get turned away. The thought pressed fear into Blanca's veins like venom, and anxiety seeped from every pore. *But we're Americans,* she thought. Surely their ID cards would prove that?

With those dates? Who would believe you?

Blanca rubbed a hand over her face.

Of all the places, of all the times, of all the eras the world had seen and God had judged, why this place? Why had they come here, and why to this war? Blanca pulled

one hand off her rifle and shook her wrist to bring down
the rosary beads. Once the cross was in her hand, she
pressed it against her lips once and recited her prayers, just
as she'd been taught all those years before.

The church had been a magical place to Blanca and
Mateo. They'd stumbled upon a service one night while
wandering, and with each step, the children's wonder
increased tenfold. The inside was stunning with its
intricate ceilings, soft seats, and lovely paintings; Blanca
felt as if she could not see enough with her own two eyes,
and she wished she had more so she could look in all
directions at once.

There were lit candles on silver cases, tall mirrors with
detailed etchings, and pictures everywhere she looked.
The air was warm and it smelled so nice, like a thousand
flowers mixed with *clean*.

They sang songs from a book and shouted joyfully.
They held hands – everyone! – and wished all around them
well. There were lights and colors and hugs and smiles.
And even though no one knew Blanca or Mateo, they
didn't treat them like strangers. They patted their heads
and gave them candy. They told them "Merry Christmas"
and "God be with you." A man held their cold hands,
closed his eyes and asked God to watch over them.

"He will keep you safe," the stranger in robes told
them. "My name is Father Gregory. I am a priest here."

"I don't know what that means," said Blanca baldly.

Father Gregory tilted his head. "It means I help guide
this church and all the people in it. We come together to
worship and praise God for his many blessings. We help
each other in times of trouble, as God would want us to
do as his children."

"You aren't a child," observed Blanca. "You're old."

He chuckled again. "Yes, I am, but it doesn't matter how old you get. You will always be a child of God because he loves you."

Blanca narrowed her eyes. She didn't feel loved, and she resented this man for lying to her.

"I can see you are feeling sad. You are afraid you have been abandoned," he said gently. "But you have not. Please remember, you can come here at any time. You are welcome in the house of God. In many ways, a church is your home."

Blanca felt a lump in her throat. That word stuck out in her young mind – *home*.

For the next two years, as long as she and Mateo lived in the area, Blanca walked them both to Mass every Sunday. It was their favorite day of the week; Mateo enjoyed it because they could eat a good meal and play with other children.

Blanca, on the other hand, worshipped the consistency and ritual. In the church, she could let the burden of responsibility slip off her tiny shoulders, if just for a few hours. It was only there she could truly *breathe*. She didn't always understand the wise words of Father Gregory, but she hoped that by being there and giving all her effort, she might absorb something that would make her good.

She wanted so much to be good. She wanted to be strong and capable and worthy.

Please, God, she would pray. *Help me be good enough for Mateo. I want him to be happy. Help me take care of him.*

One day, Blanca learned she and Mateo were being moved to a group home in another part of the city. In tears, she told Father Gregory they would not be able to come back to the church.

"Here," he said, pulling something from his pocket. It looked like a necklace of beads, and at the end was a small cross. "These are rosary beads, my child. Do you remember your prayers?"

Blanca nodded vehemently.

He closed her fingers tenderly around the beads. "You say them, and you keep this in your hand. The beads will guide you and give you strength. Do you understand?"

Blanca looked down at the rosary beads, and she felt a deep power as she clutched her hand around the crucifix. "Yes, Father," she whispered, desperate for some tangible reminder of her time there. She hugged it to her chest.

Together, they said one last prayer, and then they left. She never saw Father Gregory again.

Over the years, her faith waxed and waned, but the rosary beads at her wrist never left. Their weight was an old and familiar comfort, and on the days when she felt like she could no longer stand on her own two feet, she would kneel instead – in a street, at an altar, on her own bedroom floor – and say the prayers Father Gregory had taught her.

She never became fully convinced she was as loved as he said, but it was a nice thought.

Maybe one day, she thought every day for the rest of her life.

The next full day of travel was gratifying. They had purpose and direction. Unfortunately, what they did not have was food.

Otto grew dizzy and sick again, probably from the traveling, so they stopped and waited inside an abandoned train depot. "We are all going to die out here," he muttered. Nearby, Priya staggered and dropped into a dusty chair. She wrapped her arms around her stomach and whimpered.

"I've never been so hungry in my life," she whispered. Blanca studied her; Priya wore name brand clothes and expensive jewelry. Her long black hair was glossy, even after days in the woods, and she'd had a half-dozen credit cards with her when they'd landed in that dark pocket of forest. It was clear she'd come from a home of privilege; real hunger was new to her. Mateo, on the other hand, kept quiet.

Blanca looked up to see Iain scanning the train depot speculatively. After a moment, his face lit up. "Ah-ha!" He dug through a pile of rubble and emerged with an old rotary phone. "Hmm, if I can just find some wires…"

Blanca was too exhausted to ask what he was up to. She'd learned Iain could be a little erratic, frantic in the way really smart people often were. A half-hour later, Iain reappeared from a dingy room in the back of the depot, his arms full of wires. "Come with me."

Blanca glanced at the others before standing and heading outside with Iain. They were still near the river, and Iain raced straight for the water. He had a pair of plyers, a bundle of wires, and the rotary phone, which he quickly disassembled. Blanca rubbed her eyes blearily.

"You callin' us a pizza?"

Iain didn't answer. He was busy looping the wires from end to end, which he then connected to something in the phone. He tossed one end of the wire into the water and backed away with the other, careful not to touch the river. "Don't try this at home," he muttered. With a single digit, he turned the rotary dial on the phone. For a moment, nothing happened. Then the water bubbled, and to Blanca's astonishment, fish began to float to the surface. Iain let out a happy yelp.

"Wha – What the hell did you do?"

Iain set the phone aside and held up an arm to keep her back.

"Careful, don't get shocked. It's an old fishing technique – I mean, it's illegal, technically, but desperate times and all that." He began to fashion a net with the cords from Otto's parachute. "Rotary phones have a metal component called a magneto, and it can be used to generate shockwaves that briefly paralyze fish, causing them to float to the surface. Pretty nifty."

Nifty was one word for it. Within an hour, they had a dozen fish roasting over an open flame. Blanca couldn't remember ever enjoying something so much, but it was Priya who cried tears of happiness.

"You are the best!" she proclaimed, squeezing Iain with all her might. Blanca's lips lifted at the Irishman's bright red flush. Priya bounced away, happy once more. Even Otto had nothing scathing to say; he'd eaten his share of fish and immediately fallen asleep. After a while, Blanca took a seat next to Iain. He was sitting on his own, drawing on his left hand with a black ink pen. He'd made a dark loop around his ring finger, which he seemed intent on darkening.

"You seem pretty smart," she remarked.

Iain stopped drawing and looked up, surprised. "Me? No, no. I just… I read a lot."

"Can you think of anything we should know about this era?" she asked hopefully. "Anything we should avoid?"

"Mm, no, I'm afraid not." Iain scanned their bags. "You'll probably want to look at that textbook of Mateo's, though. It might mention something useful."

Blanca flushed, embarrassed. She'd forgotten all about the book. "What's up with that?" she asked, pointing at the black circle he'd inked on his left ring finger.

Iain shrugged. "Just an old habit."

Blanca waited to see if he would elaborate, but he didn't. Instead, he looked up at Otto and said, "He is wrong, by the way. Irishmen fought in the war, even though the country was officially neutral."

Interested, Blanca asked, "Really? Then why did he say the army is staying behind?"

"Most did, but some soldiers deserted the Irish Defense Forces to join the British so they could fight. My grandfather was one of them." Iain's smile dropped. "They weren't treated well when they returned, though. Many considered them traitors."

"That's rough. Your grandfather made a tough decision." She paused before going on haltingly, "I hope it was okay for him later."

Iain smiled, looking delighted at her awkward attempts at comfort. "It was, yes. After a few years of being jobless, he managed to start his own automobile-repair business. And then in typical Irish fashion, he got married and had too many children, one of which was my mother, Aoife."

Blanca grinned. "Aoife? That's a new one."

Iain chuckled. "It's very old, actually. In Irish, it means 'beautiful.'"

"I—Wait, is Irish a language?"

Ian looked amused, and Blanca flushed.

"Well, hell. I thought Irish people spoke English."

"We do," he explained kindly, "but we also have our own language. Most call it Gaelic."

"I, uh, did not know that."

"It's alright. You're not Irish," he pointed out gently, and his genuine tone made Blanca even more flustered. When she shifted uncomfortably, Iain tilted his head. "May I ask what 'Blanca' means? I've never heard it before."

Blanca picked at the denim of her jeans. "Means 'white,'" she said after a pause. "It's kinda like naming someone 'Pearl.'"

"Ah," he said, smiling. "I like it."

"Whatever, it sounds like an old White lady's name."

Iain laughed at this, and Blanca's lips twitched upward at the corner. "I should go look at that book." She managed an awkward nod before shuffling off.

Night fell soon after, and the temperatures plummeted. Blanca took Otto's ripped leather jacket and gave it to Mateo, who in turn offered it to Priya. Priya delicately ripped off the Nazi badges before wrapping the jacket around her skinny torso, even managing to fit her bunched up knees inside.

The group settled down for the night, with Blanca taking first watch. Otto eventually woke, and Blanca felt a mixture of relief and anxiety when she saw some of his color had returned. He was improving. Thankfully, he was still too weak to talk much. Instead, he watched them all with a calculating look that set Blanca on edge.

Despite the group's exhaustion, sleep didn't come easy for any of them. The empty night air left too much room for snapping twigs and eerie woodland chatter. In the distance, the clamor of a tank battle echoed, breeding unease. Blanca listened, mentally counting the thunderous booms until they finally faded away.

"It's pretty far off," she volunteered quietly of the fighting.

Priya frowned and curled closer against Mateo's back. He turned over and wrapped her up in his arms, helping her to relax. They spent a restless night there, and in the morning, they moved on.

A few hours into their morning walk, the group stopped to rest and eat. Priya struggled some with her thin sandals. "Making it?" Mateo asked, appearing beside her. They began walking again.

Priya shoved her hair back from her face. "Yeah, I'm just not much of a hiker. Obviously."

"Me, either." Mateo walked alongside her, taking one stride for every three of hers. "Back home, I never saw a tree that wasn't in a park."

"We used to go camping when I was little," Priya said with a laugh. "It wasn't real camping, though. It was, like, sitting in an air-conditioned RV and sometimes cooking out kinda' thing, and it was always at the beach."

"Wow. Ritzy."

"I guess." Priya fell quiet for a few minutes. "So what did you do back home? Besides school?"

Mateo shrugged. "I wanted to get a job, but I didn't have a car and I was never in one place for long. So I mostly just…hung out."

"I bet you had a lot of friends at home." Priya nudged him with a teasing smile. "Since you're such a sweetheart and all."

Mateo smiled in return, but the expression didn't reach his eyes. "I had some, yeah. Blanca never liked them, though."

"Why not?"

Blanca appeared and prodded Otto up the last section of a grassy hill. "Because they were thugs," she said flatly.

Mateo scowled. "For the last freaking time, they were not thugs."

"Whatever."

"You know what? Mind your own damn business, Blanca."

The group froze. Blanca whirled to face her brother, and Priya darted behind Iain as Blanca stalked forward, jaw clenched. "You'd better watch your damn mouth, Mateo, because I don't have time for your pissed-off teenager attitude."

"Yeah, you don't have the time for much of anything," Mateo replied bitingly. "That's why you fucked off to the other side of the world for four whole years, huh?"

Blanca's eyes widened. "I got deployed, Mateo. What do you want from me?"

"Well, I didn't want you to join the damn Army, for starters."

"Damn, Mattie, I barely graduated high school! What the hell else was I supposed to do?"

"You were supposed to *stay with me*!" Mateo growled. "I needed you!"

"All I wanted was to keep you out of trouble so you didn't end up like your stupid friends, getting locked up for drugs or something!"

"For god's sake, Blanca, I wasn't interested in any of that crap—"

"Then why did you hang out with those guys?"

"Because I wanted to!"

"But *why?*"

"*Because I had a crush on one of them!*"

Blanca balked. "I—Wait, what?"

For a split second, Mateo looked as surprised as she did. Then he shifted and shrugged his skinny shoulders. "Yeah," he muttered. "Lucas."

Blanca glanced around at the others, all of whom were gawking. "I, uh. I didn't know you…liked boys," she admitted awkwardly.

Mateo fidgeted, looking equally uncomfortable. "Yeah." He scratched his head.

For a long, tense moment, no one spoke. It was Otto who finally broke the uneasy silence. "Mateo is right, you know." He wiggled his finger at Blanca and smirked. "Women belong at home."

Blanca shoved him hard in the chest and Otto vanished with a shriek down the grassy hill behind him.

"Blanca!" Iain admonished.

"*What?*"

Otto was still falling.

"His hands are tied!"

"Who gives a shit."

Blanca stomped away. Exasperated, Iain turned and hurried down the hill to catch the falling German. He caught up with Otto at the bottom, where the other man was facedown in the grass and groaning. "Come on, you're fine." He pulled Otto to his feet.

"Take these ropes off of me." Otto held up his bound hands. "I am not going anywhere. I do not even know where we are anymore."

Iain trekked back up the hill with Otto in tow. "I'm not doing anything until Blanca says it's alright."

"Do you always take orders from women?"

"Wise men usually do."

Otto made a loud noise of disbelief. Once they reached the others, he asked curiously, "She is in the Army?"

Mateo said nothing, plodding alongside the two older men without a word. Iain glanced uncertainly at Otto, then shrugged. "I'm not telling you anything."

"What do you people think I am going to do with this information?" Otto asked with a huff. "I once tried to pickpocket a uniformed police officer. I am not exactly a criminal mastermind."

"You got caught stealing from a cop?" Mateo asked incredulously. "And you were allowed to join the Air Force?"

"I come from a *very* important family."

Mateo sighed. "Rich White boy wins again."

"It is what we do."

⸻ ∞ ⸻

That evening, a storm swelled in the western sky. Blanca turned her gaze upwards and watched the darkening clouds with irritation.

Mateo hadn't said much since their argument, instead sticking close to Priya. Blanca hadn't pushed it. She didn't have the mental energy for another fight, and she knew Mateo was frustrated and hungry like the rest of them. The river here was swollen and fast, too dangerous for Iain to try and fish. They had no choice but to tough it out.

As the group rounded a bend in the river, the wind picked up and stirred some thin branches, peeling them back to reveal a clearing up ahead. Blanca's brows furrowed when she noticed a layer of stone hidden behind some trees.

"Hold up," she told the group sharply, and they all paused.

Ahead, they saw a small grey stone castle situated on the bank of the river. It had four rounded towers, one of which was crumbling, and a few balconies dotting the sides. The eastern face of the castle sat at the top of a hill that ran all the way down to the water, and as they watched, bits of stone fell away and tumbled into the raging river.

In front of the castle, a decaying courtyard bore the scars of war. Elegant stone planters stood cracked and

barren, with only shriveled stalks and weeds left behind
in the dirt. A low wall sported vines choked with rot along
its sides. A fountain, long dry, was centered in another
courtyard off to the right, and there was a large statue of
a woman in sweeping robes in the back. Half of her face
had been blasted away, giving her an eerie, lopsided stare.

"Wow," Priya murmured as the others appeared
behind her. "This is like…a real castle."

Otto tilted his head up at the tall roof peaks. "Have
you never seen a castle before?"

"I'm from Utah, dude. The only castle I ever saw was
owned by a lady named Barbie."

Otto's brows furrowed in confusion.

Blanca looked at the castle's front doors, one of which
was mounted but open while the other dangled from a
single hinge. The interior of the castle appeared black and
empty, and although they strained to listen, they heard no
movement inside.

Overhead, thunder clapped again, and a few droplets
of rain hit their shoulders.

"Should we go in?" Iain asked, and Blanca peered back
at the others. Night was approaching, and they were about
to get swept up in a hellish storm.

"I don't think we've got much choice." She stepped
inside reluctantly, rifle raised. Behind her, Iain illuminated
the way with a small torch. The light was a paltry defense
against the heavy shadows of the windowless corridors.

Inside the castle, the rooms were in disarray. Cobwebs
decorated the corners, and old paintings hung crookedly
on the walls or lay flat on the floor. Most of the furniture
was gone, with only the occasional broken chair or table
still remaining.

"Do you know anything about this place?" Mateo asked Otto in a whisper.

Otto shrugged, eyes scanning the walls. "It was likely abandoned by a family of means when the war started."

"I don't think anyone's been here in a while." Blanca relaxed a little. The group came to a large foyer, which was empty save for a few small tables. A large fireplace sat in the center of the wall nearest the door. Tall arched windows decorated the other. Shattered glass, once ornate, lay scattered on the floor below them.

Outside, the rain started in earnest. It pounded against the roof of the castle, creating a steady hum. There was a leak in the far corner of the room, but most of the stone floor was blissfully dry. Above their heads, a broken chandelier swayed.

Blanca lowered her gun. "I think it's best if we stay in this room tonight." She nodded her head at the fireplace. "Iain, can you make that work?"

He nodded. "I'll go break up some furniture for wood." He ducked into the next room, and a few minutes later, returned with busted chairs and a few dusty pillows and blankets. He and Blanca flapped them clean and laid them out on the stone floor just in front of the fireplace. Once Iain had the fire going, radiant warmth filled the room.

Mateo and Priya stretched out in front of the fire like fat, lazy cats, glad that at least one of their worries had been taken care of. They wrapped themselves up in the blankets and played tic-tac-toe on the stone floor with a chalky rock Priya had found.

After a while, the teens fell asleep and the others started their shifts. Otto remained awake, eyes on the pouring rain just outside the glassless window. When he shifted his head to look at Iain, the Irishman raised a brow.

"Yes?" Iain asked patiently.

Otto smirked. "I am just trying to remember if I know any racist words for Irish people."

Iain rolled his eyes and returned to his task of cutting up firewood.

"I cannot think of any but give it time." Otto gaze shifted to Blanca, and his grin grew. "You, on the other hand," he went on with growing delight, "I know plenty of racist words for you."

Blanca shifted and walked over to Otto at a leisurely pace. Then she shoved the barrel of her gun against his groin, causing him to flinch.

"Go ahead. Say one."

There was a tense pause. "On second thought," Otto managed, his voice a little higher than normal, "they are... all in German. The effort would be wasted on you."

"Too bad," she murmured, before pulling the gun away with an extra little shove, causing Otto to wince and twist away so he could rub himself.

Blanca leaned back against the wall and let her eyes close. Iain pulled the cushions off some chairs and offered them to the others as pillows. The fabric felt grimy against her cheek, but Blanca accepted it anyway. Anything was better than sleeping against the cold stone.

Exhausted, she let Iain take the first watch.

———⟨∞⟩———

Everything around her was blinding, from the hot midday sun to the reflective glass of her knife. She was trying to cut a man out of his protective vest, hoping to free him, but it wasn't working. She wasn't fast enough or strong enough, and the man was dying.

"Come on, come on!"

Blanca finally made it through the strap keeping the man trapped under the rubble, and she tossed her knife back into her pocket so she could reach under his armpits and haul him out. Over her head, a tank gun blasted through a wall and sent debris flying through the air. Blanca ducked, and small rocks hit her helmet in a pitter-patter that sounded like heavy rain.

"Agh! Okay, hang on..." She started to pull, and the man grew even more panicked.

"Hernandez! Get me out of here!"

"I am, I am!" She looked desperately for an exit, but the world was blood and dust. Blanca looked back at the soldier, ready to tell him everything would be okay, only to discover the man's face was gone. It had caved in during one of the blasts and was now a gaping wound lined in blood and shredded flesh. Blanca stared in horror as the faceless man pleaded for help.

"Get me out of here, Hernandez!" the dead man begged. When she screamed, he said it again, louder this time.

"GET ME OUT OF HERE, HERNANDEZ!"

───⚛───

Blanca jerked awake, flat against the cold stone floor.

Everyone else was asleep, save for Iain. He was sitting near the entrance, just a few feet away, and when he spotted her stricken face, he got up and came over.

"Are you alright?" he asked in a soft whisper. "You're shaking."

Blanca wiped blindly at her face, and her vision slowly cleared. The fire was small and dim, and the room had grown very dark. Outside, the downpour continued. The pitter-patter of raindrops drove her to distraction for a few seconds, and she touched her head. "Weird dreams."

Iain's eyes were sympathetic. "I bet," he murmured. "It's almost your shift. Do you want me to stay up with you for a little while?"

He managed to make the question sound sensible and not at all silly, but Blanca flushed with embarrassment anyway. "No, I'm fine. Just go to sleep." She took the rifle, which Iain hadn't even been holding right, and assumed a guard position near the door. Iain watched her for a few minutes, as if he thought she might change her mind, but eventually he curled up and went to sleep.

Blanca let her head rest against the wall. The images from the dream faded, but the sounds did not. Each time thunder rolled overhead, Blanca could only hear the din of warfare: the pounding of explosions against the ground, the blast of a tank gun, the racket of semiautomatic gunfire. Adrenaline swarmed her and refused to abate.

Blanca put her face in her hand and fought the urge to cry. There was no time for this. Her eyes fell on the fireplace, and she focused on the dwindling flames. After a few minutes, a flicker of light near the doorway caught her eye.

Shifting her head dully in the direction of the light, she squinted. There it was again, that brief, bright spot, like an orb. Blanca looked around uncertainly. Everyone else was asleep. Her eyes were playing tricks on her.

But then another orb joined the first. There was a pair of them.

The lights were moving, bobbing up and down, low to the ground. Blanca watched, frozen, as they approached the glow of the dying fire.

Just then, a large gray paw stepped into the light.

Blanca's throat locked up, and her fingers clenched around her gun. She understood now; they were not lights at all, but a pair of reflective golden eyes. When they lifted, the large lupine head of a wolf was behind them. Three more pairs of eyes waited just beyond it.

"GET UP!" Blanca screamed to the others, but the massive wolf at the front pounced and took Otto by his ankle. Otto awoke with a scream and lashed out, landing a kick on the wolf's head and causing it to yelp.

Three more gray wolves rushed forward, and Blanca locked the rifle against her shoulder and shot twice, not hitting either one of them because they were too fast and too close. One wolf hit her hard in the chest and Blanca brought up the gun, crying out as she fell to the floor with the wolf's full weight on her. She shoved up the gun to catch its jaws, and it clawed viciously against her as it scrambled for purchase.

Suddenly, the weight flew off her with a kick from Iain, and he pulled Blanca up off the floor just as another wolf rounded on them. It jumped up and latched onto Iain's arm. The Irishman yelled out fiercely and fought wildly to get it off. Blanca scrambled back, and she suddenly realized Otto was beside her while Iain, Priya, and Mateo were at the opposite wall. Two wolves raced in their direction.

"RUN!" she told the others before she and Otto turned and raced through the double doors at the end of the room. Otto tried to shut the wolves out, but they barreled through the doors, nearly knocking him off his feet.

"GO!" he shouted, shoving her forward, and they raced down the shadowed corridors with two wolves at their heels. They bolted into the castle's kitchen and Otto jumped up, running across a long counter as one wolf pursued him and the other leaped at Blanca.

Blanca ducked and the wolf crashed into a wooden table covered in old cooking utensils. Otto slid to the end of the kitchen counter, snatched up an old butcher knife with his bound hands, and brought it down on the the wolf. The knife hit home in the thick, matted fur of the wolf's throat but not before it managed to snatch Otto's arm with its jaws.

A few feet away, Blanca scrambled to escape the wolf nearest her. She brought the gun up to shoot, but the rifle was too long and the wolf was too close, so she smashed it across the wolf's snout with a yell. Then she fired at the wolf holding Otto, blasting it off the counter. "Where is the other?" he panted, and Blanca looked back to see their final opponent snarling, jaws dripping, as it turned to face them.

"Shoot it!" Otto yelled, but when Blanca raised the gun and pulled the trigger, nothing happened.

"I can't!" she shrieked. "I'm out!"

The wolf sprang forward with a snarl, and Otto and Blanca turned and hurled themselves through a doorway and onto a rain-soaked balcony lined in crumbling stone. Lightning split the sky behind them, showing a frightening flash of the wolf as it crashed through the doors and raced in their direction.

The pair braced for impact, but as soon as the wolf hit the slick balcony floor, it lost control and slammed right into them. Blanca and Otto yelled out as the wolf's bulk broke through the dilapidated balcony railing, and they fell through the open air.

Blanca hit first, slamming into the wet grass with a shocked gasp before rolling down the grassy slope. Otto tumbled wildly next to her with the wolf just behind him. Without warning, they plunged into the icy water of the river, where the rain-swollen current sucked them beneath the surface in an instant. The wolf vanished from sight, and Blanca saw only a brief flash of the black night sky before the raging river swallowed her whole.

"AGH—"The cold immobilized her, locking her joints and causing her fingers to slip uselessly over every rock and branch. "HELP—" she tried again, but the current dragged her from the castle and down the ferocious river. Heavy rain pushed it higher, faster, and deeper with each passing second, and Blanca's throat burned as her body sank into a chilling numbness.

The castle disappeared from view, and murky blackness took its place. Blanca scrambled for the surface, but it seemed impossibly far. Precious bubbles of air spilled from her mouth.

Suddenly, a hand snatched her by the shoulder, hauling her above the water's surface. Blanca gasped loudly and clutched the person who'd grabbed her. It was Otto; he struggled to brace them against a rock.

"Get your damn knife!" he roared at her. Blanca numbly felt around in her pockets until she found her knife. Otto faltered on the rock behind her, nearly causing her to lose her grip. When he reached over her, she quickly began sawing at the rope binding his hands. A full-body shiver rocked her from the inside out.

"Don't...leave..." she managed between chattering teeth. "Not...a good...swim—"

"Cut the rope!" he interrupted harshly. The rope snapped, and Otto jerked his hands apart before grabbing her knife and shoving it into his own pocket. Blanca looked up, eyes wide.

He was going to leave her. All he would have to do is let go and she'd get swallowed up in an instant.

But if that was his plan, he never got the chance. At that moment, a loud creak echoed down the raging river and they looked up to see a massive tree rip free of its roots and tumble into the water with a great crash.

There was no time to react. The broken tree's wide trunk came rushing down the river with blistering speed, rolling over everything in its path and bouncing across the rapids with astonishing force.

"GET DOWN!" Otto shouted, circling his arms around her.

It was no use. Water rushed up ahead of the tree in a monstrous wave, then came down and ripped them from their perch. Within seconds, Blanca and Otto were underwater again, lost in its turbulent force. The tree rolled overhead like a black shadow, and one of its thick branches sliced through the water and caught Blanca's foot, spinning her cruelly in the volatile current. Otto's tight grip on her hand vanished.

Seconds later, she hit a rock and everything went black.

⁂

South Carolina, USA
2015

The inside of the bus was dark for most of the three-hour ride, so Blanca couldn't really see the faces of the people around her. It didn't matter, though. They had ten weeks to get to know each other. She wasn't exactly in a rush.

The others must have felt the same because the bus remained silent for long stretches at a time, and only the occasional shuffling of bags indicated anyone was there at all. Each time the bus rolled past a bright light, the people nearest the windows flinched and retreated further into the shadows. Blanca sat close to the back, glad no one was in the seat next to her. She'd been one of the last people to show up, and she'd been careful to avoid eye contact with the others as she found her place. That probably wasn't the best plan; she'd read online that teamwork was one of the biggest aspects of training.

Blanca was not good at teamwork.

Still, she would cross that bridge when she came to it. Currently, she was content to curl up in her seat and hide under the cover of the deepening night, her bag and a stack of papers sitting next to her in the adjacent seat.

Blanca's eyes flickered to her things. Her whole life was there, shoved into a single duffel bag and some plain folders. The papers were everything about her on record—where she'd been, what she'd done, and what she was made of. Reaching out, she brushed her fingers over the edge of the folder and lifted one corner; her eyes fell on the dim outline of her typewritten name.

She let it close again and shifted her gaze to the window, trying to look past her own reflection so she could focus on the state she'd never seen. It looked like everywhere else, though.

Her mind wandered to Mateo. He didn't understand her decision now, but one day he would. The recruitment officer had promised her she would be able to take care of him once her service was done. He'd be eighteen by that time. They'd be finished with foster care for good, and their lives could start at last.

The bus rolled to a stop. The others straightened in their seats as the overhead lights came on without warning.

The sudden brightness shocked Blanca into a brief panic, and she peeked over the seat in front of her anxiously.

The bus door opened and a tall man in a broad hat and military uniform stepped up next to the driver. Blanca's heart began to race, and her mouth went dry. The kid across the aisle recoiled into his seat.

The soldier's eyes swept over them.

"Listen up," he said in a loud, flat voice. "On behalf of Lieutenant Colonel Jacobson, welcome to Fort Jackson, South Carolina. I am a drill sergeant. Everyone wearing a hat like this or something similar is a drill sergeant. You will address us as 'Drill Sergeant.' From this point forward, the only words we should hear from you are 'yes' or 'no, Drill Sergeant.' Do you understand?"

"Yes, Drill Sergeant," the group fumbled. Blanca didn't speak. Ice pumped through her veins when the man's eyes flickered in her direction.

"Now," the drill sergeant continued sharply, "you are going to exit this bus. Females, you go to the left. Males, you go to the right. Line up on the yellow dotted line with your hands extended in front of you. Put your bag and paperwork directly in front of you. Stand with your heels together and your back straight. Do you understand?"

"Yes, Drill Sergeant!" Blanca joined in this time, astonished at how small her voice was in comparison to the resounding boom of the other recruits.

"You have two minutes to get off my bus. Go."

The recruits scrambled to grab their things and get off the bus. As soon as they stepped onto the pavement, other men and women in uniform were there, shouting at them to move forward, hurry, get in place, look forward, stand straight.

"Move with purpose!" the drill sergeant snapped. "Everything you do from here on out, you do with a sense of urgency! Move, now! Go!"

One of the recruits tripped, and the nearest drill sergeant swooped down on him, three inches from his face. "Get up! What are you doing? Get in place!"

Blanca hurried up behind the other female recruits, bag in one hand and her paperwork in the other. There were eight other women in the line with her, and one spilled a few bottles of makeup.

The only female drill sergeant appeared next to them in a flash. "Why do you have makeup?" she barked. "You do not bring makeup to my training camp! You will throw every bit of that makeup away, do you hear me? All of it!"

"Yes, Drill Sergeant!"

Blanca kept her face straight, but inwardly, she scowled. Who brings makeup to basic training? *Dumb bitch.*

"Now," boomed the main drill sergeant's voice once more, "listen up. Every single one of you has failed in your first task. I told you to get off that bus in two minutes. You were too slow, and you failed! Get in the push-up position now."

The recruits dropped, some looking at each other with incredulous expressions. The girl next to Blanca frowned as they placed their hands on the gritty asphalt. Blanca wished she'd tied back her hair and felt stupid for not already having done so.

"This is called the front leaning rest position," stated the drill sergeant. "If you do not follow my orders, you will be in this position a lot. If you cannot complete your tasks, you will be in this position a lot. If you don't wipe that shitty look off your face," he leaned down in front of a young man opposite Blanca, "you will be in this position a lot. Do you hear me?"

"Yes, Drill Sergeant!"

"Start doing push-ups."

It was ten o'clock at night. They'd been on a bus for the better part of three hours. Blanca hadn't eaten since the day before.

It was only five push-ups in before her arms started to quiver.

"You're all going to have to do a hell of a lot better than that!" snapped the drill sergeant, and across from Blanca, an overweight teenager dropped to his stomach.

"Get up!"

The recruit struggled, sweat already pouring from his brow. They'd been going for maybe ten or fifteen push-ups, and Blanca's were much shallower than they'd been at the start, but she didn't want anyone coming over and screaming in her face, so she kept the motion going.

To his credit, the overweight kid pushed himself back up, heaving, and kept going at a glacial speed. The girl next to Blanca whined a little, but when the female drill sergeant stepped closer, she closed her mouth with a snap.

"Listen up!" The drill sergeant paced between them. "From here on out, you will follow orders. You will not have to think. We will tell you the who, the what, the where, and the when. You do not need to know the why."

Blanca paused, eyes shifting down to the concrete beneath her red hands. Her hair, greasy from a lack of washing, hung around her face.

"Is that clear?"

"Yes, Drill Sergeant!"

"Stop doing push-ups."

The recruits froze in their positions on the ground. Blanca kept her eyes low. When the drill sergeant was done with his instructions, the group was ushered into a long classroom with white-washed walls, where they spent hours finishing up their paperwork and listening to the drill sergeant "welcome" them to their reception.

Blanca watched expressionlessly as the United States Army Soldier's Creed rolled by on a screen. Later on, she would be required to memorize it.

I am an American Soldier.
I am a warrior and a member of a team.
I serve the people of the United States, and live the Army Values.
I will always place the mission first.
I will never accept defeat.
I will never quit.
I will never leave a fallen comrade.
I am disciplined, physically and mentally tough, trained and proficient in my warrior tasks and drills.
I always maintain my arms, my equipment and myself.
I am an expert and I am a professional.
I stand ready to deploy, engage, and destroy, the enemies of the United States of America in close combat.
I am a guardian of freedom and the American way of life.
I am an American Soldier.

CHAPTER 4

They've got us surrounded
again, the poor bastards.
—General Creighton Abrams

B lanca awoke and immediately vomited.
In great heaves, she hacked up water and bile for what felt like an eternity. Her chest burned and her throat felt like sandpaper, but finally she managed to suck in a rattling breath and turn her bleary eyes upward.

There above her, she saw the sky, some branches, and a small child's face.

The child, who was tiny and White and clutching a stuffed doll with black button eyes, looked down worriedly at Blanca. As Blanca struggled to breathe, the little girl patted her head with a wise and sympathetic nod, as if Blanca's restoration was welcome but not unexpected. A man in farmer's clothes appeared and shooed the child away before kneeling beside Blanca and helping her up.

Blanca flinched at his touch, but the man held up his hands in a placating gesture and spoke swiftly in another language. Blanca couldn't understand the words, but his tone was gentle and reassuring. A woman in a plain dress with another child on her hip appeared and quickly offered Blanca a dry cotton cloth, which she used to rub at her face.

"Thank you," she whispered hoarsely. The man, who was still talking, pointed at the river and then at Blanca. He'd pulled her from the river, it seemed. A hacking cough drew her attention, and Blanca looked over to see Otto, haggard but alive, pushing himself up to a sitting position.

He spotted Blanca. "Oh, good. You are alive."

"Try not to sound so excited about it."

Otto put his chin in his hand. "I will make an effort to contain myself."

The farmer motioned to his wife, who quickly brought them a pair of blankets. Blanca accepted hers gratefully. "Can you understand them?" she asked Otto, who shook his head.

"No, they are Polish," he said tiredly. "I only know a few words."

"Do you know 'thank you'?"

Otto inhaled deeply, eyes half-lidded as he fought to warm himself up. He said something that sounded like "jen-koo-yea," and Blanca did her best to mimic it. The family must have understood because they looked delighted and nodded furiously.

The little girl hurried over, stuffed doll still tucked under her arm, and offered them both some bread and dried meat. Blanca hesitated. "What if this is all they have?" she asked Otto, who was already halfway through his meal. He rolled his eyes.

"Just eat it," he said, talking over his food. "And do not try to save it for your brother."

Blanca accepted the food awkwardly and choked it down. As she finished eating, Otto cocked his head in the direction of the Polish family's blue truck.

The farmer followed Otto's gaze, and he mimed something to Otto that Blanca didn't understand, but apparently Otto did. With a nod, Otto pushed himself up and walked with the farmer to the truck. Blanca grew instantly alert. Was Otto going to try and steal the truck? Would he use the radio to call the Nazis? What would she do if he did?

To Blanca's shock, none of those things happened. Instead, the farmer retrieved some tools from the truck's cab, and together with Otto, he replaced a dangerously low tire on the front. Blanca realized belatedly that this was probably why the family had stopped at the river in the first place. They'd been saved by a flat tire.

The two men finished their job, and the farmer smiled appreciatively and shook hands with Otto. Then he pulled something from his pocket and offered it to him. Otto refused and offered the gift back, but the farmer seemed insistent. Blanca peeked over curiously and saw it was a deck of playing cards.

The little girl gasped happily at the sight of cards, and Otto took a seat and held them up for the small child to see, tapping the picture on each one. Once he'd shown her all the cards, he laid them face down in three rows on the ground. The little girl watched with rapt attention, clutching her button-eyed doll tightly in her tiny hands. Otto held up a single finger for her to wait, and then he turned over one card to reveal an ace. He turned over another card, only to find a seven of hearts. He turned them both back over, then repeated the motion with different cards. He did this two or three times until he found a match, then looked up at the little girl and clapped his hands excitedly.

The little girl's face lit up. She understood.

She chose her cards with care, tongue between her teeth as she concentrated on the game. She would point to one, let Otto overturn it, and then she would scan the remainder of the cards, fighting to remember where the others had been. The first time she made a match, she jumped up with delight and thrust her arms happily in the air.

The family laughed, as did Otto and Blanca. The little girl's joy was contagious.

The game went on, with Otto playing against the little girl until she had quite soundly defeated him, getting all the pairs in the stack. Once it was done, she bounced in her spot, saying something in rapid Polish that neither Otto nor Blanca understood, although the sentiment was clear.

She and Otto got to their feet, and Blanca fumbled through another thank you to the family who had saved their lives. When she shook the hands of the parents, she gripped them tightly, hoping to convey how grateful she was. The family seemed to understand, and their kind faces helped untwist at least a tiny portion of her heart.

Otto shook their hands as well, and Blanca's dark eyes shifted suspiciously over him as the family piled into their truck. However, he didn't make any motion to join them, and once they were gone, he raised a brow at her.

"What?"

Blanca scowled. "Funny how nice you can be to White people."

Otto sighed loudly. "*Meine gott*, leave me alone you harpy."

Blanca stepped out from under the canopy of trees to peer at the sky. Then she shifted and looked down the river. Once she had her bearings, she began to walk.

"Come on," she said gruffly. "We have to get back to the others."

Otto made a face but fell into step next to her. "Slow down!" he snapped as he struggled with the leg of his ripped flight suit.

"No! I have to get back to Mateo."

Otto let out an exasperated huff. "He is nearly a man. Stop treating him like an infant."

Blanca stopped in her tracks. "Are you seriously trying to tell me how to take care of my brother? Because if so, shut the hell up. Your opinion means less than nothing to me."

They resumed their walk. After a few minutes—and to Blanca's great annoyance—Otto spoke up again, this time sounding curious. "Are you really going to allow him to be a homosexual?"

Blanca grimaced. "Are you really asking me that?"

"Of course I am." He finally fixed the torn leg of his flight suit and caught up to her. "You cannot let him do that."

"Why do you even care?" she asked flatly, never slowing down her pace. "You going to send him to a concentration camp?"

"For the love of god, woman, I am a *fighter pilot*. I do not send people to camps. I shoot Russians out of the sky. That is it."

"Whatever," she spat. "You voted for people who *do* send homosexuals to concentration camps. So yeah, that's on you." She looked over at him. "And that's why people hate the Nazis, you know. Because you're a bunch of prejudiced, elitist, homophobic assholes."

"The only nations that hate us, fear us," Otto countered with certainty. "We do not cause any more harm than any other warring country."

"You're delusional. You and every other racist piece of garbage that wears a swastika on his uniform."

"Only you Americans think that."

Blanca stopped and gave him an incredulous look. "Are you kidding me? Nazis are the worst war criminals in the history of modern warfare. No one else even comes close."

Otto regarded her suspiciously. "How can you make a statement like that when the Nazi party has only existed for fifteen years? And the war far less than that?"

Blanca's stomach did a flip-flop. "I… Well, it's just common knowledge. Everyone knows it's true."

Otto tilted his head. He didn't believe her, and something in her tone had caught his attention. He stepped closer. "Everyone who?" he questioned. "How can they compare us to others that way?"

Blanca fumbled, and then she managed at last, "Your government is the one with the concentration camps. They're committing genocide."

Otto did not seem impressed by this. "It is war," he said plainly. "Or do they not teach you about war in your American schools? All these things have been done before. Besides, the camps are for political prisoners. Those people have broken the law."

Blanca knew that wasn't true, but she didn't know how to contradict him without giving herself away. Somehow, mentioning her limited knowledge from history class didn't seem like quite enough. Otto really seemed to believe what he was saying though. She wondered, for just a moment, if he was being lied to—or if he was simply so brainwashed, so dedicated to his cause, that he was willing to overlook the obvious.

"You keep thinking that," she said cynically. "You and your lunatic leaders."

Otto snorted. "Again, we are not doing anything that has not been done before, so save your lectures."

He started walking again, and Blanca matched his pace. "And what about the Jewish people, huh? Systematically killing them is just part of war, too, I guess?"

Otto skipped a beat before answering. "They had their chance to leave," he said crisply. "And besides, the numbers are not nearly so high as Americans believe. Very few Jewish people go to the camps, and those that do are given the opportunity to convert. They refuse."

"Oh god," groaned Blanca. "Do you really think that's true? Or are you just stupid? Because your government officials are murdering Jewish citizens in your own country—"

"Shut up," Otto interrupted irritably.

"—not because they're traitors or political prisoners, but because of your power-hungry leader!"

"Where are you getting this information?" Otto snapped, stopping again.

Blanca hesitated, then suddenly remembered the newspaper she'd seen on their first day in Poland. "The German paper," she said hurriedly, "the one I found—I don't have it anymore, but it had horrible cartoons of Jewish kids being killed on the front—"

Otto looked doubtful. "What paper?"

"It was like…Stummer, or something."

"*Der Stürmer*?" guessed Otto incredulously, and Blanca pointed.

"Yes, that!"

"Oh, for the love of—that is not a real newspaper! It is a—a silly thing for schoolboys and poor people to read. No one takes that seriously!"

"Well, it looked pretty damn serious to me!"

"Well, you cannot read German!" Otto's eyes sharpened on her. "Have you ever even been to Germany?"

Blanca's jaw twitched. "No."

"Tell me what you know about my country."

Blanca's shoulders tightened. In a flash, she racked her brain for information. "Well, I know you Nazis believe in—"

"I did not say 'Nazi,'" he corrected swiftly, eyes serious. "Nazi is a political party. Germany existed for a thousand years before it. So...tell me what you know about *Germany*."

Blanca seethed, but nothing came to mind. Truthfully, she could not remember a single thing about Germany— past or present—that she could tell him. What else did she really know? She knew about the Berlin Wall...but only what it was and when it came down. Had she missed something in school? Had she met any actual Germans during her lifetime? Outside of World War II, she could think of almost nothing.

She wasn't even really sure of their current government. Wasn't there a lady in charge? Blanca felt shame burn her cheeks when she realized she didn't know.

Otto's head ticked to the side at her frustrated silence. After a long pause, morbid satisfaction settled over his features. "That is what I thought. So perhaps you should stop trying to tell me how my country works and how it should operate, as you know nothing about it." He pointed to his own chest. "I was born and raised in Munich, and I have seen my entire life what we suffer. We were left with *nothing* after the Great War. But now, with our Führer's help, we will become great once more."

Blanca frowned. "At the expense of millions of people?"

Otto dropped his head back to chuckle darkly at the sky. "You need to stop believing everything your American news tells you. Your mind has been clouded."

"Me? I'm not the one who's brainwashed here!"

Otto's expression tightened. "Do you know why you say these things? Do you know why you believe all that you do about Germany and her government?" He stepped closer, and Blanca realized with a tendril of fear that Otto was over six feet tall; with his spine straight and shoulders back, he towered over her.

"It is because you come from a nation of pillagers and thieves," he murmured. "Your people are nothing more than the collective offspring of a global terrorist, one that lost its empire because its lust for power finally outgrew its reach."

Blanca's fingers curled at her sides.

"I asked you what you knew about Germany. Would you like to hear what I know about your country, Blanca?" Otto went on lowly. "I know that America has never defended anything it did not *need*. I know after the Great War, it signed that cruel punishment they disguised as a peace treaty—the one that dismantled our military, forbade us from exporting resources, and burdened us with every damn expense from the war." He narrowed his eyes. "And I know as soon as America's economy collapsed, it came to Germany and demanded *all* the reparations paid in full, knowing damn well we could barely afford to feed our own people, much less yours!"

Any hints of playfulness were gone from Otto's expression.

"What do I know of America?" he continued, his voice dropping to a growl. "I know that it is a country of people that would save a fish from drowning…only to make it their meal as soon as no one is looking."

Blanca turned away from his intense glare.

"So perhaps you should stay in your own affairs," Otto finished heatedly. "If nothing else, I am sure Poland would be better off without America's so-called 'help.'"

Blanca forced herself to meet his gaze, discomfort needling in her chest. "Let's just go already," she grumbled before turning to shuffle away. Otto didn't move. When Blanca stopped and looked back at him, he remained where he was. And that was when it hit her.

Otto's hands were no longer bound.

That old and wretched fear settled in the pit of her stomach as Otto looked down at the broken pieces of rope on his wrists. With a smug look, he tugged them off and dropped them to the ground.

"It looks like," he said cockily, "I do not have to go anywhere with you after all."

Blanca held her ground, spine stiff.

Otto walked over at a leisurely pace, expression predatory. The balance of power had undoubtedly shifted in his favor. Blanca felt it close around her like the raging river had done the night before, choking her with fear.

She had no gun, no knife, and no help. And without those things, she had no safety.

Otto stood just in front of her, blue eyes looking down on her arrogantly from his great height. He made no gesture toward her, no threatening motion. Instead, he simply called upon that menace that was so easy for men of his size and strength—that invisible violence that made the threat of force as potent as the act itself.

Blanca glared up at him, eyes shining with anger at her own disadvantage. There was really nothing she could do to stop him from doing—well, *anything*. Her weakness filled her with fury. And god, she had tried. She had tried for so many years.

"I should kill you myself," Otto said softly. "After everything you have done, I should take this knife and put it in your neck. But instead, I think I will throw you over my shoulder, walk you to the nearest German camp, and hand you over to the first officer I see."

Blanca clenched her trembling hands. "You'd be in for one hell of a walk."

Otto looked surprised, but not displeased, at her response. "I am sure," he murmured. Blanca's heart hammered in her chest. Neither of them moved. For a split second, Otto's eyes flickered to the side.

Suddenly, he shoved her hard, and Blanca fell to the earth with a surprised grunt. As soon as she hit the ground, the tree branch that had been just behind her head seconds before shattered under an explosion of gunfire.

Blanca jerked up on her elbow, and that was when she realized Otto was on the ground too, having thrown himself in the opposite direction.

"What the *hell*?" A man in uniform appeared some thirty feet away, and when he saw them both still alive, he shouted to people behind him. "Who the hell is that?" she cried out, but Otto was already on his feet, and before she knew what was happening, he had snatched her off the ground.

"Up, up!"

More shouts rang out, and gunfire destroyed the tree trunk next to them. Blanca bolted with Otto, fleeing into the dense woods and away from the river in a flurry of motion. More soldiers appeared in front of them and raised their guns, and Otto skidded to a halt before grabbing

Blanca's arm and yanking her out of the way as gunfire sailed right through where they'd been only seconds before. He pulled her behind a tree and ducked low.

"Who is that?" Blanca whispered frantically.

Otto's blue eyes flashed with a malice she'd never seen before, not even on the first day they'd met. "Russians," he snarled. "What are they doing so far across the border?"

Blanca's lips parted. "Russians?" she whispered, ducking against heavy footsteps nearby. "Wait, this is—"

Damn, it's 1943.

"This is when they start!" The Russians were on their way into Poland to start the beginning of the end— the final movements on the eastern front to cripple the Germans and finish the war.

"What are you talking about?" Otto growled, but Blanca never got the chance to answer because the Russian soldiers spotted them hiding in the brush and opened fire. She swore fiercely and raced off with Otto on her heels. Together, they ran through the underbrush to escape the growing horde of Russian soldiers.

"Maybe I can talk to them!" Blanca shouted to Otto as they ran. "Russians are American allies!"

Otto stopped and looked for an escape route. "Russians are on *Russia's* side," he told her flatly. "And if they catch us, they will kill me and do worse to you."

His words rooted Blanca to her spot, but she had no time to respond because a group of soldiers suddenly swarmed them. One man grabbed Blanca and pinned her arms against her sides. She shrieked and kicked furiously, pulling up her legs with all her core strength and swinging them wildly. The soldier hadn't expected this, and he toppled over before dropping her. Blanca let out a yell before turning and slamming her fist into the man's exposed jaw. He sank like a stone, but another pair of men were on her in an instant.

Otto tried to pull them off, but the end of a rifle came soaring into his stomach and he fell back with a choked noise. The nearest soldier grabbed his arm, and Otto punched him hard in the throat, fighting like a man possessed.

It was no use. Blanca felt a fist land in her stomach, and that was all the opening the soldiers needed to twist her wrists behind her spine and shove her to her knees. The ragged forest floor pressed through her blue jeans and cut into her kneecaps.

Otto continued to fight, but the Russians managed to subdue him at last. When they jerked his arms behind him, a painful crack sounded, and Otto hissed in pain. Blanca winced, hoping his arm wasn't broken. Otto let out a brief grunt of pain as the soldiers shoved him to his knees alongside her.

The fighting ended suddenly, and the Russian soldiers, some bleeding and heaving from the altercation, looked down at Otto and Blanca with undisguised contempt. From behind the line of disgruntled soldiers, an officer emerged, his lip curled as he looked down at them.

When he spoke, his voice was low and deep. The Russian language sounded rambling and nonsensical to Blanca, but when the officer looked down at Otto and touched the barrel of his gun to the Nazi patch on Otto's flight suit, the scorn was obvious.

Otto lifted his head, a black and purple bruise swelling around his left eye, and he spat on the ground at the Russian's shoes. The hatred in his expression was staggering. As hostile as he had been to Blanca and the others, he had never looked at them like that.

The Russian officer narrowed his eyes on Otto, and he walked a few additional steps in his direction before winding up and punching Otto in the stomach with all his might. Otto wheezed and fell forward, but he didn't pass out. Blanca watched warily as the soldiers patted him down.

One of them found Blanca's knife in Otto's pocket, and her heart twisted when he kept it for himself. After a few seconds, she looked up imploringly at the Russian officer.

"Sir, please, I am an American and—"

WHACK.

Her lips parted in shock, and her head twisted sideways from the slap. The other soldiers chuckled behind their leader, and Blanca slowly closed her mouth, cheeks red with fury. She swept her tongue over the bloody crack in her lip and fell silent.

Otto looked over at her and then back up to the Russian officer before saying something scathing in German that likely none of them could understand.

The Russian officer ignored him, instead walking up to Blanca and grabbing her chin so that she was forced to look up at him. He spoke mockingly and tightened his grip until Blanca winced. In a flash, she remembered Otto's words.

They will kill me and do worse to you.

Fear pierced her heart, but she kept her gaze steady and her expression hard.

The Russian officer let go of her chin with a jerk, then seized her upper arm and pulled her to a stand. He examined her clothes, brows furrowed as he looked over her blue jeans and t-shirt. He asked a few questions to his soldiers, obviously confused by her outfit.

Without warning, Otto burst out of the lax grip of his captors and attacked the nearest two, quickly embroiling them in a brawl. The outburst was easily dealt with; no matter how well Otto fought, there were too many of them, and the only apparent result was that he was subdued again. Now, though, he was even more grievously injured than before.

Blanca grimaced when two men held Otto by his arms and a third laid into him with a fierce punch, once, twice, and then a third time before finally stopping. Heaving, Otto struggled to stay on his feet, and Blanca wondered why he had even bothered.

The Russians seemed to be wondering the same thing, but they simply hauled him up and looked to their commanding officer. The man barked an order, and the others began walking. The soldiers holding Blanca pulled her hands forward and placed a pair of metal handcuffs on her wrists, locking them in place. They did the same to Otto, then shoved him onward.

The group began to move. Where to, Blanca couldn't say. The Russian officer called in something over a radio, and a gruff voice responded. *Shit*, she thought with real panic. They'd been ordered to take them somewhere, which could only mean more soldiers. *And if Otto is right...*

Her fingers grasped weakly for the rosary wrapped up her arm, but one of the soldiers saw her reaching for it and took hold of her wrist to examine the beads. When he saw that it was a rosary, he scoffed and shoved her arm down again.

Blanca fought with herself not to fight foolishly like Otto had done. She would lose. She knew that.

Instead, she twisted her fingers to grab the crucifix of her rosary beads, and she prayed. Her throat burned again, and her sides ached. "Hail holy Queen, mother of mercy, our life, our sweetness, and our hope," she whispered rapidly, eyes closed and fingers stroking the beads. "To thee we do cry, poor banished children of Eve; to thee we send up our sighs, mourning and weeping in this valley of tears."

The Russian soldier leading her looked back at her mumbling, but when he saw she was praying, he rolled his eyes and looked forward again. Blanca finished her quick prayers, and when she opened her eyes again, her gaze landed on Otto.

He was watching her closely from a few feet away, where he was also being led by armed soldiers. As soon as their gazes met, he flicked his fingers to show her something concealed in his hand.

He had a grenade.

Suddenly, Blanca understood the tussle from before. He hadn't been trying to get away at all; the little thief had stolen a weapon. Her eyes quickly darted forward again, heart pounding.

He couldn't use the grenade with them all packed in like this, moving in a tight unit as they were. They had to spread the soldiers out, make some space. The wheels in Blanca's head started turning, and she moved her fingers continually along the beads. She tasted blood again in her mouth, just a hint, and an idea hit her.

Eyes shifting to Otto's meaningfully, she gave him the faintest of nods. He responded with the same, and they kept walking in silence until Blanca began her prayers anew, this time muttering more loudly. After a few seconds, she coughed hard. The Russian soldier behind her prodded her forward unpityingly.

Blanca swallowed and kept walking. Minutes later, she coughed again, this time hacking rather hard and gasping. Some soldiers stopped and looked at her warily, and Otto caught on immediately, pulling away from Blanca and pointing as if in a panic. He spoke in rapid German, seemingly in warning.

Blanca leaned over her knees and kept coughing, doing her best to look ill, which was terribly easy after getting tossed around in the river all night.

The Russian nearest her called out to his commanding officer, and the man turned back to them with a grunt. He pointed at Blanca fiercely, and the Russian soldier beside her tried to make her move again. Blanca continued to make great gasping noises.

The Russians quickly grew restless and uncertain, holding their guns level but moving away from her. Blanca swatted at her chest as if to stop the coughing, but then she heaved in a deep breath and stumbled, swaying on her feet. She reached out for a soldier, as if for help, and the man quickly jumped away from her.

The Russians began yelling to each other, clearly alarmed.

So Blanca finished it off with one last great hack, and this time, she bit her tongue very hard. Blood spilled into her mouth, and with that, she turned to the nearest soldier, clutched her throat, and heaved with such force that she sprayed his face with blood.

The men, terrified of disease, scattered like doves.

The soldier she'd bled on panicked and ran straight to the river's edge to wash his face while the other men jumped away and yanked their shirt collars over their mouths in fear. The commanding officer tried to corral

them, but it was obvious he didn't want to get any closer
to Blanca, either, who stood in the center of a wide-open
circle with blood splattered over her parted lips.

The commanding officer let out a shout, and then he
raised his gun.

Blanca gave one last sickly gasp. She stumbled toward
the man with outstretched arms, and then, in a flash,
jumped and rolled to the side.

Otto reacted instantly, slamming his elbow into the
face of the nearest panicked Russian and bolting. As soon as
he had cover, he took off the pin and rolled the grenade into
the cluster of confused men. Only a handful of them even
spotted it. The rest were blown sky-high, and their bodies
came back down as scattered limbs and bleeding torsos.

"Shit!" Blanca shrieked, barely getting out of the way
of the shrapnel as she dove into the brush and tossed up
her arms. Dirt and blood rained down on them, as did the
great echoing *BOOM* of the explosion. "Damn it, Zimmler!
You couldn't have waited two more freaking seconds!"

"Shut up!" he yelled from behind a tree somewhere.

Gunfire exploded through the air, and Blanca
screeched, then scrambled forward on her elbows and
knees as best she could with the handcuffs still on. The
group of soldiers was now down to six, but she and Otto
were still vastly outnumbered.

That didn't stop the German, though. He appeared
from behind a group of trees and wrapped his cuffed hands
around a Russian soldier's neck, tightening the chain
against the man's throat and then wrenching it to the side
so that it snapped. As soon as the soldier was down, Otto
picked up the gun and returned fire through the smoke
and dirt, causing the Russians to scatter.

You are not outfighting me, you Aryan son of a bitch,
Blanca thought crossly, and she leaped up to sprint toward
the nearest soldier only to find he was the bastard who'd
taken her knife. Blanca jumped on his back, slipped the
knife from his pocket, and jammed it into his neck. The
man collapsed in a pool of blood. Others turned on her,
but Blanca picked up the rifle and rushed behind a cluster
of trees. She slammed right into Otto, who grabbed her
arm, turned her around, and pointed. "Take that side!"

Without a second thought, Blanca shifted the rifle
onto her shoulder and opened fire on three soldiers trying
to get closer to them. Gunfire blazed over them, cutting
up trees and blasting through branches. One bullet grazed
Blanca's bare arm and she yelled out, then twisted back
behind the tree and clutched it. Seared skin smoldered on
her arm, and the blood felt red-hot as it trickled down her
elbow, but she didn't have time to stop.

With a yell, Blanca pulled up the gun again and sent
a bullet through the nearest Russian soldier, knocking him
clean off his feet and to the ground. At her back, Otto did
the same and took down two more, but the commanding
officer was advancing on them. At the last second, he
reached for a grenade at his belt.

"Look out!" Blanca shouted to Otto, and they were
forced to pull down their guns and run as the grenade
sailed through the air, landing where they had been
seconds before and blasting the earth apart.

Otto stumbled at the force of the blast behind him, but
Blanca caught a tree trunk and pulled him around with her. The
remaining soldiers crashed into them and Blanca was thrown to
the forest floor. The soldier bore down on her, trying to wrestle
her rifle away, but Blanca managed to bring up her knees

and kick as hard as she could, landing a blow in his stomach. The man rolled off her, and Blanca swiftly followed, coming out on top and slamming the butt of her rifle into his face.

The soldier's nose and teeth collapsed with a *crunch*, and she repeated the motion again, then twice more, until the other man's face was a bloody mess and he was almost certainly dead.

In a flash, she shifted up her gun, blasted the nearest man off his feet, and locked her sights on the officer grappling with Otto. The officer had locked an arm around his neck, trying to choke him. Blanca pressed the gun against her shoulder and aimed. Otto, seeing her, elbowed the man roughly in the ribs and pulled away just a little.

Blanca took her shot. The bullet hit the officer above his right eye—not quite where Blanca had been aiming, but she'd always been guilty of pulling to the side.

The officer's grip fell away, and he slumped to the ground. Otto staggered away from him and slapped a hand over his heart. "*Meine gott*," he rasped. A nearby soldier moved as if to get up, and Otto looked over before kicking him hard in the ribs. The solder fell still again.

Blanca lowered her gun with a shaky exhale while Otto let out a relieved laugh. "Go to hell, Russian dogs!" he sneered at the bodies.

Blanca didn't celebrate with him. In her veins, she felt a heavy pulse. Her body ached, and her grip on the gun remained tense. Dully, she scanned the area around them.

Crushed faces. Gaping wounds. The scent of blood was suddenly overwhelming.

"Blanca?"

It was a long moment before she reacted. "Yeah?" she asked, voice soft in her confusion.

Otto tilted his head at her, but he didn't question her strangeness. "Let us find a key," he said, holding up his cuffed hands. With a thick swallow, Blanca followed him, stumbling a little. They checked the commanding officer first, but he didn't have it.

"That was a good shot," Otto commented as they searched.

Blanca shrugged, not willing to say anything more. Instead, she tossed the rifle strap over her back and shoved the gun out of the way so she could look around. After searching for a few minutes, her trembling fingers closed around the key in a soldier's pocket.

As she pulled it out, a photo fell with it.

Otto wandered over as Blanca stood, key in one hand and a black and white photograph in the other. It was an image of the soldier with his wife and two young children. Otto inspected the photo and lifted both brows. "Pity," he said, without much pity at all. "Foolish Russian bastard should have just stayed home." He took the picture from Blanca and ripped it up before tossing the fragments aside. Blanca said nothing, her eyes low.

In another timeline, that man might've lived.

With a flurry of anxious motion, Blanca quickly jabbed the small key into her handcuffs and unlocked them. She shoved the cuffs into her back pocket, and Otto held out his own expectantly.

But Blanca stopped, her dark eyes lifting to his. Her expression was largely blank; she had not even considered what she was about to do or say. The need to get back to Mateo was purely instinct, and it required no real forethought.

"No," she said hoarsely. "You're keeping yours." She shifted her gun back into her hands, eyes locked on

Otto's swollen and bloodied face. He gaped at her and then scowled. He still had a rifle on his back, but Blanca brought up her own in a flash. "Make one move towards that gun, and I will blow your head off."

Otto froze, though his stare did not waver. "I saved your life."

"I don't care. Put the gun on the ground."

"You do not fight fair." It wasn't an accusation; he simply sounded puzzled.

Blanca didn't lower her gun, but her heart raced. In her mind's eye, she saw him standing over her again, expression mocking and amused. It was a look she had seen so many times on so many faces.

"You're right. I don't fight fair. Because *life* isn't fair." The two stared hard at one another, and Blanca shifted her gun up. "Now, put your rifle on the goddamn ground. I will do whatever it takes to get back to Mateo, even if that means putting a bullet in your skull."

Otto watched her stoically. Then, without another word, he shifted the rifle off his shoulder, put it on the ground, and remained where he was, expressionless.

Blanca waited for a few seconds, wondering if it was a trick. When he didn't move again, she walked over and picked up the gun. She jabbed her rifle in the other direction, and they set about picking up any useful supplies. Not a word passed between them, and each time Otto came across a weapon, he handed it to Blanca.

Blanca handed him two bags to carry, and although he was quite injured, he took them without complaint, and they began walking back upriver.

Thankfully, they encountered no more Russian soldiers.

━❦━

"What was your job?" Otto asked after nearly an hour of walking. "In the Army?"

Blanca kept her gaze straight forward. Her chest hurt, and she scratched at it absently. "I'm a combat medic."

"A nurse, you mean?"

"No," Blanca said flatly without looking at him. "A *combat medic*."

Otto looked confused. "You were in the field?" Blanca shifted her narrow eyes in his direction, face hard, and Otto's expression grew thoughtful. "I did not realize America let women on the battlefield. On the bases, of course, but in combat?"

"Yeah," she said stiffly, hoping he would leave it at that.

He didn't, of course. "Where did you fight?"

Blanca drew in a deep breath. She couldn't tell him the truth, so she tiredly sorted out the history in her brain, trying to think of something suitable. "You haven't heard of it," she said at last, too exhausted to figure out something that made sense.

"Was it against the Japanese?" questioned Otto after a short pause. When Blanca didn't reply, he went on, "I read about their attack on your base in Hawai'i. They destroyed many of your ships. A clever plan, for savages. I do believe, though, that it was a mistake on their part."

"You have no idea."

Just then, they heard a voice.

"Blanca!"

Her heart jumped into her throat, and the haze of misery disappeared in an instant. "Mateo?" she called out, hurrying along the river's edge. She looked across the water.

There, she saw Priya, Iain, and—*oh, god*—Mateo.

"Mateo!" she shouted. She rushed into the river and hurried across at the shallowest section. The water climbed all the way up to her hips, but she didn't care. She pushed herself through until she stumbled out on the other side and tackled her brother with a strangled gasp.

"I'm sorry, I'm sorry!" Mateo sobbed. "I'm sorry I yelled at you, I'm sorry!"

"It's okay, it's okay—"

Priya embraced her next, and Blanca hugged tightly in return. Iain smiled as soon as he saw her, and Blanca found herself wildly grateful he was alive, too. She hadn't even thought about him since they'd gotten swept down the river, but his gentle look—pleased, but not surprised, as if he'd been certain she would show up sooner or later—was a sudden and unexpected comfort.

Instead of hugging her, he looked across the river and raised a brow. "Still dragging around Zimmler, eh?" he asked mildly. Blanca actually laughed, hand still holding Mateo's arm. They all looked across the river to where Otto was waiting, eyes rolled skyward.

"Yeah," Blanca said. "Come on, he's not going to risk walking across. Zimmler, go to the rocks over there!"

With an annoyed look, Otto did as he was told, and he joined them shortly after.

"Damn, Blanca," Mateo said, finally noticing all the guns strapped to her back. "Where'd you get all those?"

"From a bunch of dead Russians," Otto answered for her as soon as he was close enough. He breezed right past them and leaned heavily against a tree, where he slid to the ground. "Now if you will excuse me, I need a nap. All of you, shut your mouths."

True to his word, he closed his eyes and fell asleep.

Priya stared. "Wow, you guys had a *day*, huh?"

"I said, shut up!"

⬿⬿⬿

Bavaria, Germany
1932

"*Blut und Ehre!*" chorused the boys.

The man in front of them nodded with satisfaction. Otto stood straight and proud, shoulders back and head held high. His stance drew the attention of their leader, and the older man gave Otto a look of approval. This was not uncommon; Otto was tall and strong for his age, bigger than most fourteen-year-old boys, and he had the look of a true German. Even amongst his peers, he stood out.

The boys were assigned their activities, and they spent the rest of the week in a flurry of exciting competitions. At the end of each assignment, they thrust their arms in the air and declared their allegiance to Nazi Germany.

To give their lives for country, the leaders told them, was the ultimate honor.

For the first time in his young life, Otto felt a deep sense of responsibility. Germany had struggled, but his generation would elevate their beloved homeland beyond imagining. By the end of the week, though, he was looking forward to a challenge of a different sort—a visit from the German League of Girls.

That night, the girls' leaders brought them over to the boys' camp, and they all sang together before listening to speeches about the importance of loyalty and the great responsibility of the youth to keep German blood pure and strong.

Next to him, Otto's friend Erich snickered. "I definitely plan to do my part in keeping the German population strong," he whispered, eyeing one of the girls nearby. Otto grinned and agreed.

Soon, the formal meetings ended, and the two groups mingled. The adult leaders, it seemed, had mysteriously vanished, and soon enough, pairs of teenagers were doing the same. Otto became interested in a girl he knew from school: a bright-eyed brunette named Sophie. He remembered from their classes together that she liked art, and he'd always thought she was pretty, so he talked to her about painting.

Sophie, he discovered, was quick-witted and thoughtful. He liked that.

They walked together away from the others, and Otto offered to hold her hand. Sophie flushed and let him, clasping their fingers together. Once they were away alone, he leaned over and kissed her.

Sophie accepted the kiss, but after a few seconds, she pulled away. "Otto, you are very nice…and handsome, too."

"I agree," he said cheekily.

"It's just—I know what you want…and what the others are all doing."

"Yes, I know, too. I can hear Erich all the way from here." He pointed.

Sophie's cheeks grew red. "We can all hear him," she muttered. "But I don't want to do that."

Otto huffed. "Why not? I thought you liked me."

"I do," Sophie insisted. "I just don't think it's a good idea."

Otto stepped closer and touched her arm sweetly. "But you heard the camp leaders. We're the future of Germany. That's why they brought us all together here. They say we are ready."

"How can they know something like that, Otto? About all of us?"

"They're our leaders," he pointed out. "They know what's best for us."

"But how, Otto? Don't you wonder?" she asked desperately. "How can they know all of us? How can they know me? Or you? They might know what is best for Germany, but I am not Germany. I am Sophie." She looked away, eyes thoughtful. "It doesn't seem right to me. We are not all the same. And if I am going to be with someone, I want it to be *my* decision, not Germany's."

Otto listened, and when she was done, he said grumpily, "If we go back now, everyone will know we didn't do it, and they will make fun of us."

Sophie frowned. "I know," she whispered. "I'm sorry."

Otto made an annoyed face and flapped his arms. "Fine." He grabbed her hand and led her behind a tree. Sophie grew worried and tried to pull away.

"Otto!" she exclaimed in alarm.

But he just tugged her down onto the grass, and once they were both settled away from the others, he pulled out a bag of marbles and some candy, which he offered to her.

"We will stay here for a while," Otto said simply. "Is that alright?"

A slow smile spread over Sophie's face. "Thank you." She leaned over and kissed his cheek, and Otto made a face before gracelessly shoving a piece of candy in his mouth to show his displeasure. Sophie giggled.

"The camp leaders told us not to bring games and candy," she pointed out.

Otto shrugged. "I know, but I am not very good at following orders."

"If you cannot follow orders," Sophie said slyly, "you will not be a very good soldier."

Otto leaned back against the tree and laughed.

"Probably not," he agreed.

CHAPTER 5

*It is always more difficult to fight
against faith than against knowledge.*
—Adolf Hitler

It was hard to say how the next few days passed. Blanca was sure some things happened and words were said, but mostly she could only say later that she saw Mateo smiling and relaxed for the first time in ages. They had food they'd taken from the Russians (which Otto detested but ate anyway), so their gnawing hunger was put off for a while. They also had guns, which were a great comfort, particularly to Blanca.

Unfortunately, the harsh weather grew worse as the days passed, but Blanca and Otto had taken some clothes from the Russians and given them to those who could wear them, so they managed. One of the heavy coats would have fit Otto perfectly, but he refused to wear it.

"I will die in German rags before I live in Russian furs," he told her, and he meant it.

The others happily bundled up. Blanca offered one of the rifles to Iain, but the Irishman quickly waved her off. "I don't really like guns," he told her. "I'd rather not use one if I don't have to."

Otto made a loud noise of disdain. "What do you even do?" he asked Iain. "You do not fight, you do not shoot.

Even the skinny boy and little colored girl are tougher than you."

Priya and Mateo's jaws dropped in unison.

"He just said the word 'colored,'" Priya said in disbelief, before going in a whisper, "…Like a *grandpa*."

"What?" Otto exclaimed. "'Colored' is the nice word!" Everyone else kept walking, and Otto huffed. "Colored is what my mother says, and she is a very nice person," he muttered to himself.

"Only brutes think fighting is all a man can do," went on Iain pointedly, directing Otto's attention back to him.

Otto snorted derisively. "Better a 'brute' than a…" he paused, trying to think. "Oh, what is the English? I cannot remember. A word that means a sad little man who spends more time with books than women."

Iain sighed loudly.

"Anyway, I should have a gun," Otto went on, although it was clear he did not expect to receive one. After another half hour of walking, he picked up his pace and appeared next to Blanca. "The Russians called in a report about us," he reminded her.

Blanca frowned. She'd forgotten. "Do you know what they said?"

"No," he said. "I do not speak their barbaric language. But, as a military man, I am sure they gave our details and descriptions. It is what I would have done. And once their bodies are discovered, that means the Russians will be actively looking for us. You and I, specifically."

"Do you really think they would kill us?"

Otto looked at her from the corner of his still-bruised eye. "After what you saw, how can you doubt it?"

Blanca sighed. "Well, just keep an eye out. You can't get home if you get shot or captured by Russians, and neither can we."

"I could help protect us," he said firmly, "if I had a gun. You are leaving me defenseless." He held up his hands and rattled the handcuffs.

"I already told you," Blanca growled. "I don't trust you. You're not getting a gun, and I'm not taking those cuffs off."

"What have I ever done to you?" Otto asked, as if he'd never committed a foul deed in his life.

"You said you were going to drag me to a German camp and leave me with an officer!"

Otto shrugged dismissively. "Well, I probably would not have actually done that. Too much work, and I am sure other German soldiers will dispose of you eventually."

For a split second, Blanca believed him. Then she remembered the fight with the Russians and the feeling dissipated. Otto acted careless, and his very demeanor was like that of a cocky teenage boy: reckless, and sometimes destructive, but ultimately without the intention or means of doing real harm.

And yet.

He had savagely killed those Russian soldiers with next to no remorse, and he had done it with a surprising amount of skill. Who was to say what he might do?

The most dangerous thing about Otto was how good he was at pretending otherwise. She would not let the stupid, boyish behavior fool her any longer, though. Without saying another word, she picked up her pace and left Otto behind. He didn't try to catch up with her again.

Later that night, they camped.

Blanca sat with her back against a tree and focused on cleaning the guns while also keeping an eye on Otto. Iain built a fire before settling down with something in his hands, which he fiddled with for about half an hour.

The next morning, as they prepared to leave, Iain appeared next to Otto. "Good morning," he said cheerfully, and then he took the thing in his hands and zapped Otto with it.

"AGH!" Otto jumped, cringing away from Iain. "*What the hell was that?*"

"This," explained Iain with a smile, "is a taser. I made it out of a battery and some metal wire. And from now on, every time you say something racist, sexist, or offensive in any way, I am going to zap you with it."

Otto gawked, lips parted.

"Hopefully, you will start choosing your words more carefully," Iain went on sweetly. "But if you don't, I'll just keep tasing you. Or better yet, I'll hand it over to Blanca."

Blanca grinned slowly. Otto, on the other hand, looked furious. "One day, Irishman, I will not have these binds on my hands." He waved the handcuffs. "And as soon as they are off, you will be the first one I come after."

"In that case," Iain said lightly, "don't expect to take me by surprise."

The two observed each other balefully until Otto scowled and walked off. Iain, unbothered, put the taser in his pocket. When he caught Blanca's amused expression, he winked.

Blanca bit back a grin, but it must have shown in her eyes because Iain's smile grew. They started their morning hike a few minutes later.

For some days after, their trek on foot remained uninterrupted. They traveled mostly through the woods, sticking within sight of the river, but never out in the open. They stayed far from the roads and listened to the radio Blanca had taken from the truck.

Otto translated, but only when he felt like it. He would never tell them exactly where the Germans were, only how to avoid them. When Blanca once suspected him of lying, she reminded him how their last encounter with Germans had turned out.

"You said you wouldn't help us cause harm to Germans," she reminded him with a dangerous glint in her eye. "You screw us, Zimmler, and I will kill every last German I see, including you."

Otto set his jaw grimly at this, and since then, they had not encountered anyone—friend, foe, or anything in between.

Unfortunately, the Germans weren't the only threat on the horizon. Mateo was fearful of encountering wolves again, and Priya could barely sleep at night thinking about Russians coming after them like they had Blanca and Otto. Iain remained steadfast in his cheerful optimism, but in the quiet moments when he thought no one was looking, Blanca saw fear creep into his expression.

Each new day seemed colder and shorter than the last. The sky no longer brightened in the morning and darkened at night but instead remained drab and colorless throughout the day until the dusk snuffed it out like a last lonely cinder. Each bitter gust of wind snatched a little more of their optimism, and soon even Otto grew despondent. On some nights, he would sit quietly and listen to the distant racket of warfare. "Those are not Germans," he would say, looking—as he did only rarely— truly anxious.

Blanca managed to pull out Mateo's history book one
night without being seen so she could scan the section on
World War II. She knew they were in late 1943, and she
knew the Russians were at least this far. What else could
she discover? For hours, she worked to set up a timeline for
their area. The war was winding down, she realized, but it
wasn't over. Even if they remained in this time period for
an entire year (a thought she refused to entertain), there
would still be fighting. Then the Russians would settle
there, and that was hardly any more comfort than the Nazi
occupation.

Blanca closed the book with a snap, a painful knot
building in her chest.

That night, she leaned against a tree and closed her
eyes, trying to envision what was waiting for her back in
Texas. She needed something to hope for, something to
give her courage. Mateo had friends, maybe even a crush,
and Priya had her parents. Iain, likewise, probably had a
family and a home he was missing.

But when Blanca closed her eyes and thought of
home, nothing came to mind.

There was the apartment she had rented just two
months before, which was barren of furniture and had
nothing on the walls. There were clothes still in boxes—
mostly things she hadn't worn in years—and a few
scattered photographs. There was a book she'd bought in
the airport on her way home and hadn't started, as well as
a single ratty pillow she'd had since the beginning of time,
even before all the foster homes. That was it.

The only real semblance of belonging she had was
Mateo. He was her home. Anywhere else was just a place.

"Hungry?"

Blanca looked up in surprise to see Iain, ghastly white under the pale moon, with his hand extended. Blanca tried to smile and winced instead, accepting the dried meat and eating without enthusiasm. Iain hesitated, then sat down with her.

"Things have been going well," he said, keeping his voice soft. Priya and Mateo were already asleep; Priya had been shivering like mad in her sleeping bag, so Iain had put his heavy coat over her and she'd finally relaxed enough to fall into an antsy doze.

"I guess." Blanca chewed on the tough meat without really tasting it. Her eyes lifted to the moonlight where it was scattered among the pine needles overhead. "Just feels like everything around here looks the same. Trees and the river and dirt and rocks. It doesn't feel like we're getting anywhere."

"We are, though," Iain said encouragingly. "We'll be at the coast soon."

"But how are we going to get on a boat?" Blanca asked, frustration prickling under her skin. "How are we going to pay? Talk to people? Hell, how are we even going to get into the city?"

"We'll figure it out," Iain insisted comfortingly. He reached out as if to touch her, but before Blanca could react, he jerked away, placing his hands back in his lap as he cleared his throat. Blanca eyed him uncertainly.

This wasn't the first time he'd done something like that. She had once seen him reach out to Mateo, only to pull awkwardly away before making contact. He also seemed nervous any time Blanca inspected his wounds, and he'd once asked her—with flushed cheeks—if she'd washed her hands after. *Great*, she'd thought. Combat was the last place for a germophobe.

Iain stirred next to her, and she wondered about his strange behavior, but all he did was pick up the crucifix at the end of her rosary and place it in her hand. Blanca gripped it immediately and held her clenched fists against the front of her bowed head.

Iain watched her, patient and quiet in his spot. When she looked up, he pointed to the sky. "Too bad we don't have a record player." When Blanca stared at him in confusion, he laughed quietly. "I could use some Pink Floyd."

Blanca's muddled brain finally made the connection. "Dark Side of the Moon?"

"An album suited for literally any situation," he said, and Blanca finally let out a small laugh and swatted at the teary corner of her eye.

"Yeah," she said quietly, gaze turning up to follow his to the sky. "I guess that's true."

"Reminds me of how I wanted to be an astronaut when I was small."

Blanca let out an amused huff. She was glad for the distraction of idle chatter. "So you were that kid," she muttered.

"Aye, I was." He grinned over at her. "Always into things. Always the kid with questions."

Blanca couldn't relate. Questions got you hit. Or worse, they got you answers.

"It did get me into trouble from time to time," he admitted cheekily, as if echoing her thoughts. "I was a bit of a pyromaniac. You would not believe how many everyday items are crazy explosive."

Blanca's lips twitched.

"Fortunately," he went on airily, "all that insanity matured into a love for physics, and that's what I study now." He looked over her face, expression softening. "What about you? Did you always want to join the Army?"

Blanca's smile was aimed at her knees and looked more like a grimace. "No. I, uh…" She cleared her throat. "I wanted to be a doctor."

"A doctor," Iain repeated. "I can imagine that."

Blanca's taut smile grew tighter. "I can't."

"Why not?"

"People like me don't go to medical school, Iain." She reached up and scratched absently at her scalp.

"Why not?" he asked. "You'd be great at it. You're smart, you're hardworking—"

"Medical school takes something like ten *years*," Blanca cut in roughly. "And it costs thousands of dollars. What would I have done for ten years of college? Not work? What would Mateo have done?" She let out a bitter laugh. "And it's not like I'd even get in. I was never good in school." She rubbed at her face. "Would've been a waste of my time."

Iain waited a long time before speaking.

"I still think you would have been wonderful at it," he told her sincerely. "Anything you missed in school can always be learned later. The kind of stuff that can't be taught—like how well you handle pressure, and your critical-thinking skills—those are the things you've got like no one else I've ever met." He let his head fall against the tree, his face turned toward hers. "I'd bet on you saving my life any day of the week."

"With a gun."

Iain shook his head. "With your head," he said. "And your heart."

Blanca fell quiet. A voice called out to her from a few feet away.

"Blanca?"

It was Mateo.

Blanca looked up, then stood, using the end of her rifle to push herself to a stand. Iain got up as well, and they rounded the tree to find Mateo sitting next to the dying fire. "I can't sleep," her little brother whispered. Blanca sat next to him and Mateo fell into her arms while Iain settled reclined against his bag.

"Good night," Iain murmured to Blanca.

Blanca looked across the clearing at him. She opened her mouth to say in the same, but the words caught in her throat. *Good night*, she thought, feeling that old anger.

They traveled without incident for one more day before the rain returned.

Soaked to the bone, the group continued on as best as they could. The water was freezing, and their warm jackets turned into oppressive weights, dragging them down at the shoulders so that each step was harder than the last.

Priya's sandals finally broke, and they tore away as useless strips of plastic. Blanca was the only one among them even close to Priya's shoe size, so she took off her sneakers and gave them to her. After that, Blanca trudged through the dense, sodden ground with bare feet.

"You're going to get sick," Iain whispered to her, looking concerned.

"I'll be fine," she responded gruffly.

They slogged on, finally breaking away from the trees to cross a walking bridge that led over the river and down into a valley. Here, the water sloshed up to their knees, and Iain ended up carrying Priya onto his back because the water came so high on her tiny frame. Blanca wasn't much bigger than Priya, but she refused Iain's help. She did notice, though, that Otto kept a close eye on her as they crossed. Once, when she slipped against a rock, he stopped and waited for her to recover before moving on.

They camped that night in an abandoned barn settled at the end of a marshy pasture. The roof was ancient and only intact on one side, which meant the air inside was frigid. Huddled together, they managed a small fire and then peeled off their clothes to dry near the flames. All thoughts of modesty were lost in their desperation; they had to dry fast, or else Iain's prediction would come true and they'd *all* get sick.

Blanca pulled off her t-shirt and jeans and laid them out on a plank of wood near the fire as she carefully steered clear of the many pockets of rain pouring in through the damaged roof. The warmth of the fire spread through her body like needles, painful but necessary.

Iain turned away from the others to lay out the long-sleeve button-up shirt he'd been wearing. Before he came to the fire, he pulled a sleeping bag over his shoulders and kept it over his arms, with only his hands visible. Blanca wondered if he was self-conscious about his body, even though there didn't seem to be anything wrong with it. So far as she could tell, he was just skinny, like Mateo. His pale skin bruised easily, though. She could see faint marks on his arms before he pulled the sleeping bag tighter around his torso.

Otto stripped down as soon as he was able, apparently not at all concerned with nudity. He was also completely unabashed in his inspection of Blanca and Priya in their underwear. "Are you sure you have to be a homosexual?" he asked Mateo thoughtfully, and then he pointed to Priya.

"Surely you could just date her. She has the body of a boy, at least." He snickered.

Priya picked up a stray piece of wood and hurled it at Otto's head. "Iain!" she whined, pouting.

Iain zapped Otto without even looking, and Otto yelped and fell silent.

Blanca rolled her eyes and settled in front of the fire. Honestly, she cared very little about looking at the others. To her, there was nothing impressive or appealing about a man's body. It was either an instrument of violence or a fragile, breakable thing she had to take care of.

In the pit, the flames crackled and popped, searing away the freezing-cold droplets sticking stubbornly to her skin. She rubbed at her arms, wishing for nothing more than a warm, dry sweater. The desire for comfort faded from her mind as she looked into the fire and recalled late nights in Afghanistan and how unexpectedly the temperatures had dropped at sunset. It hadn't been a cold like this, though. The chill there had been dry and arid, stagnant in the worst way. A part of her wondered what was worse: those cold desert nights, tense and unnatural, or the wet chill of Poland, which seeped into her bones and coated her lungs, making it hard to breath.

Ultimately, she decided it didn't matter. A ripped fingernail and a papercut both bled.

After a while, she took a seat on her newly dried sleeping bag and curled her arms around her knees. Otto sat near her, having pulled off his flight suit and the shirt he wore underneath. He didn't make any additional comments to Priya, who was now curled up next to Mateo and hidden under a sleeping bag. He did, however, stare quite openly at Blanca.

Unfortunately, he wasn't leering at her. That she could deal with. Instead, he was looking at her scars: the circular burns on her forearms, the thin white lines near her wrists, the poorly healed puncture wounds around her ribs from a grenade she'd been too slow to escape. The list went on and on.

The group was quiet when she pulled an arm around her head and looked at him between the gap in her elbow. "Can you not?" she muttered at last, almost pleading.

Otto blinked at her, then looked away like she asked.

Nearby, Iain sat down and stoked the fire. When he was done, he reached around in the pockets of his drying slacks and pulled out a ballpoint pen. As Blanca watched, he drew a circle around his ring finger again, darkening the line that was already there but had faded in the rain. *Of all the things for him to do on a night like this, why that?* She thought about asking him, but old habits forced her to internalize the curiosity instead.

<hr />

In the morning, the rain stopped, and they were able to move on.

One afternoon, they came across the ruinous remains of a railroad station. The building was in shambles, and the tracks in front of it had been destroyed by an explosive blast. Human remains, flesh worn away to bone, dotted the area.

Blanca glanced at Otto, who had the decency to shift his eyes away. Clearly, the Germans had taken the station out of commission for one reason or another. In this era of warfare, transport was everything, and the railroads were the lifelines of the country. Without them, supplies and troops were difficult to come by.

They poked around the battered station in search of anything useful. Fortunately, Blanca was able to pull some workable shoes from a discarded suitcase; this meant that she was no longer barefoot. The shoes were ill-fitting and uncomfortable, but they were better than nothing.

They left the railroad station behind and continued on. The nights grew desperately cold—Blanca couldn't help but wonder when it would finally snow—but they were often able to occupy themselves to the point of distraction.

Otto was the best at this; he taught Mateo and Priya how to play poker using the cards he'd gotten from the Polish family, and each night when the sun had vanished and their camp was set up, they would all gather around the fire to play. It soon became a regular competition, one that had no real stakes—except bragging rights, of course.

"No, no!" counseled Otto, now behind Mateo and looking at his cards. "See, here…" He pointed at a card before his eyes flickered up to Priya and Blanca, who were watching the two men with snarky expressions. Otto whispered something to Mateo, and then more loudly, he proclaimed, "It would be a shameful dishonor to lose to Priya!"

"You lost to her two rounds ago!" Mateo protested with a laugh.

"Yes, but I lost with dignity. You just got lucky."

Blanca whispered instructions and tips to Priya, who drank in the knowledge eagerly. "You are going down, Mateo!" she crowed, laughing, and Blanca grinned.

"Hell yeah! Beat him!"

"Hey, you're supposed to root for me!" Mateo exclaimed.

"Not while you've got Zimmler as your coach."

"Ignore her," Otto said arrogantly. "Soon, your training will pay off, and you will make us both a lot of money when we are not playing with broke peasants."

At last, the two remaining players unveiled their cards, with Mateo going first. "Two aces and two kings!" he declared proudly.

The words were barely out of his mouth before Priya slammed down her cards. "BOOM! Full house!" she exclaimed, and all the guys groaned while Priya burst out laughing. She flipped up both middle fingers before high-fiving Blanca, who laughed harder than she had in ages.

"Eugh," Otto said, shaking his head. "Defeat. Defeat and dishonor."

"You lost, too!"

"Irrelevant."

Their laughter was cut short by the sound of gunfire. It was far away, but not as far away as they would have liked. The group fell quiet, and Blanca picked up her gun and walked to the edge of their warm circle of light.

More gunfire, heavy and rapid. They peered out at the dark forest, but the pitch-black night kept its secrets. "Where is the radio?" Otto asked from behind her, and Blanca pointed to it on the ground.

Otto picked it up and listened. Only static greeted him at first, but German voices soon followed. Blanca couldn't understand the words, of course, but they sounded rushed and frantic. Otto frowned as he listened, and the rapid German continued.

Then there was a shout, and the radio went silent.

"What is it?" Mateo asked, coming up to them.

"They are not sure what is going on," Otto said of the radio, turning it off. "But it certainly sounds like an attack."

He walked up to Blanca and stepped further, peering into the darkness. The gunfire started once more, and now they could see flashes of light in the distance. Otto pointed.

"What is in that direction on the map?"

Iain picked it up and looked, tilting the map toward the glow of the campfire. "A village called Radymno."

"Radymno," Otto echoed, rubbing his jaw. "I remember hearing of that place. The Polish officer in charge of it fled like a coward as soon as our army arrived."

"So then what's going on right now?" Blanca asked, looking tensely at the far-off battle.

Otto shrugged. "I do not know. Polish resistance soldiers, perhaps. They are all in this forest, even now." Otto looked around at the dark trees, as if he might spot one even as he said it. He turned on the radio again, but there were no further communications from the Germans. The group opted to stay where they were, but they extinguished the fire and kept the talking to a minimum for the rest of the night.

When dawn broke, they left their camp. It didn't take long to spot the smoke from the village, and although they attempted to go far around the area to avoid being spotted, the river was high and wouldn't allow them to cross.

Within a half hour of walking, the cover of the forest thinned and a wide cobblestone street steered them in the direction of the village's smoldering remains.

Early morning light struggled through the dim sky and heavy smoke. Not a single ray of a warmth touched their faces as they walked in a slow, quiet dread. Around them, there was only stillness. The silence was strangely grating; their footsteps sounded overly loud against it.

At the front of the village stood a pair of brick columns meant to support a sign, but the sign itself was on the ground in pieces. The bricks were riddled with bullet holes. Blanca kept her guns poised and ready, eyes tensely searching the area. At last, the village came fully into view.

"Oh, no," Priya breathed.

The skeletal remains of a dozen houses and businesses lined the cobblestone street. Storefronts stood shattered and empty. On one black wall, a silhouette in the shape of a hunched man stood out as the only spot of white. Mateo stared at it, eyes wide, until Blanca gently tugged on his elbow and made him move.

Otto stooped down and picked up a bullet shell, which he turned in his fingers with a grim look.

All around them, shattered homes struggled to remain standing. With each icy breeze, wood groaned and shifted. A bird disturbed a nearby roof, and Blanca snapped her rifle in its direction when the beams crumbled and fell. The noise was outrageously loud, and they all froze in their spots. A few minutes passed, and nothing else happened.

"Where are all the people?" Priya whispered. "I don't see anyone." The words were barely out of her mouth when they rounded the corner, and her question was answered. "Oh my god!" she gasped, before running behind Mateo with a sob. Her fingers tugged at his shirt and she buried her face between his shoulder blades, tears pouring down her cheeks.

Iain was equally shocked, and Mateo stood frozen, lips parted in disbelief.

What seemed to be the entire population of the village lay in a haphazard pile, set upon each other in a great stack with all the same respect given to trash on the street. There were young women and old men, small children and even dogs.

Some were crushed. Others were burned. Most had been shot.

Blanca felt her stomach turn at the vacant expressions locked on their faces; many still had their eyes open, and frost tipped their eyelashes. A toddler slumped prominently in the front, and the vulgarity of it made bile rise in her throat.

"Jesus," she exhaled in a distressed fury, shoving her hand roughly through her hair.

Littered around the pile of corpses were the bodies of German soldiers. Otto came up behind Blanca, any hint of playfulness gone from his features. He looked from the soldiers to the Polish civilians, and that menace Blanca had noticed before—the one that called on an aggression he rarely demonstrated—simmered noticeably under his skin.

Then Blanca noticed his eyes move away from the bodies and darken even further. The change in his expression made her look, too, and that was when she spotted it.

The blue truck.

They moved at the same time, walking quickly at first and then picking up speed as the rest of the group looked on, bewildered. Otto reached the truck first and hurried around so he could rip open the driver's side door.

The farmer from the river fell out, hitting the ground with a nauseating crack.

Otto rushed to catch him, but it didn't matter. The man been dead for hours. Gently, Otto lowered him to the ground with the slightest tremble. Blanca's shining eyes looked to the crushed house next to the truck, and she rounded the corner to step over the broken remains.

Her expression crumbled before she could even decide what she was looking for: a hint, a hope, a confirmation.

She found, instead, a little doll with black button eyes. It was next to a tiny soot-covered arm, the only visible part of a body buried under the rubble. Blanca picked up the doll, squeezing it tight in her fingers. Her vision blurred.

Behind her, Otto slammed both fists on the hood of the truck. "DAMN IT!" he yelled furiously while the others looked on in horrified confusion. Blanca climbed shakily off the ruins of the house as Otto rounded to face her. "Those Russian dogs did this!" he exclaimed heatedly, marching right up to her. "Those goddamn Russians—" and then he lost all English, cursing instead in a torrent of rapid German. Finally, he shoved his cuffed hands at her. "Get these off me."

"I can't," she managed shakily, but Otto did not relent.

"Take these off so I can get to a plane and kill these Russian bastards! Now!" he demanded, and when Blanca said nothing, he seized her by the arms and yanked her to him.

"We – we can't, you could report us –"

"I do not care enough to report you!" Otto argued, shaking her. "All I want is to get back to my countrymen so I can kill these Russian demons and stop them from taking more German lives!"

"Guys, guys!" Priya said suddenly, pointing. "There's soldiers over there!"

Otto looked up and cursed again. "Russians! Get down!"

The group split and quickly dove for cover. Most everyone jumped to the right and ducked behind some debris, but Priya panicked and went left. She curled behind a collapsed wall, shaking violently.

The Russians approached, and behind the footsteps, clanking of guns, and shouts from officers, Blanca heard something else that made her blood turn cold—the gritty, heavy roll of an army tank. She shifted enough to peek out.

Two tanks, not one, rolled along the cobblestone street with soldiers flanking their sides. Trucks drove behind them, and each one had a machine gun poised at the top with a soldier behind it. There were probably more than a hundred men there, enough to occupy the whole village.

Most of them were laughing and smoking. Next to her, Otto trembled with rage, and without thinking, Blanca gripped his bare hand in hers. He looked at her, blue eyes like steel. "Do *not* attack," she whispered, fighting to keep the tremor from her voice. "You will get us all killed."

Otto's expression remained rigid and furious, and the effort to stay hidden seemed to test the very limits of his self-control, but he did as she asked, and the first group of soldiers strolled on without taking notice of them. A few feet away, Priya squeezed her eyes shut as the tanks passed, tears rolling down her cheeks.

"They will come down this way eventually," Otto whispered. "Someone needs to get her."

"I'll go," Blanca murmured.

"Give me a gun," Otto whispered back. "I will cover you."

Blanca hesitated, trying not to lose herself in the raw, visceral fear that welled in her chest. Otto lowered his head so their eyes stayed locked. "Trust," he whispered firmly, "must start somewhere."

Blanca held his gaze for a long moment. Finally, she reached over and unlocked his cuffs. Then she passed him a rifle, and Otto instantly drew it into his hands and nodded to her. "Go," he said.

Blanca glanced at Mateo, who nodded quickly, and then she picked up the rifle and hurried across to Priya, who instantly jumped into her arms.

Otto and Iain peeked over their wall, but the soldiers were walking in larger groups now, some straying from the strict march to peer curiously over bodies or items of value. One came dangerously close to where Blanca and Priya were hiding, and Otto raised his gun.

However, the Russian stayed only briefly before turning and heading back to the others. Otto exhaled, then gestured rapidly to Blanca and Priya. With Priya shielded behind her, Blanca hurried her back to the others, and they ducked behind the debris.

"Come on, let's go—" Blanca started, but a pair of trucks turned on their road and the group had to scramble back into their hiding place. Blanca turned swiftly and shoved them all back, and Priya managed to squeeze under a pile of rubble to make more room as the others ducked against a piece of roofing.

The group scarcely fit, and Blanca felt Iain at her side and Otto at her back, both of whom were gripping her and pulling her as far from the road as possible. At the right angle, they would be spotted, and there was nowhere to go. Blanca pulled her knees as close to her chest as she could, and for a split second, Otto's words flashed through her mind.

They will kill me and do worse to you.

A truck stopped just near them and a pair of boots appeared. Blanca felt her throat lock up. Her heartbeat pounded in her ears, and her eyes could do nothing but follow, with grim reluctance, each movement of the boots.

Behind her, Otto shifted just enough to aim his gun over her shoulder. It wasn't much comfort; a bullet would only stop the first person who looked. The rest of the army would be on them in seconds.

Blanca thought back to the small button-eyed doll, and she bit back the hateful noise that threatened to burst from her throat. *Sons of bitches,* she thought with a fresh wave of rage, the kind that felt sick and raw and unpredictable. Blanca knew this feeling well—better than she might have ever wished. It wasn't the type of anger she felt at an insult or offense. It didn't make her shout or yell or curse.

Instead, it was a cold fury that plagued her, a destructive force with all the callous indifference of a viral infection. It always started in her chest and spread through her limbs, and if she let it, the sensation would crawl up her spine and settle behind her eyes, making it hard to tell friend from foe, real from imaginary.

It was, in Blanca's opinion, the lowest and most contemptible form of violence—the sort that, once released, destroyed without distinction.

She had only ever really acted on it once, and it was a moment she hoped never to relive. Blanca had prayed for forgiveness; she had begged God never to ask that kind of anger of her again.

As the soldiers marched nearby and the tanks rolled on, she realized with a sinking feeling that her prayers would go unanswered. She was at war again, and that day would come. She knew that now.

A few feet away, the pair of boots paced. Otto moved his gun just a little, preparing to shoot.

Suddenly, loud machine-gun fire blasted over them, and Blanca jerked. The boots disappeared and shouts rang out. Everyone ducked, curling their arms over each other as gunshots sprayed through the air above them.

Clank! Thud! Clank!

Iain jumped with a hiss as a bullet grazed his arm, and more gunfire pierced their shelter and created pockets of light all around them. "What the hell is going on?" he yelled over the deafening blasts. Otto snatched up a piece of broken glass and lifted it, looking behind them through a gap in the debris before letting out a happy shout.

"Germans!" he exclaimed triumphantly. "The army is here!"

A tank boomed just a few feet away and the ground beneath them trembled.

"We've got to move!" Blanca shouted, pulling up her gun and darting out. "Come on!"

The others tumbled out of their hiding spot, with Mateo and Priya at the center of the group. Otto pulled out last and aimed immediately for the nearest Russian soldier. He shot two dead before they'd even made it three steps.

"Zimmler! Stop shooting and follow us!" Blanca commanded, tugging at his sleeve.

The group hurried away from the rubble, ducking behind fallen buildings and piles of wreckage as the battle raged all around them. They came to a screeching halt when a tank turned in their direction, and Blanca's head snapped to the left only to see a German tank on the opposite end of the street.

"SHIT, GO!" she screamed just as the tank fired a shot through the air right next to them. Otto hit the ground on his stomach, expression stricken, but then he popped back up and ran after the others with his rifle in hand. Blanca turned every corner first, shooting anyone who spotted them, German or Russian.

They raced by an overturned truck, and as soon as they rounded it, machine-gun fire pierced its side and the truck exploded into a furious blaze. The force of the explosion knocked Priya, Mateo, and Blanca off their feet, and Blanca smashed into the cobblestone road with a pained gasp.

She'd been on the ground only a few seconds when strong hands yanked her up, and she dimly registered Otto at her side.

Blanca clutched her side, where every breath felt like a stab in her lungs, but the insistent grip on her arm urged her forward. She hurried up to Mateo, who was bleeding from his head. "Where the hell do we go?" he called out just before another explosion erupted right behind him, blasting a tall cinderblock wall to pieces.

"Here!" Iain shouted, and the others all turned and scrambled to catch up with him. They scurried like rats across the cracked floor of a ruined bakery, where small tables lay shattered and cooking supplies littered the floor. The wall facing the street was open, gaping in the center like a wound, and uniformed men clashed just a few feet away. More gunfire ruptured the wall and sent bricks flying over them, causing Priya to scream and duck her head.

Iain gestured them over to a crawlspace just as a barricade burst into flames across the street. Priya did not jump but rather fell into the crawlspace, landing on her hands and knees at the bottom. Mateo leaped in after her, and the others followed.

Otto stopped, aimed his rifle out of the wall, and shot another Russian.

"Get in here, Zimmler!" Blanca shouted.

Otto didn't listen to her, of course. He was too lost in that cold fury Blanca knew so well.

She grabbed his collar from behind, and he rounded to face her, as ready to kill her as he'd been any Russian that wandered too close. But when he saw her, his vision seemed to clear. He was, to Blanca's astonishment, able to pull away from that rage. He lowered his gun.

Then he jerked to the side with a gasp, clutching his right side.

"Damn it!" Blanca hissed when she saw blood pour from his ribs. Wrapping an arm around his middle, she dragged him the few feet to the crawlspace and all but shoved him inside before dropping down after him.

Iain jumped up to pull a piece of wood over the crawlspace's broken entrance, but it was too heavy for him to move on his own.

Otto sat up with a wheezing pant, and when he saw Iain struggling, he tried to stand. A jolt of pain knocked him backwards. He reached over and grabbed Mateo by the collar of his t-shirt.

"Why are you hiding?" he demanded. "Go help them! Now!"

Mateo made a terrified noise, lips parted in fear. "I… But—"

"Now!" Otto snapped fiercely. "Be firm! Go!"

Mateo blinked rapidly, and then, as if snapping out of a daze, he nodded jerkily and rushed forward. Blanca reached out, eyes wide. "Mateo!" she shouted instinctively. "Get back!"

Mateo ignored her. Instead, he jumped up with Iain and gripped the wood's end. Bullets filled the air all around them, narrowly missing their shoulders, arms, and heads, but Mateo had an expression of resolve like Blanca had never seen on him before, and he didn't back away.

"One last pull!" Iain shouted, and both men heaved at once, pulling the protective barrier over their hiding space at last. The gunfire was instantly muffled; without the cannon blasts and furious shouts, the noises outside sounded more like an uneven rain hammering down on a tin roof.

Blanca didn't exhale until Mateo was back inside safely, and as soon as he was close enough, she yanked him to her. "Damn it, Mateo! What did you go sticking your head out there for?" she exclaimed, deeply upset.

The fierce resolve faded from his face, and some of the fear entered again. Still, he pushed her away gently. His hands felt bigger and rougher than she remembered. "Because I had to," he murmured, voice quiet against the constant soundtrack of battle above. He moved away from her and joined Priya, who was sobbing.

"God," Blanca breathed, pushing her hand over her face.

She looked to Otto, who had pushed his fingers against the wound at his side. Before she could stop him, he pulled out the bullet and looked at it with a grimace. "Damn Russians," he wheezed, tossing the bullet away.

Blanca dropped to her knees next to him and pressed her hand up against his wound, making him hiss. "Get my bag," she ordered to anyone who was listening, and someone handed it to her.

Up above, an army tank rolled over the debris and crushed a lifeless body left forgotten. There was a terrible squelching sound, and blood spilled through the broken floorboards, dripping on their hair and clothes. Priya sobbed louder, burying her face in Mateo's front as drops of scarlet slipped down her coat. Some of the blood fell on Blanca's arm, followed by more on her shoulder, but she barely noticed. A heartbeat later, she was coated up to her elbows in Otto's blood, and whoever was above them— their blood looked no different than his.

"I killed five of them," he wheezed through the pain.
"Stop talking."

"Five Russians," he groaned, eyes fluttering. "Dead.
Damn them to—to hell." He coughed, and Blanca shoved the
bandage up against his side and began to tape it. Something
above them exploded, and they all flinched, waiting to see if
the ceiling would cave in on them. It didn't.

Finished with Otto, Blanca fell beside him and turned
her head up to watch the faceless figures rush by the gaps
in the floorboards, ignorant of their audience. No one
came upon them, and the war raged on.

⸺ ❧ ⸺

"*Vorwärts, Vorwärts, schmettern die hellen Fanfaren...*" Otto
sang softly to himself.

Next to him, Blanca slumped a little, and he looked
over to discover she had fallen asleep. Her arm was pressed
against his, and her head had dropped in his direction so
that her temple rested on his shoulder. He observed her
quietly, trying to determine how deeply she was sleeping.
Then he reached into her pocket and pulled out her knife,
which he used to dig at a splinter in his fingertip. Blanca
did not stir, and he smiled to himself. He would give the
knife back, but only when he wanted to.

Nearby, Iain sat with his head cradled in his hands.
Mateo and Priya dozed fitfully in the corner. Otto exhaled
slowly, and he could see his own chilled breath even in the
limited light. His side hurt, but it would heal. Maybe.

A far-off boom caused the slightest tremor beneath
their feet, and Blanca jerked awake. Otto quickly hid her
knife in his pocket and folded his hands innocently in
his lap. Blanca touched her head and looked over at him

in confusion before she stood hurriedly and moved away. Otto rolled his eyes but didn't comment.

Groggily, Blanca wandered over to Mateo and Priya. Stooping down, she touched Mateo's head and gently ran her fingers through his hair. Mateo's eyes flickered open. Priya shifted a little in his arms, but she didn't wake up.

"You alright?" Blanca whispered hoarsely.

"Yeah." Mateo squeezed her hand. "Just hungry."

"I know," she whispered back. "We'll get out and find some food soon."

He nodded, and at Blanca's urging, went back to sleep. She went and checked on Iain, who had been quiet since the battle. "I'm okay," he told her, but his eyes were glazed over in a terribly familiar way.

"I know it was a lot," Blanca said quietly. "It never gets easy, being in combat." Her eyes moved over a cut on his head and she picked up her bandages. "Here, let me—"

"No, no." Iain jerked back, surprising her. He took the gauze from her and cleared his throat. "I've got it."

Blanca huffed. "Damn it, Iain. I know what I'm doing."

He frowned guiltily. "I know, I just—I'd rather do it myself."

Irritated, she shoved the rest of the bandages at him. "Alright, fine. Here."

Iain looked ashamed, but he took the supplies anyway and didn't change his mind. "How are you?" he asked uncertainly.

Blanca eyed him. "Just ready to get the hell out of here."

There was a pause.

"Me, too," he said simply, not sounding as if that was what he had planned to say at all.

Blanca made her way back to Otto. He had pushed up his undershirt and shifted into a pocket of light so he could examine his wound. The bullet had only touched the flesh, thankfully, so there were no broken bones to heal. Still, even though Blanca knew it must hurt, he didn't seem bothered. Otto was annoying but resilient. She had to give him credit for that much.

Falling to a seated position next to him, Blanca swatted away his hands and began looking at the wound once more. Otto let her poke and prod him, wincing only occasionally. "You got lucky," she told him stiffly, keeping her voice low.

"I usually do," he exhaled. "Three times I have been shot down. And three times, I have lived."

"Luck's gonna run out one day, Zimmler."

Otto looked amused, his eyes on the broken floor that served as their ceiling. "That is what my mother says."

"Well, she's right." Blanca secured the bandage a little better than before, and then she took a piece of freezing-cold metal and placed it against the wound to numb the pain. After a few seconds, Otto exhaled in relief. To Blanca's surprise, he reached up and put his fingers over hers. Her eyes shifted up in confusion.

"You are very good at this," he said kindly.

Blanca felt heat rise in her cheeks. She yanked her hand away from his. "For a brown person, you mean."

Otto let his head fall back against the wall behind him. "That is not what I said."

"But it's what you meant," she pressed. "You meant I do a good job for someone who's less than human."

"I never said you were less than human."

"But your leader did," she pointed out gruffly, and Otto frowned. Blanca jabbed a finger above her head. "Do you hear that shit? That battle? This whole war is on you and that damn dictator of yours."

Otto shook his head. "I do not understand your hatred for us. Why must we bow to the will of the English? Why are we not allowed to shape our own country's future? To make Germany the way *we* want?"

Blanca stared at him in disbelief. "Look around you, Zimmler. We're not in your goddamn country!"

Otto opened his mouth and then shut it, blue eyes narrowing at a distant corner.

Blanca tossed down the bloody bandage she'd taken off him, exhaustion tugging at the last of her frayed nerves. "So, don't tell me I do a good job," she went on, frowning. "You're not allowed to give me a compliment."

"Even if I mean it?" he asked softly.

Blanca's dark gaze flickered up to his. "You don't mean it. You can't, not when every night you say a prayer to a man that thinks Jews and gays are worth less than garbage on the street."

"We only want to regain our stolen glory. We want to be a great and powerful nation again."

Blanca leaned very close to him.

"You will never make a country great by putting innocent people in cages."

When Otto didn't respond, Blanca shook her head.

"And you know what pisses me off the most, Zimmler?" She pointed at him. "You're smart enough to know that. I know you are." She pulled away and buried her face in her arms. Otto watched her for a very long time, but he didn't say anything else.

―――∞∞∞―――

A few hours later, they emerged from their refuge. Iain actually staggered when he saw the devastation. The village had been utterly eradicated. Otto stood near Blanca, favoring one side and standing crookedly because of it. His expression was hard and grim.

"Damn Russians," he spat, shaking his head in misery. Blanca thought about reminding him that the Russians were only in Poland because of the Germans, but she opted to remain quiet. No one else responded to Otto's disgust.

In miserable, halting steps, the group walked over the rubble of the destroyed bakery and made their way back down the cobblestone street. The corpses were so thick in number that it was nearly impossible to take a step without treading on a body. Russians, Germans, Polish. They all looked the same in death.

A sudden noise alerted them, and they all looked quickly to an overturned truck. A voice called out in German, and Otto and Blanca stooped down to peer inside.

A young soldier was trapped inside the cab and bleeding profusely from his stomach. Blanca sighed as she heard that raspy, tell-tale wheeze. Training had called it "agonal breathing," but in her head, she thought of it as "the death rattle." It was a clear sign to any medic that the only treatment was a false promise.

"Can you help him?" Otto asked worriedly.

"It's a gut shot," she whispered back. "He's dead. I'm sorry."

Inside the truck, the German soldier let out a cry. Priya appeared next to them. "He looks so young," she said to Otto sadly. He nodded grimly.

"He probably is."

Priya hesitated before dropping to her hands and knees so she could wiggle inside the truck cab. Blanca tried to stop her. "He can't be saved, Priya. There's no point."

"He's afraid! He shouldn't be alone!"

Without waiting for permission, the young girl
squeezed under the wreckage and made her way past
another unmoving corpse to reach the injured German.
Everything around him was soaked in blood, but when he
saw Priya, his eyes lit up with a look of hope.

Priya smiled tearfully before reaching out to him. "Shh,
it'll be okay," she murmured soothingly, and the German let
out a soft sob as he held on to her. Reaching up, she gently
wiped away his tears and cupped his cheek. The young
man tilted his head into her touch even as he convulsed.
"Otto," she called out shakily. "Ask him his name."

Otto leaned against the truck, eyes low. "*Wie ist dein
Name, Soldat?*"

The man's eyes flickered in the direction of Otto's
voice, and then he looked to Priya. "Wilhem," he answered,
voice cracking.

Priya smiled again, eyes shining. "Wilhem," she
repeated. "That—that's a great name. Hello, Wilhem."
She stroked his face.

Wilhem managed a small watery smile, looking
terribly pale. When Priya was close enough, he reached out
with the hand that wasn't holding his stomach and curled
it loosely at her waist. Priya rested her forehead against his
as he began to cry in earnest. "Shh," she crooned, brushing
a hand through his hair. He knew he was dying, so she
didn't try to convince him he wasn't. The light behind his
eyes began to fade.

He asked a question, and Otto translated quietly from
outside.

"He wants to know your name."

The young girl smiled tearfully. "Priya," she murmured,
pointing to herself.

EPOCH   143

"Pr-Priya." Wilhelm bowed his head against her shoulder so his cheek pressed against her hair. "*Danke*, Priya."

"You… You're welcome," she said, desperate to bring him comfort. She glanced to the truck's opening. "Otto, how do I say—" But then she looked back to discover that Wilhem's eyes were already closed, and his grip had grown loose. He was gone.

"How do you say what?" Otto asked from the outside.

Priya brought up her trembling hand and curled her fingers against the young man's face. "Goodbye," she whispered. After a long stretch of silence, Otto answered. "*Auf Wiedersehen.*"

<hr>

Nuristan, Afghanistan
2017

They were heading to a mansion.

Well, it had been a mansion once upon a time. Now it was the structural center of an American military base, and it served as their first real stop in Afghanistan. Here, their dominance was well-established, and the journey from the airport had been uneventful. Blanca sat in the back of an open truck, loaded down with gear. The dry air was stifling, and breathing was something of a chore. Her lungs felt like they were coated in dust, and Blanca was drenched in sticky, gritty sweat even though they'd hardly done anything. The breeze from the moving truck helped a little.

On the streets, Afghani citizens, dressed in robes styled to mitigate the oppressive heat, watched placidly as the soldiers rolled by. They probably saw this sort of

thing every day. All newly arrived soldiers went through
this installation first.

Blanca observed the city and its landscape with intense
curiosity and tried not to show her amazement. The city
was quite large, and although it bore the obvious scars
of war—busted windows, broken pavement, abandoned
vehicles—there was a startling grandeur to it. The earth
here was old. Many of the buildings seemed organic, as if
they had emerged directly from the mountains a thousand
years before.

Next to the street, an Afghan man in a business suit
led a group of children into a school. They stopped and
waved at the truck as it rolled by. Blanca waved back with
a smile. Most of the other soldiers ignored them.

After nearly twenty minutes, the truck brought them
to the mansion, which was housed beyond a tall, white-
washed wall with iron fencing lining the top. Blanca and
the others hopped out, trying not to choke on the dusty
air. Her eyes turned up, and she shifted her sunglasses so
she could squint against the blinding sun. She wanted to
see this place.

The mansion, to her satisfaction, certainly proved
impressive, but the massive holes in the outside walls took
away from aesthetic a bit. Still, it had probably been quite
the sight not all that long ago.

The soldiers were led inside and moved around.
Blanca stepped on some glass near a broken window and
wondered why no one had cleaned it up. Large, open
rooms that had once been used for entertainment were
now sectioned into offices, and the lead combat medic—a
fellow called Holbrook—ushered Blanca into a wood-
lined space and doled out her instructions. She was to be

sent to an outpost north of their current location, where she would help local villagers by working in a newly established clinic.

"The fighting there is done," Sergeant Holbrook told her. "Our goal in that area is to help rebuild. Do everything you can to foster a positive rapport with the locals. It's essential we maintain a good working relationship with the village leaders."

He didn't tell her why a relationship with such an isolated village was so important—they never did, of course—and Blanca amused herself by imagining the United States Army just wanted to be nice.

"Yes, Sergeant."

A few days later, she left the mansion. The ride to the village was a long one. They started out on paved streets with metal signs, but eventually, the convoy switched to skinny dirt roads and winding mountain paths. The rugged peaks seemed to grow in front of Blanca's eyes, tall and jagged with bare sides dotted with only a few trees. They passed farmers herding goats and working in fields, and sometimes the people would stop and watch them as they passed, their faces shielded from the sun by worn linens or their own weathered hands.

Finally, they came to the village and Blanca was released, along with a few others. There were around twenty soldiers stationed there, most of whom were holed up in a tall building at the southern entrance. There was no real fence or barrier, not around the village proper, although there was one around the building where the soldiers stayed. Of the villagers, there were fewer than sixty.

When Blanca dismounted the back of the truck, the people there looked at her warily. Some shuffled away without making eye contact. There were a few children, like before on the way to the mansion; they did not, however, greet her or wave. The air was undeniably tense. It made the hair on Blanca's arms stand up.

This area was not as well-protected as the one she'd come from, but that was the point. Someone had to come and get things started. Shifting her heavy gear, Blanca went with the others to the makeshift clinic on the far eastern corner of the village and began her work.

Initially, it was not an easy task. Blanca had been given new supplies for treatment, but many of the conditions she encountered in the village were simply beyond her abilities. There had, she learned, been more than two hundred villagers just six months before. Whatever had taken place between now and then, the population has been decimated.

Still, Blanca did her best. She treated burns and broken bones, infections and nasty coughs. Some people came in with injuries that had sat too long without healing properly, and she had to manufacture splints until they could get elsewhere. For other injuries and illnesses, she recommended transport to a larger facility. Many of the locals refused to leave. In her first month in the village, two people died, despite all her efforts.

After a few months, though, things began to improve. Blanca found a routine. She became more confident. She established relationships with some of the villagers, particularly the women. The men did not care for her much; she barely even saw them. The women and children, though, would come to her often for help and advice. She would teach them English when she could, sometimes while patching up a soldier's busted knee or twisted ankle. The children wanted to be near her, seemingly out of curiosity, but they would scurry away like little mice any time she tried to approach them directly.

One night, as Blanca was returning to her bunk after a long day, she overheard one of the American officers talking with the local village leader. An Afghan soldier translated between them. "The villagers are afraid," the Afghan soldier explained. "They know there will be consequences for cooperating with American military."

"We'll keep them safe," the American officer promised. "That's what we're here for."

Blanca kept walking, eyes averted. That night, she reclined against her stiff bed and tried to think of something fun she and Mateo could do when she saw him next. Her eyes closed.

The next day, Blanca worked away most of the daylight hours and found she was satisfied with everything. Just as she started to close up shop, a fellow soldier limped in, making a whining noise. He jumped up on Blanca's table even though she was obviously finishing up, and Blanca huffed, putting a hand on her hip.

"What, Bryant?"

"Hernandez, check this shit out." He pulled up his pants leg. "Something freakin' bit me!"

Blanca looked exasperated and pushed up her sleeves so she could pull on some gloves. "You been stickin' your dick in weird stuff again?"

Bryant made a face at her. "Man, it's my knee. I was out takin' a piss and something just jumped up and got me." He grumbled when she put some antiseptic and a bandage on it. "Goddamn bugs out here, man, they're crazy."

"Mmhm." She inspected the bite. "Doesn't look like venom or anything. You'll be fine." She patted his shoulder, and Bryant scowled and hopped up, favoring one leg like he'd just gotten out of major surgery. Blanca rolled her eyes. *Babies.*

"You sure you don't want to give me some pain meds or something?" he tried, grinning as he went to leave.

Blanca pulled off her gloves. "Nope. Take some Motrin and—"

"—change my socks, *I know.*" He made an annoyed noise. "Geez, you are no help."

Blanca chuckled. "Get the hell out of here, Bryant."

"Yeah, yeah. Some medic you are." Bryant stepped outside the clinic and was immediately blown off his feet by a mortar shell.

Blanca froze.

Machine-gun fire exploded through the area, and Blanca jerked back, lips parted and hands up. Outside, screams pierced the air, and then a bellowing voice shouted:

"WE'RE UNDER ATTACK! COMBAT POSITIONS!"

No, Blanca thought in a single, blinding moment of terror.

The truck parked nearby burst into a monstrous ball of flame, rocking the ground and shattering the windows of the clinic. Blanca scrambled to the side and tossed up her arms, glass raining down on her as she tripped over her own feet and fell. For a split second, she couldn't move. Then she heard more shouts outside, and her focus sharpened. Springing forward, she gathered her rifle and med bag and sprinted to the door so she could fall against it and peer out.

The night sky was dark and starless, but the village was already on fire, and the burning truck lit up the area with a heated pulse. Blanca's head snapped to the north, and she saw flashes of light coming from the mountains.

Gunfire burst through the area, thickening the air with bullets. Blanca jerked back to avoid being hit, then looked to where Bryant was sprawled on the dirt. Gritting her teeth, she rushed out across the narrow road and dropped next to him. His body was in shambles, destroyed beyond recognition. There was nothing she could do for him.

"Damn it!" she growled, head jerking up at the sound of shouts. Pulling her rifle forward, Blanca hurried through the dark village, pulse racing as she ducked behind a low barrier and looked out. Six American soldiers crouched behind a barricade with the munitions, but they were pinned down by gunfire from the hills ahead of them. Blanca looked to the east and saw two more soldiers near the outskirts of the village, writhing in pain. In the distance, Taliban fighters approached, firing rapidly.

Blanca burst from her spot, pressed her rifle against her shoulder, and opened fire. One of the insurgents was hit instantly, and he dropped to the earth in a cloud of dust. The other scrambled away. Time seemed to slow around her, and Blanca was assaulted by panic. The soldiers cried out again, reaching for her, and Blanca's movements slipped into a blinding, mindless state of automation.

She pressed forward, shaking violently.

God, what's happening?

She could barely see. She shot anyway.

This can't be real.

She was next to the soldiers. One of them was missing a leg below the knee. The other was bleeding heavily from his shoulder. They were both riddled with shrapnel.

Where are the villagers?

She had to stop the bleeding.

Where's the CO?

She had to get them out of there.

What do I do?

An explosion rattled the earth right behind her, and Blanca thought she might be bleeding, too. It was hard to tell.

God, please help me.

Her vision was blurring.

I don't know what to do!

Her hands were shaking.

Please help me!

Insurgents had infiltrated the village's school and were firing down on them from the second-story windows. A rocket-propelled grenade blasted by her and lit up the munitions post, creating an immense burst of white-hot hellfire that washed over Blanca in a scorching tidal wave of heat. The flash of light blinded her for a few seconds, and Blanca looked back, sweat pouring over her face as she fought the urge to cry.

The soldier in front of her, Ellison, gripped her arm with blackened hands. His eyes were wide and frantic.

"Get me out of here, Hernandez!"

Blanca's eyes snapped to his face. "I got it!" she yelled out over the chaos, and then she lifted his arm over her shoulder and pulled him up. Reaching out with her other hand, she grabbed the other soldier's uniform. "Come on, this way!"

Ellison felt like a solid stone, and he hobbled for only a step or two before his strength gave out entirely. Blanca cried out against the sudden sinking weight at her side, but she dug in the heels of her boots and pushed on, dragging him through the dirt. They rushed through the street, tripping and falling but moving forward, bit by bit. Gunfire dogged their every step, lining the path with divots and clods of dirt.

Blanca reached the clinic, shoved Ellison inside, then reached back for the other man, who stumbled in after her and fell to the floor. She quickly set up a tourniquet for Ellison, each movement instinctive and, at the same time, excruciating. *Plug here, cover here, wrap here, high and tight, stop the bleeding, stop the bleeding, stop the—*

A grenade went off nearby, and Blanca jerked, eyes wide. *Stop the bleeding, stop the bleeding, stop the—*

A building collapsed across the road. Someone cried out. *Stop the bleeding, stop the bleeding, stop the—*

The door blasted off its hinges and flew over their heads. It snapped when it met the corner of a wall, causing them all to flinch. Blanca's head jerked up, and she leaped forward, scrambling for the radio and listening in. AH-64 Apache attack helicopters were on their way.

A Taliban insurgent appeared at the door with an assault rifle, and Blanca turned sharply, raising her gun with a snap and blasting him away from the doorframe. A voice crackled over the radio. "Break, break, break. Medevac requested immediately. Our coordinates are—"

Blanca jumped to her feet. "Medevac's coming, we've gotta move—they can't land here."

She shoved gauze and padding over the second soldier's wound, wrapped it up with a violent twist, and then hauled Ellison into her arms. Together, the three of them staggered out into the dangerous open air.

Blanca's muscles screamed in protest, and her side ached. A bullet grazed her arm. She ignored it. The second soldier managed to keep his gun level, and he shot an enemy fighter that got too close. They fought for every step, sweat pouring down their faces and mixing with blood as Blanca heaved and prayed, heaved and prayed, heaved and prayed.

The helicopter was nearby. She could hear it.

God, please, don't let one of those grenades hit the medevac. Please.

The helicopter was having trouble landing. The smoke was too thick. The world around them was on fire, and as Blanca fought to reach the landing point, she saw more dying men, all scattered on the ground like stones. They tripped up her feet and grasped for her ankles. They moaned her name and sobbed for their mothers.

The medevac finally came to a landing, and the air medics jumped forward, yanking Ellison and the other soldier from Blanca's grip. Over their heads, two Apache helicopters, dark and menacing, swooped down on the scene and unleashed hell on the mountainside.

"I have to go back!" Blanca called out hoarsely, turning and sprinting back into the village. Chaos continued all around her, sucking her in like a vortex. Her body throbbed, and her throat burned. Blood pooled in her mouth, bitter and foul.

That night, Blanca dragged eight more injured men and women to the medevac. She uselessly fretted over the lifeless remains of four others. In the process, she shot and killed three enemy fighters.

In the end, none of these efforts felt like accomplishments.

Months later, a well-meaning friend would comment to Blanca that the attack was probably "a total blur" for her. Blanca had simply smiled and nodded. "Yeah," she'd muttered. "A blur."

But that wasn't the truth. Blanca understood the idea; traumatic events were often converted into hazy, shapeless memories centered around an unfocused sense of terror. That was how the brain coped.

Combat wasn't like that, though. It didn't become diluted by time, but was instead cruel in its perpetual clarity. Each time Blanca thought back on the attack, she discovered—not an indistinct haze—but a new, soul-splitting detail.

The grotesque shape of a shattered arm.

The trail of blood left by a frantic grip.

The sound of a dying man's last gasp.

A blur? Hardly. She'd give anything for a blur.

CHAPTER 6

The soldier above all others prays for peace,
for it is the soldier who must suffer and
bear the deepest wounds and scars of war.
—General Douglas MacArthur

The next morning, they awoke to guns in their faces. Otto shot upright first, hands raised, only to realize he was looking at German soldiers. Relief burst through him. "*Halt, halt!*" he shouted, and the soldiers looked to him with excitement. The nearest one, the commanding officer, held up a hand to the others.

"Identify yourself," he told Otto sharply in German.

"Lieutenant Otto Zimmler of the Luftwaffe." He turned suddenly at the sound of Mateo's shout. The soldiers had yanked him up from his sleeping bag, and the others had all been shoved their knees. Mateo was pushed roughly next to them, and Blanca was on the other end, hands in the air, with a deadly glare on the men. Two soldiers had guns pointed directly at them and the third enlisted man was rummaging through their bags.

Otto stared until the other man's voice drew his attention once more.

"Otto Zimmler?" repeated the officer. He looked to the others with a laugh. "There was a notice about you from your squadron! You have been missing in action for two weeks."

Otto looked away from the others. "Yes, I was shot down."

"And who are they?" one of the soldiers asked, prodding Blanca roughly with the end of his gun. She glared at him, that dark and narrow look Otto knew all too well.

Otto hesitated. "I don't know. They have not told me anything."

Blanca's eyes flickered to Otto, but the conversation was in German. She wouldn't know what he was saying. Otto looked away from her.

"You have not learned anything about them?" the officer asked curiously.

"No," Otto replied stiffly. "How is my unit doing? Do you know how many survived? Where are—"

"I haven't heard," the officer interrupted, looking over the captives again. "We have been scouting this area for a few days, trying to find the direction of the Soviets."

"They were in the village of Radymno," Otto told him. "I saw them last night. They attacked after sundown."

"Do you know where they went after?"

"No." Otto walked to the back of a nearby truck (how they hadn't heard the soldiers come upon them, he would never know) and took a long drink of water from a canteen. He avoided looking at Blanca and the others, all of whom waited at gunpoint. One of the soldiers paced nearby, his hungry gaze lingering on Priya who trembled at the center of the line.

"We are working out of a base south of Warsaw," the officer told Otto. "You can report in there."

Otto nodded and allowed one of the other men to break the cuffs off his wrists. He rubbed the chafed skin absently. One of the soldiers came forward with his pistol and tossed it to him with a laugh. "I think you will want this back, Lieutenant. It seems like you've had a rough few weeks."

Otto caught the pistol and turned it over in his hands before placing it on the back gate of the truck. "Yes." He cleared his throat. "I am ready to go home."

"Here, we will load up the captives and take them to Sergeant Wagner," the officer said. "He commands a garrison nearby."

Otto finally looked up and let his eyes find Blanca's. When the German soldier yanked her to her feet, she pulled sharply. The soldier responded by jabbing his gun between her shoulder blades, and Blanca winced. Mateo reacted immediately, jerking free and swinging an arm at the German, but he was easily blocked. The soldier grappled with him half-heartedly for a few seconds before shoving him to the ground and kicking him in the stomach. Otto turned his head.

A few minutes later, the prisoners were all bound with their hands behind their backs and gags shoved in their mouths. Mateo looked quickly to Otto, eyes wide and pleading even as he tried to talk behind the gag. Otto gritted his teeth and said nothing.

"Sir," said the soldier nearest Priya. "Do we need to rush back? I would like some time with this one." He snatched her arm and yanked her against his torso.

Otto looked up sharply, waiting for the officer's refusal. To his dismay, the man in charge simply shrugged. "It is early," he said, as if that were the deciding factor.

"What? No, you moron," Otto cut in. "We do not have time for that. Put the girl in the truck with the rest."

The soldier looked up in astonishment, then scowled. "Why should I? It will not take that long—"

"I would not be surprised if it takes you half a minute," Otto replied scathingly, "but the girl is property of the German military now—"

"And I *am* the German military," the soldier said snidely. "Which means that, for the time being, she is mine." He slipped his arm around Priya, who began sobbing, and Blanca burst up from her spot only to be forced back with two guns pointed directly at her face. "Get back down!" snarled one soldier.

Otto rushed forward with his hands up. "Just put the damn girl in the truck, and we will not have to deal with all of this!"

"Why are you whining?" the officer asked suspiciously. "Just let him go and be done with it."

Otto looked to the other man in disbelief. "You are really going to let him rape that girl?"

The officer's eyes flickered between each of the captives, ending with one long, cool look at Priya, who was quickly growing hysterical. He turned back to Otto and shrugged.

"What girl?"

The other soldiers watched Otto coldly. The one with his hands on Priya was impatient, groping along her front as he delayed. At last, Otto looked back to the commanding officer and held up his hands in defeat. "Fine," he said with an annoyed grimace. "Just hurry up. I am ready to go."

While the response was in German, his concession was clear. Blanca and the others began to writhe and fight against their restraints, crying out over the gags in their mouths, but it was no use. Two soldiers waited with guns pointed directly at them, and the leading officer lingered nearby with his rifle ready.

The last soldier took Priya in his arms with a pleased grunt and hauled her off out of sight. "So," said the officer to Otto as he turned to face the captives, "what is the first thing you plan to do once you have returned to the homeland?"

Otto walked to the back of the truck. "Drink a beer," he answered casually, and then he picked up the pistol and blew a hole in the officer's head from barely two feet away.

Blanca and the others jerked back in shock, but Otto raised his hand and caught the nearest guarding soldier with a quick bullet before anyone else could react. Iain lashed out and kicked the third soldier's legs out from under him, allowing Otto to shoot the fallen German with barely a glance in his direction.

The soldier with Priya had not even managed to undress yet, and he'd left his weapons at the truck. When Otto advanced on him, he had no defense.

"*Nein, nein, nein!*" the soldier cried, waving his arms frantically.

Otto shot him four times, one after the other, never once halting his steps.

Priya screamed and curled up in a ball on the ground. Otto stopped next to the corpse and let out a frustrated yell. "I COULD HAVE GONE HOME!" he roared at the dead man, and then he shot him again.

Heaving, he looked over at Priya and made a face. "Come here, you stupid girl," he snapped irritably. Priya rose shakily and let Otto undo the ropes on her wrists. As soon as her hands were free, she pulled her arms around him with a teary cry.

"Thank you, Otto!" she sobbed.

Otto scowled and peeled away her grip with an annoyed grunt. Placing a knife in her hand, he turned her by the shoulder, jabbed her in the spine with his finger, and then pointed to the others. "Go," he ordered.

Wasting no time, Priya hurried forward, dropping first to Mateo and cutting off the ropes. Mateo yanked her to him, clinging for a few seconds before he steadied himself and went to release the others.

Otto, meanwhile, was poking around the bodies of the dead Germans. Blanca approached him from behind.

"Zimmler?"

Otto ignored her, instead bending down and rummaging through the soldier's pockets. "Ah-ha! At least you are good for something," he muttered in German before standing with his new prize—a tin box of cigarettes and some matches. He tucked a cigarette into his mouth, lit the end, and took a long, satisfied drag.

"What?" he asked when he saw her staring.

"You told us you would never hurt other Germans," she said quietly. "Why did you do that?"

Otto turned his head to the side to blow out some smoke. "Rapists," he told her, "are no kinsman of mine." He took out the cigarette and dangled it between his fingers. "Are you going to tie me up again?"

She shook her head.

Otto popped the cigarette back into his mouth. "Good." He brushed past her.

"Zimmler?" she said again.

He stopped and looked back.

"You are better than what you've been taught."

Otto's brows furrowed. For a split second, he looked uncomfortable. Then he shed the discomfort like an old skin and resumed his cocky walk. "Why are you all standing around?" he called out when no one moved. "Get your shit! Let us go, already!" He grabbed Mateo by the shoulder. "And you, what kind of punch was that? That is not what I taught you."

"I'm sorry, I panicked…"

"That was pathetic, and I expect better in the future."

"I will, I promise…"

Iain appeared next to Blanca, looking stricken. "I would like to learn how to use a gun now," he told her very softly.

Blanca shifted her eyes to his, and her gaze grew soft. "I'll teach you," she promised.

———— ⠳⠦ ————

Although Otto was no longer bound, he rose the next morning with the rest of them and resumed the trek without complaint. As they walked, he carried a rifle carelessly over his shoulder and used his free hand to light a cigarette. When he was done, he tossed the match on the ground.

Mateo was keeping pace next to him. "Smoking is bad for you," he said to Otto.

Otto looked over at him. "What? Who told you that?" He took out the cigarette and used it to point ahead of him. "Was it your know-it-all *sister*?"

"Well, yeah."

Otto rolled his eyes. "This is why he is a homosexual, Blanca!" he called out, gesturing to Mateo. "Because you will not let him be a man!"

"Shut up, Zimmler!" Blanca threw a rock at him, and he scrambled out of the way.

"Do not listen to her," Otto continued to Mateo, putting the cigarette back in his mouth and talking around it like a grizzled old man. "Smoking is good for you. It puts hair on your chest."

Mateo snickered. "Okay, Otto."

A few minutes later, Otto left Mateo behind and caught up with Blanca. "This country is uncivilized. Where the hell are all the towns?"

"We've been avoiding them on purpose, you idiot." She pulled out the map and showed him. "The closer we get to Warsaw, the more populated the areas get." She shifted to show it to Otto, who pointed to a spot just north of them.

"I do not know how you expect to get past here. I have no help to offer you." He dropped his hand. "There are Germans everywhere. If I get caught with you, I am not saving you again. I will deny everything."

"Yeah, that's about what I expected."

They stopped to take a break and eat.

"What do you want from me, you harpy?" Otto continued.

"I want you to shut up, and—" Blanca patted her pockets. "*Where the hell is my knife?*"

Otto paused for half a second before sprinting away. Blanca raced after him. "Get back here, Zimmler!"

Otto raced past Iain, who looked up from a flashlight he was working on but didn't make a move to stop him. Blanca rushed by a split second later and tackled Otto to the ground. They fell into the dirt with a crash, causing a cloud of dust to envelope them. Mateo and Priya nibbled on some dried meat they'd gotten from the Germans and watched the scene with mild interest.

"Give it back to me!"

"I do not have it!" Otto laughed wildly. They rolled in the dirt and Blanca kneed him in the gut, making him grunt.

"Yes, you do!"

Blanca aimed a punch at his face, but Otto managed to throw up both his forearms to block her. He quickly grabbed her fists in his hands and held them just tightly enough to keep her from pummeling him. She countered by aiming a kick very near his groin, and he jerked his legs closed with a shriek.

"Agh—What the hell!" Otto exclaimed when Blanca ripped her hands free and shamelessly searched his pockets. "I would get tased if I did this to you!" He sighed in defeat when she found her knife in his side pocket.

"I knew it, you lying bastard! How many times are you going to steal this?"

"I was going to give it back!" He let his head fall back against the ground. "And you are crushing my penis."

"I ought to cut the damn thing off."

"Why? So you can add it to your collection?"

Blanca pushed off him roughly, making him groan.

They ate and packed up, leaving behind as little trace of their existence as they could. When the group spotted some Germans in the distance, they tucked back into the woods and disappeared from sight until the soldiers were gone. Otto, Blanca noticed, did not speak up or make any attempt to join them.

One day faded into the next. No one bothered them, so they bothered each other instead.

"Why are you always in a tree like a damn monkey?"
Blanca called to Otto. The spray of the river had become
unbearable, stinging at them like icy insects, so they had
tucked back further into the woods. For whatever reason,
Otto had taken to seeing how far he could go without
touching the ground. He had successfully gone nearly forty
yards without ever leaving the cover of the trees.

"Why are you always on the ground like a snake?" he
countered from his high branch. "Oh, yes, it is because you
are Medusa, hideous snake goddess with a face that turns
men to stone."

Blanca rolled her eyes.

Otto pointed vehemently. "There, that look right
there! That is the one." He put his hands to his throat,
gasping dramatically while Mateo and Priya laughed.
"Oh—*meine gott*, here it comes!" He made a loud, theatrical
noise of death and fell over the branch. Blanca jerked
reflexively to catch him, but he held the tree limb by his
legs and ended up swinging upside down with a frozen
look of horror.

Blanca bit her lip very hard to keep from laughing.
"Idiot."

Otto unfroze his face and grimaced before pointing
at Iain as he walked by. "Do not tase me!" he ordered, and
then he pulled himself up and dropped to his feet on the
ground.

"You are immature as hell," Blanca told him.

Otto shrugged. "So? You are short." He waved his
hand over her head.

Blanca punched at him, and he scurried out of the
way. "You know what American I really like?" he asked
out of the blue. "John Wayne. I have seen all his movies."

Blanca raised a brow at him.

"I really appreciate the way he," Otto made a pistol motion with his fingers, "kills all those Indian people."

There was a collective groan.

"What? None of you are Indian people. Right?" He squinted at Priya suspiciously, and Iain tased him. "Ow! *How was that racist?*"

"Zimmler?"

"Yes, Blanca?"

"Shut the hell up."

He huffed. "Fine."

A half-hour later, the group came to a halt when Otto held up his hand. "A house," he said, pointing. Blanca peered at the gaps in the wood line.

"I don't see anything else around here," she said. "I don't think it's a village. Must be a lone family."

"Should we try to see?"

Blanca looked around. "Stay here with the kids," she said to Iain, and he made a face, but did as she asked. Blanca and Otto moved away from the others, bodies low and guns in hand.

A few minutes later, the trees fell away and a clearing opened to reveal a small brick home with two chimneys. It had a red door and two windows with curtains visible inside. There was no smoke coming from either of the chimneys, and even though they waited nearly ten minutes, there was no sign of anyone in or around the house.

"The windows are dark," Blanca murmured. "Do you see anything?"

"Not yet." They stood, moving stealthily around the home. There, they found a gray stone well, a dying vegetable garden, and a wooden shed with a metal roof.

While Blanca peered through a window of the home, Otto moved around the well. "Blanca, I think I found our homeowner."

Blanca stepped up and looked down at an old man's corpse. He was on the ground near an ax, and he'd hardly decomposed at all. His thin white hair was still intact, and his hands were curled as if holding the wooden handle. Blanca leaned down and inspected him. There were no exterior wounds; he hadn't been shot or attacked. Instead, he looked rather peaceful.

"He must've had a heart attack, or a stroke or something." She stood.

Otto looked around. "Old man, out here living by himself in the winter. That is no surprise." He stepped over the man and peered at the shed, prodding open the door with his gun. Once inside, he let out an incredulous laugh. "Blanca, come here!"

Blanca stepped in behind him, only to jerk in surprise. The shed contained four large hooks holding thick slabs of meat kept fresh by the frigid air. There were also furs set aside on a table, probably from deer, and hooves cut up in chunks. A hunting rifle was mounted on the side wall.

Blanca let a slow smile spread over her face. "Well, I'll be damned."

"Mm," Otto said grandly, "I know what I am eating tonight."

They left the shed quickly, gave the area one more quick inspection, and then agreed to tell the others. "We have to bury the man before we eat," she told Otto, who groaned.

"Why? The ground is going to be cold and hard."

"Because burial is important, Otto."

"We could burn him. It would be faster."

"No."

"Why not?"

"Burial puts your soul at rest, that's why."

Otto caught her wrist, fingers brushing the rosary beads. Blanca rounded to face him, annoyed, but he wasn't dissuaded—as usual. Instead, his expression grew gentle. "So you would like to be buried?" he asked.

"Of course." She eyed him suspiciously.

"With a Catholic priest?" His fingers brushed the crucifix on her beads.

"Yes." She paused and then muttered, "I'll probably burn in hell anyway, but I'd like to try."

"Someone like you, in hell?" Otto tilted his head at her. His fingertips brushed the inside of her wrist, and Blanca felt strangely focused on the light touch. "I do not think so. You try to do good. More so than most people, I think. That has to count for something."

Blanca gave him a bemused look. "If you say so."

Otto kept her hand, pulling his fingers over hers as his pensive look shifted into a coy one. "And what of me?" he asked slyly. "Would you show a care for my soul and bury me, too?"

He was standing very close to her. Blanca looked up at his face and tilted her head in an imitation of his. Then she leaned in, and Otto drew nearer as well. "I'll bury you right now if that's what you want." She shoved his chest and moved past him. Otto chuckled quietly to himself before following her.

The wind picked up just as the group closed in on the house, and as soon as they were past the locked door, Priya jumped inside with a shriek and a dance. "A house!" she declared happily. "And a couch! A real couch!" She leaped onto it and bounced.

The home was a cozy little space with a living room, one bedroom, a kitchen, and a bathroom. The dying light outside coated the rooms in shades of gray and black, but once they got the fires going in both the living room and bedroom, the little house filled with warmth and color.

"There's a well outside," Iain pointed out, before he went to the wide metal kitchen sink. Turning a knob, he paused to listen as a groan sounded throughout the house. The frigid pipes rattled, and for a long moment, nothing happened. With a gush, water suddenly poured from the faucet. Iain grinned.

Priya gasped. "Wait, wait." She hurried to the bathroom. "It works in here, too! We can take baths!"

"Water won't be hot," Iain pointed out. "But we can heat some up in the fireplace and dump it in there."

"We'll get to all that. First things first—burying the man and bringing in the food." Blanca gave out orders and the others hurried to task. Iain cut up the meat and lugged it inside while Otto chopped wood for the fire. Blanca had Mateo help her bury the man, and Priya set about filling up pots and canteens with fresh water.

By the time Blanca and Mateo made it back inside, the home was toasty and inviting. "Buuurggg," Mateo grumbled, hurriedly rubbing his arms and planting himself in front of the living room hearth. The others entered just a few minutes later, Otto with an armful of chopped wood and Iain with plenty of meat for a stew. They found vegetables to throw in with it, and Iain began digging around in cabinets to see what else they had.

"Oh, look at this—let's see, and…flour! Perfect!" He pulled out the jar and inspected it. "I can make bread with this."

"Really?" Blanca asked eagerly, her stomach rumbling at the thought.

"Definitely. Although it'll be tomorrow before we can eat it. Takes a while." He stopped at the sink and began washing his hands, which seemed to take a lifetime. Then he inspected his fingers very carefully. Blanca waited. She was a medic; she understood the importance of hygiene. Even so, she was starting to think Iain would never be satisfied with his cleanliness. When he saw her waiting, he flushed.

"Just making sure."

"Yeah, I got it," she deadpanned.

"Come, I'll show you." He explained the ingredients to her. "You just need yeast, a little oil... You've got to knead it, there, like that." He wiped at his face, leaving a streak of white flour, and Blanca chuckled.

Otto walked in and let out a bark of laughter. "Of course you bake," he said to Iain. "You really are one pair of stockings away from being an actual woman."

"Otto, get out!" Blanca threw a spoon at him.

"Ow!"

"Go!"

"Fine, fine."

Once he was gone, Blanca looked back at Iain. "Just ignore him."

"I do my best," Iain replied wryly. He turned back to their dough and helped Blanca get it into a pan before he poked around the woodburning stove to make sure it was in working order. Together, they finished their work. "I haven't cooked in a long time," he admitted a few minutes later. "Hardly seems worth it when you live alone."

"Were you—I mean, it just seems like—" Blanca paused, wondering if she should continue. Iain's eyes flickered to hers and then back to his flour-covered arms, which he began to wash. Again, he seemed almost fanatical in his efforts at cleanliness.

"Aye?" he asked questioningly.

Blanca balked. "I just—I'm surprised, you know. That you're not married."

Iain hesitated before asking casually, "Why is that?"

How could she explain it?

Iain just seemed like he *belonged* in a family, like he'd been the type of kid who'd always had a smiling mom to pick him up from school, and clothes that fit, and money for treats. That had never been a way of life for Blanca. There had only ever been Mateo and a distant, dreamy vision of her mother. But Iain had the face of someone who would look for love simply because it seemed strange to live without it. She couldn't imagine why he, of all people, would live alone.

"I don't know how to say it," Blanca mumbled, cheeks red. "You're just so—"

"Try one word," he offered gently. "Say the first one that comes to your mind."

Blanca looked up at him. "Warm," she managed at last.

Iain looked briefly surprised, and then his features softened into a smile. "Warm," he repeated.

"Does that seem weird?"

He shook his head. "No, I don't think so."

"So then why aren't you with someone?"

Iain studied her, looking truly blank for a brief, strange moment. He'd always been so readable before, so terribly transparent in everything he said or felt. For a second, though, there was something else—a glimpse of emotion terribly close to anger. It was subtle, but Blanca spotted it.

Then it broke, and Iain's expression relaxed again. "Jus' didn't work out that way, I guess."

Blanca hesitated, discomfort welling in her chest. Then she heard a crash and Mateo's voice, followed by Otto's, talking in the living room.

"Oops, we broke it."

"So? It is not ours."

Blanca cleared her throat. "I should probably go in there."

Iain seemed normal again. "Sure, I'll keep an eye on the bread."

Blanca managed a shaky nod, then hurried away. In her head, she berated herself. She knew better than to ask questions. She *knew better*. Answers had never helped her before…and yet, for the first time since meeting Iain, she didn't believe him.

Blanca shoved the thought aside and yelled at Mateo and Otto for breaking the lamp. Soon enough, Mateo and Priya were circling the kitchen like dogs, whining about hunger pains.

"Okay, okay—look, there are the bowls, set the table—"

Moments later, the kitchen was full of people. Blanca felt her anxiety fade away as everyone poured in and the excitement grew. Across the room, Priya dashed to the window.

"Look! It's snowing!"

The others all looked to see flecks of white falling gently outside the frosted glass. From inside their comfortable sanctuary, the scene was terribly beautiful. Blanca paused to look at it. She'd never seen real snow before.

"Wow," Mateo breathed, looking out. Behind him, Otto—who was uninterested in snow—fiddled with a radio he'd found. A jaunty, upbeat tune by Nat King Cole played from the arched speaker.

"Food's ready!" Iain called out.

He lifted the big pot off the stove and put it on a mat in the center of the table as a mouthwatering aroma filled the air. Otto found a large spoon to use for the stew. He handed it first to Priya, who beamed.

Laughter and chaos filled the room, hands grabbing, utensils clanging, and then quick, murmured prayers from Blanca and Mateo, along with the sign of the cross before they dug into their food with ravenous enthusiasm. The song on the radio changed to Bing Crosby.

"Look what I found," Otto announced with a grin as he pulled out a bottle of wine. After weeks of drinking flat water, it was an exciting change.

"Blanca, can I try some?" Mateo asked, and Priya clapped her hands together pleadingly.

"Please, please!"

"I don't know…"

Otto rolled his eyes. "Really, Blanca? They are eighteen. Let them live a little."

"Jesus drank wine," Mateo pointed out, and Blanca finally laughed.

"Fine, here. You can both have half a glass."

Mateo and Priya accepted their wine eagerly. Priya drank hers down to the last drop. Mateo, on the other hand, took one sip and grimaced. "Oh, god. This is horrible! Why did you let me drink this?"

The table erupted into laughter, and Blanca looked smug. "That's what you get."

Mateo ended up giving his to Priya, who happily accepted it. Everyone else had a bit for themselves. Otto took over the conversation by regaling them all about the time he'd gotten kicked out of school for taking all the hinges off the doors. Apparently, he'd done things like that quite often.

"Did you get in trouble at home?" Mateo asked, laughing.

"No, I hid at a friend's house until my father left for a business trip."

"I pulled a fire alarm at school once," Iain volunteered, and Blanca snorted.

"You did? Why?"

"Because it was a dare, and I'm stupid."

"Well," Otto said grandly, "I had very little time for school growing up. I was doing more important things, like driving around with my friends and going out with girls."

Iain rolled his eyes. "Like any woman wants anything to do with you."

"For your information, I had many women back in Germany."

"Oh yeah?" Blanca asked. "They charge you by the inch or by the hour? Either way, I'm willing to bet it didn't set you back much."

She grinned, and Otto kicked her under the table. She kicked him back, and the furious battle only came to a halt when Mateo threatened them both with a wooden spoon.

Outside, the storm raged on into the night, coating the edge of the window with soft white powder. Wind rattled the hinges of the door, and tree branches swayed and scraped the glass. Inside the home, though, they were safe and warm and happy.

"At least the storm means no one's likely to come around," Iain pointed out. "Better cover for the smoke in the chimney, too. It'll be a pain when we leave, but I think it's a good thing for now."

Blanca was forced to agree, although she was already dreading the moment they would have to leave their little sanctuary. The sight of Mateo's happy face made the knot in her chest loosen, and her gaze moved to the others. Everyone was talking, moving, eating, sharing, and waving their hands. No one was angry, and there were no harsh looks or words. Blanca felt her throat tighten. It was beautiful—too beautiful. Discomfort poured into her chest.

On the radio, the music faded away and a cheerful voice took over. "I hope you all have a wonderful Christmas Eve!" it declared, and Mateo grew excited. "It's Christmas Eve! Hey, this is like our Christmas dinner!" He looked around the table. *"Feliz Navidad*, everyone!"

Blanca's heart fluttered. *"Feliz Navidad*," she said with a nod, lifting her cup.

"Fröliche Weihnachten," Otto added with a quirk of his lips, raising his cup as well.

"Nollaig Shona," Iain said with a smile.

"Krisamas kee badhaee!" Priya declared jubilantly.

They clicked their cups together, and for just a little while, they were exactly where they wanted to be.

Once the kitchen was cleaned up, they got water from the sink and heated it in the fireplace before filling the bath. "We've all got to use that tub." Blanca eyed the boys sternly. "So don't go in there and work out any 'tension' you might be having."

Otto looked at Mateo curiously. Mateo gestured, and Otto snickered. "You are a thief of joy," he told her.

Once the tub was ready, Priya bathed first, and the others followed. Blanca chose to bathe last, pulling in her own water and pouring it into the tub so that wispy steam filled the air. Sinking into that tub was one of the highlights of her life. She had never taken hot baths for granted, but this one was by far the best.

Since everyone else had gone, she took her time working the hard sponge over her skin. Dirt and blood flowed from every crevice and slipped off every strand of hair. She watched expressionlessly as it changed the color of the water, polluting it with grime. Eventually, she stopped scrubbing and set the sponge aside so she could stir the misty swirls of color with her fingertips. Her head fell back against the edge of the tub and rested there.

After a while, she raised her hands and saw they were stained with blood again. The water in the tub was red, and it stuck to her palms. She stared at them for a long time.

A knock came at the door. "Blanca?" It was Mateo.

"Yeah?"

"Is it okay if me and Priya sleep in the bedroom?"

Blanca looked down at the dirty, red-stained water. "Sure, Mattie."

"Okay! Thanks!" A pause. "Are you okay in there?"

Blanca lowered her hands back into the water. Her fingers were starting to wrinkle.

"Y – Yeah, I'm good." She choked back a sob and climbed out of the tub. Iain had discovered some green flannel pajamas that were only a little too large for her, and Blanca pulled on the clothes numbly before heading out into the living room.

Everyone was there waiting for her, snuggled into various spots in the comfortable living room and looking drowsy. The fire in the hearth was blazing, and Otto was stretched in front of it on his stomach, eyes half closed. Priya rested in an armchair under a heap of blankets, and Mateo lay curled up on one end of the couch. Iain sat on the opposite end, a pillow trapped in his arms and his cheek resting against it.

Blanca dropped to the couch with Mateo and curled up in his arms. He rested his head against the top of her damp hair. "Blanca?"

"Yeah?"

Mateo's arms tightened around her. "I love you," he whispered.

She closed her eyes, but a few tears escaped and fell down her cheeks. "I love you, too, Mattie."

Blanca couldn't see his face, but she felt his smile and her heart fluttered on response. She wished—for a brief, painful moment—that she could keep him locked away in this tiny house until the world was safe.

But you don't exist here, her brain reminded her. *You aren't a person in this place. You're a trespasser. A parasite living off a land that isn't yours.*

But maybe this little home could be…?

It's borrowed time, and you know it.

Time, Blanca thought with a heavy dose of irony. She had never measured her life in hours, days, weeks, or years. Life for Blanca had always been divided into movements. This place to that one. One school and then another. An unfamiliar family, and the next day, someone different. Even when she'd joined the Army, there had been no settling in, no real sense of security or belonging. She'd fought through every damn test, waiting for the day when she'd done enough, but the foundation of her life rested on shifting sands, as it always had.

Eventually, she closed her eyes and forced herself to forget.

‒‒‒‒⊗‒‒‒‒

Later on, Mateo and Priya left the living room behind and curled up in bed together. The sheets were cool and soft, and the pillows were clean. A heavy quilt lay over them, welcome and reassuring. For a while, they whispered in the dark.

"Mateo," Priya whimpered. "Are we really going to get home?"

He reached over and pulled her into his arms. Her tears fell against his chest and dampened his shirt. "Yes, Priya. Blanca is going to get us there. I know she is." He stroked her hair. "She promised me, and she always keeps her promises." He paused. "Well, most of the time anyway. She did lie once."

"What? When?"

Mateo frowned. "My high school graduation. She swore she'd be make it. She said she'd get home from Afghanistan with plenty of time to spare, but on the day of the ceremony, she just wasn't there." He lowered his eyes. "No one was. I walked across the stage, got my diploma, and then I just sat down. No one cheered, no one clapped. There wasn't a single person in that audience who even knew who I was."

"I'm sure she had a good reason for missing," Priya murmured consolingly.

"She said her flight got delayed," Mateo explained with a sigh. "But when I looked it up online later, it didn't say anything about a delay. She just…missed it." He shrugged. "Anyway. It's not important." He fell asleep a few minutes later, and Priya slipped out of the bed and tip-toed into the living room. Otto and Iain were asleep, but Blanca was still on the couch, staring out into the deep, dark night. When she spotted Priya, she sat up, alarmed.

"Are you okay?"

"Yeah, yeah." Priya held up her hands and smiled. "I'm fine."

Blanca relaxed and reclined against the couch again. Priya hesitated before coming over and taking a seat next to Blanca, who looked over curiously. "You wanna' talk about something?" the older woman asked uncertainly. "Because that's really more Mateo's thing."

Priya wrapped her arms around her knees and looked up at the ceiling. "He's asleep."

"So wake him up."

Priya grinned. "Are you really that afraid of a little girl talk, Blanca?"

"I'm not afraid. Just don't care to make conversation."

"Why not?" Priya wiggled closer. "Come on. Mateo has so much faith in you, and you're so... strong. I just want to know more about you, that's all."

Blanca looked over Priya's sweet, round face. "No, you don't."

The pair fell into an uncomfortable silence until Priya spoke again.

"Maybe... you want to know about me, then. Do you? Come on, ask me anything. I'm an open book."

"No kidding."

Priya pouted. "Please. Isn't there anything you want to know?"

Blanca dragged a hand down her face. "Fine," she said finally. "Your name, Priya. That's an Indian name, right? So then what's up with 'Simmons'?"

Priya's eyes widened. "I was adopted," she explained after a pause. "My parents got me from an orphanage in India when I was a year old and named me Katie. I changed it to Priya as soon as I turned eighteen."

"Why?" Blanca asked, now curious.

Priya shrugged. "I just – I spent my whole life wondering about India. I wanted to know more about it, more about where I was born. My family back in Utah, they're all White. They said it didn't matter, that I was an American now and I didn't need to revisit the past." Her gaze dropped. "They meant well. They were trying to make me feel included, like I wasn't any different than my siblings. I was, though. No matter how colorblind they tried to be, I was still the oddball.

So I learned all I could about India. I practiced Hindi and watched Bollywood movies and did everything I could think of. I even tried to find my birth family, but the adoption paperwork only had one name. My birth mom's name."

"Priya," guessed Blanca.

The young girl nodded. "I have no idea why she gave me up or whether she's still alive. I guess I'll never know." She turned her gaze longingly to the window. "All I wanted was a small piece of India, something to remind myself that I didn't just materialize from nothing."

"It's hard," Blanca acknowledged solemnly, "being a part of two worlds. Being other."

"Apocryphal."

"What?"

Priya smiled sadly. "Apocryphal. It means 'of doubtful origin.' It's meant to describe urban legends, ya know, stories that may or may not be true. As soon as I saw it, though, I felt like I'd finally found a label that applied to me. I'd never thought of myself as American or Indian, daughter or sister, but this, this I could relate to. Apocryphal. Of doubtful origin."

Together, the two women gazed out into the blustery night, each lost in their own thoughts.

⸻ ◈ ⸻

The next morning, they all awoke later than usual. Blanca peered outside and saw the storm had only intensified, creating a total whiteout. They resolved to stay put, but Otto seemed bothered by the delay, and he stood at the window with his arms crossed, listening tensely to a German radio station for most of the morning. Blanca watched him for a while before walking over and grabbing his sleeve.

"There's nothing you can do right now," she pointed out. "It's not like you could fly in this anyway."

Otto grimaced. "The Russians are made for weather like this. They could use it to their advantage and attack our army. The men need us."

Blanca felt a small pang in her chest. "Are you going to leave?"

He hesitated before answering. "No. I said I would see you to the coast, and I plan to do that." His expression eased some, and he reached up, knocking a curled finger gently against her jaw. "You would perish without me." He jerked his head in the direction of the porch. "Come."

Together, they wrapped up in coats and headed outside. Otto pulled out his tin box of cigarettes and lit one before leaning against the porch railing. For a while, they looked out meditatively into the hellish storm without a word passing between them. Eventually, Blanca reached over and took the cigarette from Otto's mouth so she could pop it between her own lips and take a huff.

"Don't tell Mateo," she ordered, and Otto chuckled as he blew smoke away from them.

"Let me guess," he said. "Your time in the army?"

"Yeah," she admitted with a wry smile, flicking some ash off the end. She passed it back to him.

"You do not seem to do much sleeping," he noted. "Is that from your time in the army as well?"

Blanca shrugged. "Sleep and I have never gotten along."

"You have nightmares." There was no judgment in his voice.

She twisted her head in his direction. "Do you not?"

Otto seemed to seriously consider the question. "I do not have...fearful dreams, no. Not anymore. But I do have sad ones."

The air was bitterly cold. Blanca liked it. It made her feel more aware.

"Like what?"

Otto breathed in deeply, huffing on the cigarette and then passing it to her. "When I was young, I had a very close friend named Erich. He was like my brother. We dreamed of being pilots all our youth, and when we were finally accepted, we were so happy." He smiled, and it was one of the most miserable expressions Blanca had ever seen.

"While training, we met two other boys—because that is all we were at the time, boys—and their names were Klaus and Jannik." He kept his gaze trained on the bleak wintery sky. "The four of us together—oh, you would have hated us." He chuckled, eyes lowering, and Blanca couldn't help a small smile. "We were such trouble. But we had so much fun, and we were so close. For three years, we lived and worked together every day. We shared everything. We were family."

Otto's eyes shifted to his hands on the railing, and his fingers brushed the snow piled there. "On our very first mission, we said goodbye and left. That day, I shot down two Russian planes before returning to the base. I was so proud, and I could not wait to tell them all about it." He paused, and the pit in Blanca's stomach grew.

"But when I returned—and I saw my captain's face—I knew something was wrong. And I was right." He met Blanca's gaze. "I was… the only one who had made it back. All three of them had been shot down and killed." He inhaled deeply, grimacing and knocking his fist against the snowy railing. "I could not believe it. I had never—*we* had never even imagined such a thing. We thought we were invincible. We were wrong."

Blanca moved closer, and they turned their backs against the harsh winter wind, staying shoulder to shoulder. Otto looked up at the aged wooden roof and sighed deeply.

"So sometimes, when I dream, I dream of them. And I miss them."

"I'm sorry," Blanca murmured, surprised to find that she meant it very much. "What did you do after you found out?"

Otto looked over. "I killed every Russian I could find. And I have been doing it every day since."

Blanca nodded. She could understand that. Snow flurries fell around them, and she held out her hand so she could catch some in her palm. "Do you ever get tired of it?" she asked quietly. "The fighting?"

Otto watched her hand twirling in the wintery breeze. "No," he answered. "But I am not like you. My battles are ruthless, but I do not have to look my enemy in the eye." He tilted his head in her direction, and their faces were close. "My job takes skill, but yours requires perseverance, and that is something you cannot teach. I could not do what you do. You save people."

"Not all of them." She curled her fingers tensely and crushed the snowflake waiting in her palm. "Otto?"

"Yes?"

"Does everyone in Germany…" she paused, trying to find the right words. "I mean, do they all really support Hitler?"

Otto settled an odd look on her. The space between the question and its reply seemed to stretch on for ages.

"We are not so single-minded as that, Blanca," he said at last.

∞∞∞

Bavaria, Germany
1939

The line for the market stretched the length of the street and wrapped around the corner. Otto sighed and took his place at the end. Next to him, Erich stood with his hands shoved deep into the pockets of his coat. It was a cold, blustery day in Munich, and a persistent fog hugged the area and kept the sun at bay. Otto shifted in his spot and tried not to look as tired as he felt. The man in front of him was reading the latest issue of *Der Stürmer*. When he was done, he offered it to Otto, who declined. Erich took it and laughed at something on the cover.

With nothing better to do—and nowhere to go for a while—Otto looked around.

The neighborhood was mostly made up of aged brick walls and dilapidated storefronts, many of which featured empty displays and broken doors. The ghost of industry lingered here; it had been a busy area once. The grave reminder of what had existed before Germany's collapse only compounded the nation's collective misery.

Around them, the sidewalk was littered with trash and people alike. A pair of children sat on the stoop of an abandoned building. Otto told himself they were probably just waiting on their mother. He didn't see any likely candidates, though.

The queue shuffled forward. People appeared behind Otto and Erich, unsurprised to see the monstrous wait ahead of them. Some of the women had purses overflowing with German marks, but it hardly mattered. Inflation had destroyed the value of their currency some years before, and a suitcase full of cash was barely enough to buy a meal.

After a while, Erich tossed the paper aside and hunched against the wind to share a cigarette with Otto. After a few puffs, Erich said nonchalantly, "Factory got closed down."

Otto frowned. "The one your father and uncle work at?"

"Yeah."

Otto paused. "How'd he take it?"

"Pa?" Erich laughed humorlessly, dark eyes shifting over the battered skyline. "About the way he takes most things. He drank until he started fighting, and he fought until he started falling."

Otto sighed. "I'm sorry."

Erich shrugged. "Yeah, but…you know, it's actually alright. That job was a dead-end anyway. And besides," he clapped Otto on the arm, "we're nearly done with training, right? Pretty soon, we'll be in the sky, best pair of German aces the world's ever seen!" He laughed, and the sound was more genuine this time. "And I'll be sending my whole salary home, you know, so it'll be fine."

"Sure," Otto agreed, although he knew money was useless when there was nothing to buy. He didn't mention this to Erich. "Where do you think they'll be sending us?"

"Probably to France, I'd wager," Erich said, kicking a rock as they walked. "Heard they're going to be declaring war on us soon, official-like. On account of their friends, the Polacks."

The line inched forward, and Otto and Erich did the same. Eventually, they got close enough to the storefront to hear a radio. The voice that bellowed from its speakers was guttural, emphatic, and unmistakable.

"In connection with the Jewish question I have this to say: it is a shameful spectacle to see how the whole democratic world is oozing sympathy for the poor tormented Jewish people, but remains hard-hearted and obdurate when it comes to helping them, which is surely, in view of its attitude, an obvious duty..."

Otto listened with vague interest.

"The Americans act as if they pity the Jews," a woman behind said with disgust. "Why don't they just take them all if they like them so much? We'd gladly ship them out!"

Her companion nodded. "I heard the Americans make Germans in their country wear swastikas on their coats, as a protest for the treatment of the Jews," she added.

The two women exchanged scandalized looks and shook their heads. The voice on the radio raged on.

"Today I can only assure these gentlemen that, thanks to the brutal education with which the democracies favored us for fifteen years, we are completely hardened to all attacks of sentiment. The German nation does not wish its interests to be determined and controlled by any foreign nation..."

The wind picked up, wrapping them in a chill they had no choice but to endure. Otto had been in line for nearly two hours.

"...France to the French, England to the English, America to the Americans, and Germany to the Germans!"

"Germany to the Germans," Otto echoed reflectively, and he smiled.

At last, they were inside the store. The family in front of Otto received their groceries, and then Otto stepped forward, asking for bread and milk. Erich got the same, and he cradled them in his arms like a pair of infants. Together, they stepped aside and replaced their billfolds. Behind them, an old man came forward and asked for bread, gnarled hand clenched tightly around a wad of German marks.

The grocer sighed and shook his head. "I'm sorry, but that was the last bit. Supplies have been cut short by the bombings."

Otto looked over his shoulder as the old man groaned in disappointment. Otto frowned and looked down at the loaf of bread he carried. Erich's hold on his own food tightened.

"Excuse me, sir." Otto stepped forward and extended the bread he'd gotten. "Take mine."

The old man looked up in surprise. "Oh, no...I couldn't take that from you. You're a strong young man. You need it more than I do."

"I don't," Otto insisted, placing the bread in the man's weathered hand. "I'll be back at the base soon, and they'll feed us more than we need. Really. Take it."

The old man looked at the bread with clear eagerness, but he resisted valiantly for a few more minutes. Otto remained persistent and the old man eventually took the bread with a grateful noise that sounded dangerously close to a sob. He gripped Otto's arm with trembling fingers.

"Thank you for your service."

Otto managed a small smile. The elderly man wandered off, holding his bread like a proud hunter carrying his bounty. Otto sighed deeply.

"That was stupid of you," Erich remarked. "We won't be back at the base for another week."

"I know," Otto said wearily.

Erich knocked shoulders with his taller friend, and they walked to the steps of an old schoolhouse. It had once been filled with boisterous children, but Allied bombings had forced mass evacuations some years before. Only the poor and the proud remained in Munich now.

Otto took a seat across from Erich, who began to unpackage his bread. Otto quickly held up his hands. "Erich, save that for your family, you idiot."

Erich broke off a piece and handed it to him. "You are my family. Idiot." He laughed.

Otto huffed, but he took the bread and shoved some in his mouth before reclining against the splintered red wood. In the distance, the same radio broadcast as before continued to play, and the wind carried the words far and wide.

"In the course of my life I have very often been a prophet and have usually been ridiculed for it... Today I will once more be a prophet: If the international Jewish financiers in and outside Europe should succeed in plunging the nations once more into a world war, then the result will not be the victory of Jewry, but the annihilation of the Jewish race in Europe!"

The speech was met with thunderous applause. On the steps, Otto and Erich stuffed the bread into their mouths so they could clap, too.

CHAPTER 7

A lie told once remains a lie, but a lie
told a thousand times becomes the truth.
—Joseph Goebbels

The storm lasted through the next day and thickened the air with snow. Frustrated, Blanca paced the house like a caged animal before announcing she was going outside to chop wood for the fireplace.

After she'd returned and dumped the wood in the basket, she spotted Otto standing in the bathroom with the door open, this time examining the still-healing wound on his side. He was wearing her green flannel pajama pants and nothing else.

"Those pants are mine, you little thief," she told him, picking up the gauze and swatting away his hands.

"Actually, they belong to neither of us," he pointed out. "And they are clearly for men, as the hole in the front indicates—*meine gott*, your hands are freezing!" He jumped away from her touch, and Blanca grinned.

"I was outside chopping wood," she told him proudly. "I'm like a Latina Paul Bunyan."

"I have no idea who that is." He picked up her small cold hands and pressed them between his own with a smile.

"He's a lumberjack."

"Ah."

Tingly, borderline painful heat rushed through her palms and fingers, and Otto rubbed gently at her digits to encourage circulation and chase away the last of the chill. Blanca kept her gaze on their joined hands. Otto's movements slowed, the rough pads of his fingers pressing over hers tenderly.

Her eyes flickered up to his. Hastily, Blanca pulled her hands away from Otto's, rubbing them instead on her own hips. "Here, let me put a new bandage on." She finished quickly, and Otto watched without a word.

When night fell, the activity calmed and the group dispersed, falling into various spots to sleep.

Blanca knew she needed rest, but anxiety kept her stomach in knots and her mind racing. Finally, she got up and walked around the house so she could check on everyone. As she paced, a soft tune caught her attention, and she followed it into the kitchen. When she peered beyond the doorway, she found the room bathed in blue-gray shades of moonlight pouring in through the window.

Sitting at the dinner table was Otto, and he was toying with a radio in his lap. When he looked up and saw Blanca, his lips quirked. "I am trying to listen for news," he explained, voice low to avoid waking the others. "But there is only music. I suppose it is because of the holiday."

The house was uncomfortably quiet, and the unnatural stillness seemed to magnify every uneasy thought in Blanca's mind. She felt alien and out of place in the relative peace of a comfortable home. Otto, on the other hand, completed the familiar scene as if he'd been posed there. Blanca had the sudden mental image of his portrait, antiquated in shades of sepia, set against the glossy page of a history book.

Lieutenant Otto Zimmler, Luftwaffe pilot, it would read, along with the dates of his life. In her time, he was almost certainly dead, and the world would only know him as a photograph. They would see his sharp features and serious expression, and they would assume the details of his personality. They would not know about his sense of humor or the sound of his laugh. They would not guess he was good with children or skilled in card games. They would not know anything about him that mattered.

They would only know that he had lived and died as a Nazi.

Truthfully, it was a legacy well-deserved. Otto believed in his ideals. He was wrong in so many ways. Still, there was more to it than that. An entire life behind the uniform. A beating heart under the insignias. A host of memories beyond the cool gaze.

Blanca struggled against the sudden mental image of herself standing at attention in full military uniform, wilting under the scrutiny of Afghanistan's wary locals. *Who was the villain of that story*, she wondered. Her heart raced at the thought.

Otto noticed her frozen stare, and he gestured to a chair. "Sit," he offered softly.

Blanca took a seat. "Isn't it strange they get English-language stations all the way in Poland?" she asked, pointing at the radio. Otto shook his head.

"Oh, no. England broadcasts their stations all over Europe. It is possible to hear them in the very heart of Germany, although it is illegal to listen." He paused before telling her in a mischievous whisper, "I must admit, I do like the music."

Blanca rested her temple against her hand and watched. In an odd way, the strangeness of the night soothed her. If she could pretend this was all a dream, perhaps she could forget about the consequences...for a little while, at least.

Otto didn't seem to sense her mood. He adjusted the dial on the radio again. "Ah, like this woman here, she is wonderful. You must know her?" He turned up the music just a little. To Blanca, the song sounded terribly old-fashioned, and she didn't have the slightest idea who was singing. It was the beautiful, crooning voice of a woman, but the tune was unfamiliar.

"No idea," she murmured, eyes on Otto.

You'll never know just how much... I miss you... You'll never know just how much I care...

"She is called Vera Lynn," Otto explained. "She is very popular in your country. You are sure you have not heard of her?"

Blanca's eyes flickered over his face. "I haven't been home in a while."

Otto set the radio aside and stood with his hand extended. "Dance with me," he said, and Blanca snorted.

"I don't dance, Otto."

"Yes, I could have guessed as much," he teased. "But if you will allow it this one time, I will teach you something important. It may even save your life someday."

Blanca eyed him suspiciously. "What is it?"

"I am not telling unless you dance with me." When she hesitated, he added quite softly, "Please."

Blanca hesitated. Otto's expression seemed startlingly genuine. Even so, Blanca stayed where she was, frozen by the absolute certainty that this was yet another thing she would ruin.

But then the music shifted into a dreamier tune, and the darkness of the kitchen transformed into a wonderful disguise, cloaking them in something like peace. Blanca unclenched her hands from the chair and rose, fighting the urge to cross her arms.

"I don't really know what to do," she told him at last, making an awkward motion with her hand. "Never done this before."

Otto's lips turned up at a smile, and he took both of her hands, placing one at his shoulder and clasping the other between them. Tenderly, he laced their fingers. "It is quite simple," he told her. "You hold me here, and I hold you…"

Blanca gave him a sharp look, and Otto's mischievous smile grew.

"… here," he finished lightly, putting his hand demurely at her waist.

"You'd better watch yourself, Zimmler."

"I will be on my best behavior."

"That's not saying much."

He chuckled. "True." He turned her gently, and they swayed to the music.

Soon, their joined hands moved a little closer to their bodies, relaxing from the more formal stance. The motion brought them closer together, and Blanca's eyes lowered to the collar of Otto's shirt. A peculiar calm settled over her. She liked the quiet, the solitude, the soft flutter of piano from the radio. It reminded her of the church and the way her worries fell away for a precious few hours. It was cathartic, this moment of unfiltered interaction.

"What were you going to teach me?" she asked without looking up from Otto's shirt.

"A sentence," he whispered. "It is in German. Are you ready to hear it?"

Blanca nodded.

"*Ich bin Italiener,*" he said slowly.

"What does that mean?"

"It means," Otto said, "'I am Italian.'" His hand had shifted behind her back and settled at the base of her spine. She could feel each individual fingertip, and the sensation made it hard to concentrate on his words. "And if you are ever caught by Germans while I am not around, I want you to say it to them."

"Why?" Blanca fought to focus.

"If you tell them you are an American, they will kill you," he informed her, and his fingers reached up and traced along her collarbone until they found the chain around her neck. Blanca felt every nerve in her body follow the motion as he pulled out the ID tags, catching them in his fingers. "Especially if they find these. But many Italians are our allies. If you tell them you are Italian, they will likely treat you with respect and not harm you."

Blanca's eyes lowered as she considered his words. "And then what? What would I do from there?"

"You are clever. I am sure you can figure something out." He let her ID tags drop. "Try to say it. *Ich bin Italiener.*"

"Ick bin—" she fumbled, and Otto listened.

"*Ich,*" he corrected.

"Ick—uh."

"*Ich.*"

"That's a hard noise to make."

"It is not."

Blanca relaxed in his grip, suddenly fighting the urge to laugh. "*Ich,*" she managed, and Otto nodded.

"Better."

"*Ich bin Italiener.*"

"There, that almost sounded like German. Except for the 'r.' Why do you make that bird sound at the end?"

"Bird sound?" Blanca repeated a little too loudly, startled, and Otto hushed her. "What are you talking about? What bird sound?"

"You know, like… Oh, I cannot make it."

"Are you talking about rolling my tongue?" She did it, and Otto grinned.

"Yes, that!"

"Oh god," she muttered, and they laughed quietly.

"*That* is a strange noise."

The song changed, and neither of them noticed. They continued to sway.

"It's not hard," Blanca told him, amused. "You could do it. You just—ya know—press your tongue to the roof your mouth and—" she paused, trying to figure out how to explain it. "I don't know, make the noise."

"I think you are lying to me. I have never heard English like that."

"It's not English." She reached up and absently brushed a hand against the collar of his shirt. "It's Spanish."

"Spanish," Otto repeated thoughtfully. "Your family is from Spain?"

She shook her head. "Mexico, before I was born."

"Really? Does Mateo speak Spanish?"

Blanca thought about it. "Nah, he—he did when he was really little, but not anymore. I tried to speak it to him for a while, you know, so he wouldn't forget, but the foster homes kinda beat it out of us, so I stopped."

"Beat?" Otto asked. "You mean 'hit'?"

"Yeah," she said, shrugging. "I guess they thought—I don't know, maybe that we were trying to keep secrets from them or something. But it wasn't like that. I just wanted him to know Spanish because…" she paused, eyes low and unfocused on his front, "because that was the language our mom spoke. And I really wanted him to remember. You know, for her. That was…" her voice trailed off to a whisper, "…that was all."

A lump formed in her throat. The world around them seemed out of focus, and sentient shadows seemed to lurk in every corner. She scarcely noticed Otto's hands as they moved around her back, pulling her deeper into his embrace. His fingers traced sweeping, tender patterns just below her shoulder blades.

"What happened to her?" he asked very softly. "Your mother?"

A long pause.

"She got sent away," Blanca whispered.

"Sent away? Why?"

"Because she didn't exist."

They stopped swaying, but their bodies remained close. "For the longest time," Blanca continued, "I was afraid Mateo and I would get sent away, too. I was afraid… we weren't safe. That any day, someone would show up and tell us we didn't belong." She kept her face hidden in his shirt. "I think that's one of the reasons I joined the Army." She looked up at Otto's sympathetic expression, and her voice cracked. "I mean, what's more American than that?"

Otto swept his thumb over her fingers. "Nothing," he said simply. "You are the best of your people, Blanca."

They met gazes, and for a while, nothing was said.

"Do you want to know why I speak English so well?" Otto asked suddenly. At Blanca's nod, he leaned close. "It is because my mother spoke it to me."

He leaned against the kitchen table, Blanca still in his arms. "She is German," he explained, "but she grew up in a colony in South Africa. There, she spoke English nearly all her life, and when I was born, she taught it to me." He traced a curled finger along the inside of Blanca's wrist. "My father always hated it. He does not speak English at all, so he did not trust our words. He even commanded her to stop. But my mother is proud and stubborn, like you. So, she refused to listen."

Blanca chuckled quietly as she conjured up a mental image of Otto as a young boy, sitting at his mother's knee as she shared her language with him.

"So now when I speak English, I think of her," Otto went on, "and it fills me with joy, because I love her so much. I miss her."

Blanca felt her chest tighten. "Where is she?"

Otto frowned. "In her last letter, she told me she plans to flee Munich with my aunt because the English have been bombing the city nonstop. That was over a month ago. If she has written to me since then, I have not been there to receive it."

Blanca bit her lip. "I hope she's alright."

Otto took a moment to answer. "So do I," he said at last. He watched Blanca's face for a long time, and then he straightened away from the table, once more towering over her. "Now, what do you say if you are caught by Germans?"

Blanca made a gun motion with her fingers. "Pow."

"No. Try again."

"*Ich bin Italiener.*"

"Very good."

Belatedly, Blanca realized how close they were. Otto's hand at her back had drawn them together quite subtly, and the space between them had vanished. Unconsciously, she curled her fingers against the hard planes of his stomach.

"I do not think there are other women like you, Blanca."

The calm she'd felt before slipped away at his words, affectionate though they were. When she looked down at her feet, her forehead rested against his front and her eyes were hidden. "There are plenty of women like me, Otto," she said to his chest. "You just don't know any because your government kills them all."

He lowered his face to hers. "That is not fair," he insisted heatedly, and Blanca turned her head away, moving to pull herself from his grip.

"You're right, Otto. It isn't fair. But that's life."

He held on to her. "I refuse to believe that is all there is to it."

"What else is there to say?" she asked. "Tell me. What can you say to make all this Nazi craziness seem 'okay'?" Otto opened his mouth, but Blanca cut him off. "Would I be safe in Munich?"

His expression shifted to uncertainty.

"You know I wouldn't, and not just because I'm an American. If the Nazis had their way, it would never be safe for someone like me—or Mateo or Priya—to ever live in your country. We couldn't walk your streets. We couldn't shop your stores. And we sure as hell couldn't live in your houses." She caught his shirt in her fingers. "We would be killed. Look at me, Otto. I would be dead or a prisoner under Nazi rule, and so would Mateo."

Otto breathed in deeply, blue eyes serious. He seemed ready to speak several times, but the words never materialized.

"Is that what you want?" Blanca asked earnestly. "Is that what you fight for?"

Before he could answer, a noise at the door drew their attention.

"Uh—"

It was Mateo, standing in the doorway to the living room. Blanca pulled away from Otto roughly, and he stepped back as well, clearing his throat and folding his arms. When Blanca glanced at him, he refused to look at her.

"What're you doing up, Mateo?" she asked gruffly.

Mateo pointed. "Getting some water."

"We should sleep," Otto mumbled, and then he brushed by Mateo, who watched him go.

Blanca was left alone with Mateo. He raised a brow at her. "So, uh, what was that all about?"

"Nothing," she muttered crossly.

"Really? Because your pelvises were touching."

Blanca clenched her fists. "Just get your damn water and go back to bed!"

"Fine." He got his drink and returned to the bedroom. Blanca paced the kitchen listlessly for almost fifteen minutes before finding a distant corner to sleep in alone.

⸻

The next morning, the group loaded up cooked portions of the meat from the home's stash, and then, with gritted teeth, they stepped out into the powdery snow and frigid air. Priya sighed heavily, and as they walked away from the little cottage, she turned and waved.

"Bye little house," she called out mournfully.

They walked all day, trudging through the snow and fighting for every step. They pulled scarves over their faces and wore wool hats on their heads, but the harsh winter air cut through it all, biting at them like a million stinging insects.

All the while, Otto stayed unusually quiet and speculative, speaking little and thinking very hard. Each time Blanca tried to talk to him, he made an excuse to get away.

That night, the group stopped at the sounds of shouting in the distance. They peered into a clearing and spotted a cluster of German soldiers gathered nearby. The uniformed men were ushering groups of civilians out of trucks and onto the platform of a train station.

"What are they doing?" Mateo asked worriedly. He looked at Otto, who shifted tensely and picked up the radio. He already knew what was going on, but he listened anyway.

"The soldiers are transporting them out of the area," he told the others. "They must come from a village nearby."

Priya bit her lip. "Are they going to kill them?"

"I do not know," he lied resolutely and without hesitation.

"Well, where are they heading?" Mateo took the binoculars and looked at the train. The soldiers were now going through the civilians' luggage, separating items of value and tossing them into crates. Many of the villagers were women and children. "Otto, where are they going?"

"Treblinka," the German answered quietly. "It is a work camp."

"We've got to help them!" Priya piped up immediately, but Iain touched her shoulder.

"We can't, Priya. I'm sorry."

"There are too many soldiers," Blanca agreed. "We don't need to start any fights."

"But Otto, you—you could talk to the soldiers, make up an excuse, tell them not to take those people away—"

"I am not their commanding officer," Otto growled. "I have no authority over those men. They have no reason to follow my orders."

"So we're just going to let them all die?" Mateo asked harshly.

"I'm sorry, Mattie." Blanca ran a hand over her face. "This is the way it has to be. You know that. We can't do anything."

Priya looked back at the train and sniffled. "They're all so afraid…"

"Come on." Blanca took Mateo's bicep in her hand and tugged him away, and Iain stood behind her, motioning to Priya.

Otto turned and left with them, distracted by his own thoughts. That night, as he kept watch, his eyes drifted over to Blanca's sleeping form nearby, and the desire to curl up next to her nearly overwhelmed him. After a while, the others all fell asleep, and Otto knocked his gun lightly against his head, eyes closed and head bent.

Close to sunrise, his decision was made. He stood up, shouldered his bag, and walked quietly over to the spot where Blanca slept. Behind his back, the horizon grew lighter as the break of dawn approached. Otto placed the map in Blanca's bag, and then—quite against his own will—he reached out and touched her dark brown hair. Blanca curled closer in her sleep, threatening to shatter Otto's resolve with one tender motion.

Fighting against the turmoil in his heart, Otto stood and stepped over her, sliding his gun away from his front as he came to the sleeping bag Mateo shared with Priya. Otto wanted to leave him something important, something to remember him by, but he didn't have anything.

I am sorry, Mateo.

Frustrated, he started to stand. Just as he pulled away, a gust of wind blew over their campsite and stirred the sleeping bag. Otto's gaze sharpened on it. Something wasn't right. Brows furrowed, he leaned over and pulled back the dirty material.

The sleeping bag was filled with coats. Mateo and Priya were gone.

Otto's stomach lurched. Frantically, he pulled away all the bags and coats, hoping to find something. A train whistle blasted shrilly into the early morning air, and his head snapped up. "*Quatsch!*" he hissed, before sprinting in Blanca's direction. "Blanca, get up! Get up!" He grabbed her and she jerked awake.

"What—What's happening?"

"Mateo and Priya are missing. I think they went after those prisoners."

The color drained from Blanca's face, and she snatched up her gun before racing off through the woods. Otto and Iain followed quickly. They dropped to their knees and peered through the branches to see the German officers ushering people into train cars.

"Where are they?" Blanca growled anxiously. "I don't see them!"

"There!" Iain pointed, and they looked sharply to see Mateo and Priya in the distance.

Otto cursed fiercely. "They were caught! Idiots!"

Iain pointed. "Shite, the train's leaving!"

"Like hell it is!" Blanca snarled before sprinting out into the open.

"Blanca!" Otto jumped up and raced after her with Iain hot on his heels. German soldiers spotted them, shouted, and raised their guns.

"*MOVE!*" Blanca roared, snapping up her gun and spraying the area with bullets. Soldiers dropped at her feet and she leaped over them while the others rushed after her.

"BLANCA, WAIT!" Otto shouted, but she didn't seem to hear him.

The train was moving faster now, picking up speed, and Blanca still outran them all. The ground beneath their feet became asphalt and railroad tracks. She didn't slow, didn't shoot, didn't even look in the direction of the remaining soldiers.

Instead, she jumped.

Otto's heart seized as Blanca flew through the air and grabbed the back of the train, feet locking onto the lowest rung of a ladder for barely half a second before she powered her way up.

Otto jumped after her, catching the ladder just as Iain slammed into the side next to him and latched onto a tiny railing. "Bloody hell!" Iain yelped, looking back at the speeding tracks with a terrified gasp.

Blanca was already near the top, jaw set and teeth bared in a growl. She gripped the railing and scrambled up only to get knocked back by the icy gusts rolling over the train car's roof. Undeterred, she dropped to her stomach and crawled across the frosted metal with manic determination.

"Blanca!" Otto called out again, but she was already at the small roof door to the train car. Without warning, she reared back with the handle of her gun and struck as hard as she could.

"*OPEN—THE—FUCK—UP!*" she screamed, bashing it against the door.

Inside the train car, German soldiers jerked in surprise at the thuds and clanks overhead. Priya and Mateo, bound and crammed in with the other captives, looked up with wide eyes. At the sound of Blanca's voice, Mateo's face turned white.

"They're here!" Priya cheered.

"Oh, god," Mateo groaned, looking nauseated.

The Germans inside scrambled, confused, then opened fire on the roof, peppering the metal with bullet holes. Blanca jerked aside and tumbled straight off the edge of the train. Otto leaped forward and snatched her wrist, and she slammed against the freezing cold metal with a pained gasp.

"Hold on!" Otto shouted as he locked his other arm around a metal piece of roofing. Inside the rattling train car, the Germans heard his voice and fired through the car's walls, filling the metal with holes just inches away from where they held on for dear life.

"*Shit!*" Blanca screamed, looking down below her feet.

The ground was gone.

Otto whipped his head around to watch as the train car left the Polish countryside behind and sped out onto a narrow train bridge spanning a vast mountainous gorge. Below them was nothing but misty air and jagged peaks. Blanca kicked fiercely and found her footing just before Otto hauled her back up to the top of the train. She gripped him for the barest of moments before looking around frantically.

"Iain!" she shouted over the rushing wind.

"I'm here!" he called from somewhere below. "We have to find a way to disconnect the car!"

"Get down!" Otto shouted suddenly, shoving Blanca to her stomach as gunfire pierced the air just above her head. Two German soldiers pulled themselves out of the top door and aimed their rifles, and Blanca rolled over with Otto to avoid the shots as they blazed by.

Blanca raised her gun with a snap and fired. One of her shots landed, but the other missed, and the remaining German soldier levelled his rifle at Blanca's head.

Gunfire pierced the German's chest, jolting him, and then he slumped back, spine curling grotesquely as he went limp. Blanca rolled onto her back, lips parted in shock as she and Otto locked gazes. He lowered his gun shakily, expression stricken.

The train lurched, hurling itself around a corner in the direction of a gaping tunnel set against the mountainside. Otto's focus sharpened once more, and he hurried to Blanca's side. A wave of darkness enveloped them as they sped into the tunnel, and Otto curled his arms protectively over Blanca's body.

A voice called out to them.

"Mateo?" Blanca called out hoarsely.

"GET IN HERE, BLANCA!" he shouted in reply.

Light blasted over them as the train flew out of the tunnel. A final German soldier appeared and leaped at Otto, drawing him into a brutal fight for control of his gun. Blanca threw herself at the German soldier and they crashed at the front of the car, landing with such force that the roof collapsed. Inside the car, terrified prisoners screamed and jumped out of the way. Otto landed behind her and smashed his gun against the German soldier's head, causing him to drop.

"Where's Iain?" Priya exclaimed, and Otto pulled open the heavy doors so he could peer out. He was astonished to see Iain standing between the two train cars, feet perched dangerously on the metal pieces connecting them.

"We have to get this car away from the rest of the train!" Iain called out, smashing a metal hook against the connecting rod. "Hold on to something!"

Otto ducked back into the train and grabbed Blanca with one arm and Mateo with the other.

Outside, Iain brought down the metal hook one last time and hit the connector as hard as he could. It broke, and inside the train car, something snapped and the train rocked, tossing them all to the floor. There was a metal dragging sound under their feet; something had fallen off onto the tracks below them. The passengers were thrown against the wall, and there was a terrible screeching noise as the rest of the train left their car behind.

Screams rang out as the train car skidded wildly out of control and leaped off the tracks with a metallic shriek. The passengers were thrown around like ragdolls, bodies flying from floor to ceiling and back again as the train car slammed into the earth. It rolled rapidly, flipping once, twice, and then a third time before finally crashing on its side and sliding to a stop on the snowy grass.

Wearily, Otto opened his eyes and breathed in a shaky breath. Blanca wheezed next to him, and he reached down, gently tugging her to her feet.

"B—Blanca—"

They looked up to see Mateo with Priya at his side. "I think I'm okay, but…Priya…"

Blanca quickly went to Priya and found her sobbing in pain as she clutched her side. Blanca couldn't see what was wrong in the darkness of the train car. The other people started to move and cry out. "We need to get Priya out of here, I think she broke a rib."

They glanced around to see other people stirring, groaning, and crying. There were some beneath their feet who were almost certainly dead. Otto looked back at Blanca. "Your head is bleeding," he said worriedly.

She shook her head quickly, wincing as she did so. "No, I'm—"

"You need someone to look at you—"

"Not now," she told him firmly. "Come on, we have to get these people out of here."

"But—"

"*Otto.*"

He scowled. "Fine."

One by one, they pulled people out of the overturned rail car. Fortunately, the other train cars hadn't stopped, and no one was coming back for them—yet. As soon as Blanca's feet hit the snowy grass, she looked around desperately. "Iain!" she yelled out, swallowing over her dry throat. "Iain!"

"I don't see him, Blanca," Mateo said anxiously as he helped Priya lower herself to the ground.

"Otto, see if you can find Iain."

Otto looked at her gravely and nodded. "I will return soon." He took his gun and left, jogging back in the direction from which they'd come.

Blanca began attending to the people as they climbed out of the train, and Mateo did his best to help her. Blanca worked like a woman possessed, eyes dark with focus as she set bones with bits of cloth and plugged gushing wounds with her bare fingers.

The chaos settled. The minor injuries were attended to, and the greater ones were managed, except for those that weren't. Blanca dropped her head as a woman slipped away in her arms, last rattling breath echoing in the open air.

"Blanca! Get over here!"

Blanca's head jerked up just in time to see Otto and Mateo round a corner with Iain between them. Blood soaked the Irishman's shirt, and as soon as Blanca stopped in front of him, the reason for the gore became immediately apparent: Iain was missing his left hand. It had been completely ripped off.

"Jesus Christ," Mateo murmured in horror.

"I tried to...to hold the train," Iain rasped. "Caught my...hand under a chain..."

Blanca sucked in a deep breath. "It's okay, hey—we've got this, it's going to be fine. We've got to sterilize it—Iain, stay awake, come on. Mattie, get the alcohol." Blanca leaned over Iain and touched his face. "Hey, Iain. Look, we've got to bandage up your arm, okay?"

Mateo poured alcohol over the bandage. Iain shuddered, swallowing and kicking tensely at the ground. "B-Blanca," he gasped.

Otto paced restlessly behind them.

Without looking away from Iain, Blanca took the bandage from Mateo. "Just a few seconds more," she promised him, head snapping back in the direction of his wrist, which now ended at a bloody nub lined with a few shredded pieces of skin. "Okay, let's go." She pushed the bandage over the nub where his hand had been, and Iain let out an agonized shout and twisted on the snow. Blanca quickly pulled the bandage up around the end of his arm and wrapped it while Mateo fought to keep him still.

After a few minutes, Iain fell back limply against the ground, tears streaming down his cheeks.

Priya hobbled over and held his head in her lap while Blanca finished up with his arm. "It's okay, Iain," she whispered, pressing her cheek against his forehead. While he was distracted, Blanca secured the bandage and sat back with an exhausted sigh. After taking a moment to push past her paralyzing grief, she stood.

"I will go check the car for any others," Otto told Blanca numbly, turning away and climbing back into the shadowy steel shell. He looked around slowly. Most everyone in there was already dead. Otto rubbed his temples and fought to steady his breathing. A ringing sound in his ears kept him from concentrating.

"Z-Zimmler?"

Otto looked up sharply.

A grievously wounded German soldier sat slumped in the corner. Otto walked over cautiously, jaw set. The German's nametag read *Goten*.

"How do you know my name?"

Goten twitched involuntarily. There was a great deal of blood around his stomach. "Y-Your picture," he said in German. "It is…at the base. They are…looking for you." Goten looked at him suspiciously, his face streaked with blood and dirt. "You…you shot at German soldiers. You… killed them."

Otto narrowed his eyes.

"Why?" Goten asked angrily. "Why…did you do that?"

"I am a prisoner."

"You…do not look like…a prisoner… to me."

The broken door opened and Blanca stepped in. When she spotted Otto, she hurried up to him. "Otto, we need to—You're bleeding." She didn't notice the German soldier, and she reached out. "Here, let me see—"

Otto pulled away from her. "Stop."

The injured German scowled, and Blanca noticed him at last.

"A prisoner?" Goten asked Otto in German, and Blanca looked at Otto uncertainly. Goten let out a mocking laugh that was interrupted by a cough. "You are no prisoner. You are a... traitor."

Otto clenched his hands.

"A traitor," sneered Goten, "who betrays his country for nothing more than a wet place to put his—"

"*Shut your mouth!*" Otto snarled suddenly, and Blanca jerked back in alarm.

"If I could live...just one more day," rasped the German soldier, "I would...see you...in front of the firing squad..."

Otto pulled Blanca's knife out of her pocket.

"...and your bitch starved to death in a camp where she belongs!"

In a flash of movement, Otto sliced the German's throat. Blood spilled from the gash, pouring down the man's neck as his vicious tirade ended in a gurgle. Otto continued to stare, hands curled tightly at his sides.

"...What was that all about?" Blanca asked quietly.

"Nothing," he grunted, brushing past her and leaving the car.

Blanca watched him go and remained where she was. The sound of her own breathing seemed monstrously loud. Then the cries for help and wails of pain from outside the train car returned, flooding her with anxiety, and she forced herself to go out. Mateo quickly found her.

"Blanca, what're we going to do? We've got to find help!"

"*Where*, Mateo?" She quickly lowered her voice. "What the hell are we gonna do with all these people?"

A few feet away, a young man around Mateo's age lingered uncertainly. He was less injured than the rest of them, and he seemed to be waiting for a chance to speak. Blanca swatted in his direction. "See what he wants."

Mateo turned to face the young man. "Do you need help?"

"You—You are soldier?" asked the stranger in a thick accent. He looked at the gun sitting behind Mateo's shoulder.

Mateo followed his gaze, then looked back at him. "Uh…well, sort of. You speak English?"

"Some," said the unfamiliar young man, looking nervous. "I learn in university. My name is Jan."

"Oh, hi, Jan." Mateo smiled unsteadily. "My name is Mateo."

Jan relaxed and returned the smile. "You are—help us?"

Mateo hesitated. "Yes, but we don't really know what to do," he admitted. "We're lost, and we don't have a place to take everyone that's safe."

Jan grew excited. "I can show—I know where we go. To be safe. You will take us?" At Mateo's doubtful look, Jan stepped a little closer. "Please," he pleaded softly. "We are…we will die. But we go here, to this place, we find soldiers. Soldiers of *Polska*."

Mateo's eyes widened. "Really? You can take us to the Polish Army?"

"*No!*" Jan answered happily, and Mateo's brows knitted.

"…Uh. Okay?"

Jan dragged a hand down his face, looking embarrassed. "I apologize, I mean—yes. Yes, I know army. Do you have the map?"

"My sister does—hang on, we have to talk to Blanca." Mateo tugged on Jan's arm and they hurried over to where Blanca was kneeling next to Iain. As soon as she saw Jan, she stood and regarded him suspiciously.

"This is Jan," Mateo explained. "He can take us to the Polish army."

Otto lingered nearby, listening but not commenting.

"He says we can take all the people there, and they'll be safe," Mateo continued before looking at Jan, who stepped forward.

"Please, we need help. When we are with soldier, we can be safe." Jan pointed at the map, and Blanca swore.

"Shit, he means Warsaw."

"There are soldiers in Gęsiówka," Jan told them. "They come together to fight, everyone. They say 'Poland is not yet lost.'"

Otto paced restlessly. "This will end badly. The Führer has been waiting for a reason to utterly destroy Warsaw." He eyed Jan. "If your army continues to fight, your city will be lost forever."

Jan fell silent and said nothing.

"How many German soldiers are stationed there?" Blanca asked Otto, who grimaced.

"SS, Gestapo, and Wehrmacht combined? Over thirty thousand. So, enough to repel an invasion, but not enough to make it fast." He sighed. "Going to Warsaw would be incredibly dangerous."

Mateo frowned. "We can't abandon all these people."

"If you had listened to your sister," Otto said harshly, "we would not have these people's lives on our hands."

Mateo tucked his head and looked away. Blanca shoved her fingers through her hair until the tangled knots snagged her fingers and yanked at her skull. At last, she motioned to the others. "Get the survivors ready to go."

The others nodded and scattered as Otto turned away and headed to a snow-covered tree. He placed his forearm on the frosted bark and rested against it with his eyes closed. Blanca appeared behind him.

"You're not a prisoner anymore, Otto."

He turned to face her. "I know."

Blanca stepped closer but didn't touch him. "If you...
need to leave—if you feel like this is a step you can't take,
I won't try to stop you." She shifted uneasily. "I don't want
to ask you to attack your own people again."

The mental image of his horrified expression on the
train hovered at the forefront of her mind.

"How can I let you go alone?" he asked weakly. "How
can I let you leave, knowing you would not be safe?"

Blanca hesitated. "I'm not your responsibility."

Otto looked over her face.

"What man on this earth is not responsible for those
he cares for?"

Blanca dropped her gaze, biting her lip hard. A
fingertip at her jaw urged her to look up once more. "But
before I do this, I need to hear the truth." Otto's expression
grew serious. "Why are you here, Blanca?"

The air left her chest. Blanca thought very hard about
the question.

Why are you here? It was a question she'd asked herself
a thousand times since arriving in Poland. Truthfully,
though, she knew the answer.

"Because I deserve to be," she told him at last.

<hr />

Nangarhar, Afghanistan
2018

Blanca's squad left the base in the early hours of morning.
There were a dozen soldiers in their group, but Blanca
was the only medic. Some platoons had a couple; it just

depended on who was available and where. For some time though, she had been the only 68 Whiskey around. Just dumb luck, she supposed.

The morning was bright and sunny. Their squad had done this same route maybe twenty times, mostly just on patrol. Today, however, they were looking for specific signs of insurgent activity. Blanca kept her eyes sharp and focused. Complacency meant a bullet to the head. She wasn't going out like that, no matter how many times they took the same dull walk.

Feeling anxious, Blanca patted the vest pocket where her knife was kept. Her friend and fellow soldier Jerome had given it to her after she'd admitted to failing a physical training test. "You can't always be the biggest cat in the fight," he'd told her, "but you can sure as hell be the meanest." Blanca had taken his words to heart, and she hadn't let the knife out of her sight since.

On the road, a figure appeared. Blanca felt her heartbeat spike, but then she saw it was just a child—a boy, maybe six years old. She waited to see what Sergeant Davies would do. The child was alone.

"Sir?" Jerome questioned from near the front. The group stood immobilized when the little boy started to cry. He lifted his arms to the group, expression pleading.

Oh, god, no. Please.

Blanca looked nervously at Davies, who hesitated. The little boy began to stagger in their direction. Blanca fought to keep herself still, and she saw some of her fellow soldiers look at each other warily.

"Sir?" Jerome questioned again more loudly, holding up his rifle.

The boy came closer. Blanca's lips parted.

"Sergeant, he has an explosive device on him!" she called out just before her attention was diverted by movement near their left side.

Three men, two in white and one in brown, ushering a covered cart in their direction. This, too, was laced with explosives, and before Blanca could open her mouth to yell out, the cart rolled down to the distracted platoon.

The ensuing explosion rocked Blanca and the others off their feet, blasting them off the main road in a cloud of blood, rocks, and bodies. Blanca crashed to the earth with a shocked cry. After a few dazed seconds, she managed to lift her head. The simple act of breathing coated her lungs in sticky grime, and the world jumped across her vision in nauseating bursts.

With a pained groan, she pushed herself up. Next to her were a half-dozen mismatched body parts. One unanchored arm belonged to the child. The rest of him was nowhere to be seen.

Sirens wailed in the distance. Someone was calling for them on the radio. With a hiss of pain, Blanca shoved her dislocated shoulder back into place with a gritty pop.

"Agh!" she cried out. "Son of a *whore!*"

Panting, she turned in a circle and looked all around, unable to see far in the dusty circle left in the aftermath of the bombs. Davies was face down in the dirt, half-gone and dead. Blanca stumbled forward, only to trip and fall over a body. When she looked down, she saw it was Jerome. He'd caught the brunt of the bomb, and the ruined features of his face were almost unrecognizable. Blanca let out a sob.

But when three men came rushing by—two in white and one in brown—the tears dried, and Blanca's eyes followed them with a predatory fervor. Logic evaporated.

Her mind splintered and went dark. There was nothing else but this—this pursuit.

Reaching down, Blanca snatched up her rifle and hobbled after the men, more furious by the second. She didn't see. She didn't think. She didn't consider anything other than the three figures trying to lose her around every corner.

They darted into a building and ran up a flight of stairs. Alone, Blanca followed them, sounding heavier than she was in her armored gear. The men hurried into a room upstairs and tried to shut the door behind them. Blanca rammed her body against the aged wood and burst inside, rifle raised.

The three men dropped to their knees, hands raised and expressions panicked. They ducked their heads in surrender, babbling continuously in a string of unintelligible words.

She advanced on them, rifle at the ready, unable to see three men and instead only knowing this was the end. This was where her life had been heading. Her breathing was so loud, so ragged, it seemed to echo for miles. Blood ran down from her injured temple, staining her vision with red. She prepared to shoot.

The sound of a woman's pleading scream suddenly broke through the cloud of white-hot fury, and Blanca's dark eyes flickered to the side.

She saw three women and two children. They were squatted in the corner, crying and reaching out to the men, who tried to shoo them away. Their words were meaningless, but the desperation was potent. The women clasped their hands and shook them in the air, sobbing and begging as the two children squalled at the top of their lungs. Their little faces were red and streaked with tears. They were calling out to the men. They wanted their fathers.

For a half second, pity—the precursor to mercy— entered her mind.

Then, like the intricate internal gears of a clock, Blanca's features shifted in sync to form an entirely new expression, one that was contorted, broken, and warped.

With a snap, she twisted back in the direction of the men and opened fire.

CHAPTER 8

Leadership is a potent combination of
strategy and character. But if you must
be without one, be without the strategy.
—Norman Schwarzkopf

Early morning arrived in the form of foggy gray air and brash winds. Snowflakes stuck to their lashes, making them white and stiff. Blanca didn't have gloves, and her fingers moved sluggishly on her gun. More than once, Otto pulled her hands into his and rubbed them for warmth even as his own fingers trembled.

Iain struggled. Healthy color drained from his face, and he could barely keep up. Mateo often had to hang back and keep him on his feet.

The people from the train were not faring any better. Wary travelers regularly collapsed and did not get up. A four-year-old girl breathed her last in Blanca's arms. That night, Blanca slipped away from the others and sobbed under the cover of darkness. When she came back, a pair of hands drew her into an embrace.

"It will be alright, *Schatz*."

Blanca surprised herself by curling into his embrace. They were alone, and she felt powerless against the desire to sink against his warm body. Otto's grip felt like the only thing keeping her from breaking apart entirely.

His fingers curled against hers, drawing her down to the ground with him so she was settled between his legs. For some time, Blanca simply sat in the circle of his embrace, uncertain. Then, her heart pounding, she reclined against him and placed her temple against his chest.

Otto's arms closed around her, and she noted distantly that he'd found a blanket somewhere. He secured it around her with the utmost care before resettling his arms around her.

Across the ramshackle camp, the remaining Polish civilians cried miserably and groaned in pain. Blanca clenched her eyes shut tight, wishing she could shut off her mind. Each time she tried to breathe, the pressure building in the center of her chest grew worse. Panic ripped the air from her lungs and she whimpered.

"Blanca," Otto whispered worriedly, tilting her chin up with a fingertip. "Stop, stop upsetting yourself."

Raspy noises escaped her, growing worse by the second as Blanca struggled against the pain, the panic, the icy injection of fear that so ruthlessly assaulted her. Otto pressed her open palm against his chest.

"*Schatz*, look at me," he whispered soothingly, and Blanca made a choked noise before looking up at his face. "See how I breathe?" He inhaled deeply, letting her feel the movement of his chest under her hand. "Breathe like me. Think of nothing else. Focus on that."

"I can't—" Blanca sobbed.

"Yes, yes, you can. Focus on me." He breathed in deeply again. "Match my breathing." Blanca's trembling hand stayed on his chest, and she tried to mimic him as he inhaled, but the motion caught in a painful bubble in her chest.

"Try it again, with me." He repeated the motion, taking long, exaggerated breaths with her hand pressed against his warm torso. She could feel the cool rush of air as he drew in each gulp, the steady rise and fall of his breathing. She fought to match it, shaking violently.

"Better, better." Otto's shadowed expression changed to a tender smile. "More, though, a deeper one. Ready?" He put his hand over hers on his chest and repeated the motion countless times, guiding her to a steady pace.

Each breath got a little easier. Blanca wiped furiously at her wet face with a shoulder. The knot in her chest began to loosen, and the tension eased, bit by bit.

"There you are," Otto murmured proudly, tucking some hair behind her ear with his free hand. "Keep going."

At last, Blanca felt some semblance of relief. Lips parted, she slowly lowered herself against him again, eyes closing as she listed for the steady beat of his heart. It grounded her, keeping her from that awful place in the dark corners of her mind.

As he pulled his hand away, she followed the motion, bringing her face near his. Their lips came together, and Blanca closed her eyes and held tight.

As they kissed, an impossible vision materialized in her rattled mind.

In it, Blanca saw herself in a bed curled up in the arms of someone who would have been lost without her. This was someone she could rely on—someone to make her laugh and see and understand and feel.

Someone who made her feel like she didn't have to do every damn thing alone.

For a few seconds, Blanca managed to press away her anxiety and live inside this false memory even as she created it. Otto's hands, so gentle, traced along her lower back and pulled her up against him.

And then the brilliant vision faded away, evaporating into tendrils of smoke, and the darkness invaded once more. Blanca pulled back, wishing to god she could just do something right and easy and nice for once, but she was crying again and the moment was broken. Otto, far from being bothered, left one more loving kiss on her lips and then another on her cheek. Then he made a gentle noise of comfort, fingers in her hair again.

"Good night, *Schatz*," Otto whispered, and he kissed the crown of her head.

He had called her that before. Blanca didn't ask what it meant.

"Good night," she whispered, fingers curling in his shirt.

After three more days of walking, they came within sight of Warsaw.

"We'll rest here tonight," Blanca told the others. "We need a plan to get into the city."

Everyone agreed and prepared to make camp. Iain collapsed against a tree, and Priya rested next to him with an exhausted sigh. Mateo covered them both with a blanket while Jan looked on with a frown.

A few minutes later, Mateo joined Blanca and Otto at their fire.

"You shouldn't get attached to that boy," Blanca told her brother with a nod in Jan's direction. She'd seen them late at night, cuddled together and whispering lowly.

Mateo prodded the fire with a stick and kept his eyes low. "I can't help it. I really like him."

Otto wrinkled his nose, but after a pointed look from Blanca, he smoothed out his expression. Still, he said, "I do not understand why you cannot simply date Priya. You like her, do you not? She is pretty enough?"

Mateo rolled his eyes. "Yes, Otto. I like her, and she's pretty, but I just don't feel that way about her." He dropped the stick. "Besides, what difference does it make to you? Why do you care so much if I'm gay?"

Otto considered Mateo's question. "I want you to have a good life," he answered after a moment. "I want you to have a future. A house, a career. You cannot do that if you are a homosexual."

"Maybe not where you live," Mateo replied.

Otto looked skeptical.

"Would you hate me?" Mateo asked curiously. "If I said I was going to be gay forever, would you hold it against me for the rest of my life?"

Otto lowered his eyes. "No," he murmured at last. "I would not hate you."

"Do you think Blanca would?"

Otto shook his head. "No."

Mateo relaxed and nudged Otto's shoulder playfully. "Then what do I have to be afraid of? If I've got you and Blanca and maybe even a real boyfriend one day, what else do I need?"

Otto smiled a little. "You have conviction. That is something to be proud of."

"I mean, come on. Look who I was raised by." Mateo nodded at Blanca, whose lips quirked.

Otto chuckled. "That is true," he murmured with an affectionate look at Blanca.

Mateo stood up and dusted off his hands. "You can't choose who you love, Otto. You should remember that."

He clapped a hand on Otto's shoulder and walked off, leaving the stunned German behind.

⁂

The next morning, Blanca awoke with an immediate feeling of dread. Something wasn't right. She sat up in her sleeping bag and looked around. The morning was dim, muted, and still. When she spotted Otto pacing the fringes of her camp, she hauled herself up and went over to him.

"What is it?"

Otto didn't look at her. "We are being watched," he said very softly. "As soon as we prepare to move, soldiers will be on us."

Blanca fought against the sudden pounding of her heart. "Do they know we know?"

"I do not believe so."

"Are they German?"

"I am not sure, but they are definitely here." He turned to face her and reached out to brush a curled fingertip along her jawline. Then he leaned close, his face very near hers. "Whatever happens, do not risk your life for the Poles. You get our people out of here. Do you understand?"

Blanca nodded jerkily.

Otto brushed his lips over hers in a feather-light touch and then pulled away suddenly so he could start waking the others. He hushed them and warned against moving too quickly. "We cannot let them know we are leaving," he told Mateo in a whisper. "Bring Jan if you must. We need to go quickly."

The others began to stir and move. Blanca spotted movement in the trees. "Come on guys, get your bags – Mateo, help Iain – everyone go this way – "

The Polish citizens began to rise. Someone screamed in the distance, and a truck roared to life. Otto snatched Blanca by the shoulder and shoved her forward.

"Go, go!"

German soldiers poured out of the wood line. The remaining Polish citizens panicked and scattered.

Grim daylight enveloped them, and the air grew thick with smoke. "That truck, there!" Otto shouted. While the Germans were busy rounding up the Polish citizens, Otto shot the driver and leaped into the front seat of the truck. "In the back! Hurry!"

Mateo and Jan sprang forward and rolled into the canvas-covered bed. Iain hurried after, and Priya and Blanca scrambled in last. Bullets sprayed through the metal, causing them to jerk and fall to their stomachs. One bullet nicked Mateo's shoulder, and he let out a shout, fingers quickly staining with blood as he gripped his wound. Blanca fell over him.

"It's okay, just stay still—" German soldiers rushed at them, and Blanca slammed a fist against the truck's cab. "GO, OTTO, GO!"

The truck jerked into motion, hurtling forward with such reckless abandon that Jan nearly tumbled over the tailgate. He was saved by Priya, who grabbed him by the shirt and yanked him away from the edge. Blanca bolted into a defensive position and opened fire, causing the Germans to fall back.

"They're going for their trucks!" she shouted. "Get us out of here, Otto!"

The truck turned sharply and headed off-road, snapping tree limbs and crashing through undergrowth. Within seconds, the German trucks were visible through the gaps in the foliage, and Otto cursed loudly. Turning again, he took the truck further into the forest until he hit a trail wide enough for a vehicle. The truck bounced, tossing the others against its hard frame, but the German vehicles disappeared from sight. Blanca exhaled shakily.

"Which way?" Otto called out, and she pulled herself up to the window separating the bed from the cab.

"Northeast," she told him, pointing.

Otto turned the truck sharply and headed out into a snow-covered clearing lined with old, unfinished barbwire. Blanca heard him talking, and she leaned against the window again. "We will be close to the river again soon," he said. "What should—"

An explosion rocked the truck from underneath and sent it flying into the air, back over front.

The shocked group was launched out into the open and scattered carelessly over a snowy field. Blanca landed hard and rolled in a flurry of freezing white powder before skidding to a painful stop. Mateo was right next to her, groaning, and Jan was several feet away, moving slowly onto his back as he fought to catch his breath.

Shivering like mad, Blanca forced herself up. "What hit us?" she cried out.

"I have no idea!" Otto called. He kicked open the door and fell to the snow with a groan. They all stood quite far apart, with the exception of Blanca and Mateo. Priya was the furthest out, far behind the truck, but she was on her feet, hunched and disoriented.

In the distance, engines rumbled.

"Hurry!" Blanca yelled to the others. "Into the trees!"

They began to run, feet pounding on the rough terrain, but as they did, Iain noticed a sign just barely visible above a mound of snow. His eyes widened. The reason for the sudden explosion crystallized in an instant.

"EVERYBODY FREEZE!" he shouted, jerking to a stop. "WE'RE IN A MINEFIELD!"

Blanca, Mateo, and Jan were already down the hill and out of the field, but the others were not. "Priya, *stop!*" Otto commanded sharply, but his warning came a half-second too late.

The explosion ripped Priya from the earth and sent her high in the air before bringing her back down with a heavy, lifeless *thud*. Bits of fabric and bone followed her to the ground. A pool of scarlet seeped into snow and framed her twisted body where it rested against the earth.

"*PRIYA!*" Mateo screamed shrilly.

Otto and Iain jumped back at the blast, hands up and mouths gaping.

Blanca staggered in her spot. A ringing sound entered her head, enveloping her in a crushing wave of disbelief. She scarcely registered the hand yanking on her arm or the bullets whizzing by her head as Otto, suddenly at her side, pulled her along. "No, no—no, please—go back!" Mateo protested frantically, but Blanca and the others dragged him away from the clearing. Priya's body remained behind them, already dusted in a thin layer of snow. Soon, she would be covered.

"NO, WE HAVE TO GO BACK FOR PRIYA!" Mateo screamed. Otto grabbed him and hauled him forcefully away from the field. They narrowly missed a barrage of gunfire as they tumbled back into the forest.

The river came into view, and they sprinted across the icy layer on top, praying it would hold their weight. Jan was the last across, and he stopped them all with a shout, pointing ahead and leading them in a different direction. The German soldiers refused to cross the icy river, but they kept pace, shooting at the small group from the other side of the water and following their movements.

Blanca felt like her lungs were bursting, but she managed to push herself forward even as her feet grew numb and heavy. They barreled past another line of trees, and as they did, a row of tanks and soldiers came into view.

"SHIT!" Blanca screamed, skidding to a stop.

"Soviets!" Otto twisted to look behind him.

As soon as the Germans appeared at their backs, the Soviets spotted them. Now the Germans were caught, and before Blanca and the others had a chance to run away, the tanks turned ominously in their direction and the Soviets charged forward.

Now it was not just gunfire raining down on their heads, but also shells from the tanks, blasting through the air with trails of smoke leaving a clear path of destruction. Blanca tossed her arms over her head as if it might help and dove forward into the snowy earth. The tanks and their soldiers began to close the gap, and Blanca jerked up her head, suddenly realizing they were about to get crushed between the two clashing forces.

The German soldiers, no longer concerned about Blanca and the others, raced past them to meet the Soviets in battle. Blanca scrambled forward on her elbows and knees, dragging Mateo along with her as they fought to keep their heads covered.

"Warsaw, Warsaw!" Jan shouted hoarsely, pointing beyond the Soviet line, and they scrambled to their feet, dodging soldiers and armored tanks every step of the way.

The air filled with lights and dust, making it hard to see and breathe. Blanca turned her face up, and for a strange, feverish moment, she wished desperately to be in the sky. Life seemed cruel for tethering them to the ground, suffocating under the burden of being alive in a time when people were so intent on destroying each other.

She snapped out of her daze when a bullet raced by her head, and together, the group sprinted past the line of tanks and beyond the gunfire right up to the outermost wall surrounding Warsaw. More Germans poured out of the city to confront the Soviets. Smoke billowed from the once-proud Polish capital.

Mateo kept turning back, desperate to see Priya, but she was already out of sight.

Otto hauled him off, dragging the horrified teen every step of the way.

<hr/>

Warsaw was protected by a series of concrete barriers erected by the Germans, but Blanca and the others managed to slip through a gap created by the blast of a tank gun on the eastern side of the city. Together, they collapsed in the dusty, forgotten corner of an abandoned warehouse and waited. In the distance, mortar shells boomed, people shouted, and lives were lost. Occasionally, a bright light flickered beyond the broken windows of their hideout, and they flinched collectively.

"We can fix it, right?" Mateo spoke up at last. He looked at Blanca. "We can change this, can't we?"

Blanca stared. Otto stood next to her, looking perplexed.

"I don't know, Mateo," she said cryptically.

Mateo's jaw locked, and he looked away from her, furious that she could not promise him Priya's death might be undone. Eventually, the racket of warfare faded away, but there was no relief to be had. The stillness granted them only unease.

"I am sorry," Otto whispered at last, not looking at the others. Blanca knew he was thinking about how he'd driven them into the minefield. No one said anything in response to Otto's apology.

Morning aged into afternoon. "We have to get going," Blanca said gruffly. The others were reluctant to move, but she insisted they press on, knowing the unattended grief would only fester and rot.

They moved through the city as quickly and quietly as they could. Roads were cut into chunks, with whole intersections reduced to rubble. Buildings that had stood tall and proud for decades now lay in ruin, twisted and broken like gnarled old men. Storefront windows showed only gaping lengths of empty blackness, and the air around them was stale and uncared for.

Blanca stopped behind a broken wall. There were no people on the streets. The sidewalks were cracked and barren, and only the ghostly echo of civilization remained. The battle from earlier had gone quiet—why, Blanca couldn't say. The silence made her ill at ease.

She glanced back at Jan. "Where would the Polish soldiers have gone?"

Jan, who had been staring with glassy eyes at the ruined streets, looked back at Blanca and fought to recover his English. "The camp," he whispered hoarsely. "Gęsiówka. It is in northwest city."

Blanca looked at their map, but it contained only a few details about Warsaw. Jan peered over her shoulder and took a moment to get his bearings. Finally, he pointed.

"This way."

At Blanca's signal, the group hurried from one relative point of safety to the other. They pressed close to the crumbling walls, stopping when the sounds of rapid gunfire or mortar shells grew too close. A pair of tanks came rolling in their direction, and Blanca rushed them all through an alleyway only to discover the shellshocked remains of a city park. Gray air, thick with smoke, wrapped a children's playground in a dense fog. Wind stirred a broken swing, causing the busted chain to drag on the asphalt in a way that seemed crudely loud.

Jan turned away, eyes clenched. "I played here," he whispered. Otto's eyes flickered in his direction, and he frowned deeply.

Soon, they came to more populated streets. There was commotion up ahead, with doors slamming and people shouting. Otto pulled out the radio and listened, but he couldn't make sense of it. "Where are we?" he asked Jan, and the boy hurried forward.

"No," he breathed. "This is Wola. My grandparents live in Wola."

The group crouched behind a pile of rubble and watched through the gaps. German soldiers emerged in a heavy line and pulled civilians from their homes. They shoved them into panicked clusters, snapping guttural commands.

"What's happening?" Iain asked. "Those people aren't fighters. Why are the soldiers taking them away?"

"They are not taking them anywhere," Otto explained reluctantly. "They are punishing the city for its rebellion."

Just as the horror took root in Iain's expression, Jan made a desperate noise.

"My parents! My family!" he gasped. The citizens were pleading and screaming. Many of them were women and children. The soldiers lined them up and raised their guns. "*Nie!*" Jan sprang forward in a clear panic and raced to the civilians, just barely escaping Mateo's frantic grip.

"Jan!" Mateo jumped up, but Otto yanked him back and the others pulled away sharply so they could duck behind a building out of sight.

Jan hurried in front of his family, waving his arms and pleading.

"*NIE! Proszę nie strzelać!*" he cried out, just before the German soldiers opened fire.

Blanca jerked down as a heavy wave of machine-gun fire blasted through the area. Stones fell away like broken bits of paper, littering their heads with debris. People screamed, but their terror was short-lived. The gunfire ended as swiftly as it had begun.

Mateo's tears poured over Otto's hand, which was grasped firmly over his mouth to keep him from shouting. "I am sorry," Otto whispered wretchedly, like he had before at the warehouse.

They waited, huddled together in a trembling mass, but it appeared no one had seen them. When Blanca edged around the corner, she saw Jan staring at her from the street. His eyes were open and lifeless. A German soldier dragged him by the ankle into a pile of bodies and left him there.

She grasped her rosary with such force that the edges bit into her palm. Then, with a last exhale, she pulled up her gun again. "Come on, we have to go—"

"No, I can't—I can't keep doing this," Mateo sobbed, but Otto stood and pulled him up.

"Come, come, Mateo—"

"I can't, I can't do this—"

"Yes, you can. Come, we have got you. Let us go."

They hurried away from the soldiers, pressing on in the direction Jan had showed them.

Time slowed to crawl as they crept through the city. Together, the group pushed through the façade of a wall and found themselves inside a hollow factory. The side closest to the darkening skyline had been blown apart, with only a gaping crater where the ironworks had once been.

Suddenly, they heard shouts in English.

"DOWN, DOWN!"

People were fighting back against the Germans. Some wore civilian clothes, but others were outfitted in military uniforms cobbled together from various nations like patchwork dresses. The man at the front of the group shouted again, cursing wildly in English.

"DAMN IT TO HELL, YOU KRAUT SONS-A-BITCHES!"

"Watch Mateo!" Blanca ordered before jumping up and racing after the ragtag group of soldiers. She caught the Germans by surprise, hitting them hard from the side, and they were forced to scramble back.

The American man gaped at her. "Who in the hell are you?"

Blanca grinned breathlessly. "Just a red-blooded American soldier."

The man let out a bark of laughter. "Well," he said, replacing his cigar, "alright then. Come with me."

Blanca called over the others, and the American man led them through one last section of abandoned city before arriving at a walled-in block with sentries posted at every corner. "Ya'll here to fight?" he asked in a drawl. Blanca got a good look at him as they headed beyond the concrete walls. He was a White man of about forty with thinning brown hair, a wide jaw, and broad shoulders.

"We're not with a platoon," she explained, "but we are soldiers, and we want to help. You willing to let us tag along?"

The American shrugged. "Well, I'm not in charge, but anyone who's willing to shoot for us instead of at us seems like a plus in my book." He nodded to the other soldiers, saying something briefly in Polish, and then he led the group beyond the high walls. "This place was a city prison before the war. When the Nazis took over, they started sending the Jewish folks here—the ones they didn't kill, anyway."

Blanca glanced at Otto, whose expression was hard. He kept silent, but his demeanor was unmistakably tense.

"We managed to take the camp a few weeks ago. We even got two German tanks," the American man said and pointed to a pair of Panzers sitting nearby. He stopped. "Name's Howard, by the way. Ben Howard." He stuck out a hand, and Blanca shook it.

"I didn't realize there were any Americans stationed here."

"There's not," Howard confirmed. "I fought in the Great War, moved here to marry my wife shortly after. Didn't think I'd ever get caught up in this shit again, but here we are."

She nodded. "Yeah, I feel that."

"The Soviets were supposed to resupply us with food, but they haven't shown up yet," Howard continued gravely. "We've had a few airdrops from the British, but we can't always get to 'em on account of the Germans snatchin' 'em up." He turned his head up to the gray sky. "This can't last much longer."

Otto lifted his head, but he didn't say anything. Howard looked over him.

"You American, too, son?"

Otto paused. "Yes," he said, enunciating carefully.

Blanca shifted her gun, edging forward to attract Howard's attention. "Just let us know when it's time to move out."

Howard nodded and left. Once he was gone, Blanca stood near Otto and brushed her fingers against his. She meant to say something, to explain her logic, but all that came out was a single pleading whisper that formed his name.

"Otto."

"I know." He curled his fingers around hers and squeezed briefly, expression grave. "We need their help to cross the city."

"Yeah," she murmured.

They headed to an isolated corner and resettled wordlessly. A medic came forward with some supplies, and Blanca did her best to tend to Iain. Even in his weakened state, he refused to let her treat him.

"I've got it," he murmured gruffly. He could scarcely keep his eyes open.

Just before dawn, Blanca got on her knees, held her rosary, and said her prayers. When she reopened her eyes, the soldiers were gathering. She studied them, her heart sinking. *If these men survive the day*, she thought, *it will be luck that saves them, not experience.* Blanca wondered bleakly if she had ever looked that young.

Howard appeared by her side as she rose from her prayers. "This is a dangerous time for faith," he remarked, nodding to her rosary.

"With all due respect," Blanca replied, "this is a dangerous time to be without it."

Nearby, Otto stood with his hands on Mateo's shoulders. "We are going to lead you through the city, but you must be strong. You cannot show mercy to anyone who crosses you. Kill anyone who stands in your way. Do you understand?"

Mateo nodded silently.

Blanca appeared next to them. "Look, Mateo." She pointed out to a tall steeple far away, jutting into the sky with a sharp point. "See that? That's our rendezvous point. You get separated from any of us, that's where you go."

Mateo looked in the direction of the steeple. "I will," he promised hoarsely.

The solemn group stood together. Iain, who looked a little better than he had the day before, took up his gun with a hard swallow. They linked their arms and bowed their heads. The brief spiritual plea was broken up when a Polish officer stood up at the front of their ramshackle army and spoke. His speech was impassioned and powerful, but they couldn't understand it.

"What are our orders?" Blanca asked Howard when the speech was done.

Howard flicked his cigar. "Kill the Nazis."

Blanca shifted to look at Otto. He managed a small smile and gently knocked a curled finger against her jaw. "Let us see what it takes to reach the other side of the city. I bet you will beat us all there."

Blanca stiffened. "I hope not."

The men at the front gave their commands. The tanks started with gritty jolts. Men with flamethrowers walked behind them.

Blanca's heart raced. She kept close to Mateo, who looked no less prepared for the gruesome fight ahead than any of the other young men and women walking with them. The air was quiet, the dawn's early light subdued. They walked alongside a dozen other uniforms, all from various nations, all moving with one iron-clad purpose. Resistance in the form of German soldiers met them like a brick wall. The world went from quiet to chaos in a matter of seconds.

Explosions rocked the streets, and the tanks burst into action, rolling over the initial line of Germans with devastating indifference. The others around Blanca crouched and raised their guns. Blanca snapped hers up, and Otto, Iain, and Mateo all did the same at her side.

They let out furious shouts. The blistering hell of combat enveloped them in a tidal wave of madness. Their open mouths filled with acrid smoke and poured out venom in return, urging them forward into the throng of thrashing and fighting bodies. Blanca pushed on, shooting from behind the two tanks until the Germans reached the other side and they were forced to meet them face-to-face.

A man slammed right into Blanca, and she shoved him off with a snarl. He went down, and his head snapped back against a stone and fell still. As he fell, Blanca felt the outside noises fade away; only the sounds of her ragged breathing reached her ears. The chaos around her seemed to slow, and in her head, she heard a mantra from what felt like a lifetime ago.

I am an American soldier.

The world snapped back into place, and the soundtrack of warfare exploded through her senses.

I am a warrior and a member of a team.

The two armies slammed into each other like dueling titans.

I serve the people of the United States, and live the Army Values.

Blanca found herself shooting, thrashing, punching, and slicing as if on some feral instinct.

I will always place the mission first. I will never accept defeat.

Ahead of her, Mateo shot down two men and threw himself against a third, knocking the soldier down and ramming the end of his gun into the other man's face just seconds before he pressed on.

I will never quit.

They rushed down a street lined with businesses and buildings bearing all the wounds of war: gaping windows and busted doors, crumbling balconies and scarred brick walls.

I will never leave a fallen comrade.

The tanks fired on a group of Germans and blasted right through them.

I am disciplined, physically and mentally tough, trained and proficient in my warrior tasks and drills.

The attack rolled over the enemy forces like a thunderstorm.

I am a guardian of freedom and the American way of life.

An ancient brick high-rise, one of the few remaining structures of any remarkable height, fell victim to a tank blast. The brick crumbled and fell away, and the building let out a collosal groan before tumbling forward.

Blanca shoved Mateo forward. "GO, GO!"

The building wavered and then fell, arching over the street and casting a long shadow over the soldiers just before crashing in a booming wave of smoke and debris. The dirt and dust blasted back the soldiers it did not crush, and Blanca watched with wide eyes as it enveloped her in a storm of wreckage.

Blanca crashed to her hands and knees, and darkness swarmed her. Pain shot through her body, twisting her joints and draining away her energy, but the mantra in her head grew louder and echoed with a final booming declaration.

I am an American soldier.

With a loud cry, Blanca gripped the jagged concrete in front of her and shoved as hard as she could, stumbling out into the open with a great, loud gasp. The outside world enveloped her once more. Someone called her name, and she burst into a blind sprint.

One of the stolen tanks was caught under the rubble, but it managed to push its way through, gears grinding loudly as it climbed over the ruins and crushed anyone or anything caught below.

The resistance fighters rushed through the streets once more. They suddenly appeared at the Vistula River, which ran through the heart of Warsaw and was polluted with blood and bodies. The Germans had set up a checkpoint at the entrance to the bridge, and their position was well fortified, but they were not expecting tanks. The stolen Panzers rolled straight through the panicked Germans, and the checkpoint was breached with barely a pause.

The resistance fighters ducked behind the two tanks and let them blast apart the next barrier, sending German soldiers scattering for cover or medical attention. Polish soldiers armed with flamethrowers torched anyone who dared to flee, spreading fire into the city and igniting the

bridge's railing. Blanca and the others ran past the growing
flames, inhaling the icy air greedily as they fought to keep
their breath. Below their unsteady feet, the Vistula River
raged at high levels, fed by the melting snow and the
constant intrusion of unnatural waste. Otto appeared and
grabbed Blanca's arm.

"*Halt!*" he said. "They have anti-tank guns!"

Jerking back, Blanca took cover behind a parked car
as explosions rocked their path, shaking the pillars that
kept them high above the rushing water.

The bridge lurched, convulsing under the damage and
splitting. A crack echoed through the air, and the back half
of the bridge collapsed, sending dozens of men plunging
into the icy waters below.

"This way!" Otto shouted, sprinting forward and
ducking under machine-gun fire. He leaped over the
railing of the bridge and led them along the precarious
edges as the rest of the platform began to break away. He
jumped from the crumbling concrete and landed hard on
the other side, just above the river's snowy bank. Blanca,
Mateo, and Iain followed, and Blanca hissed at the sudden
sharp pain in her ankle, which had twisted in the landing.

As they scrambled forward, more Polish fighters
poured in from other parts of the city. It was then that
Blanca looked up and realized with growing horror that
the streets were lined with bodies strung up as if on display.
They decorated each street corner in a macabre exhibit,
one meant—Blanca could only assume—to scare the locals
into giving up their fight. The massacre at Wola flooded
the forefront of her mind, and she forced herself to look
straight again.

"This way!"

Blanca grabbed Mateo's hand and yanked him alongside her, and they crashed through a tall set of doors leading into an ornate white building. Otto moved quickly ahead of them and found a door leading below ground-level. He ushered the others through before hurrying inside after them and shutting the door with a breathless pant.

Darkness fell around them, and the sounds of battle grew muted. Otto struck a match and peered ahead into the inky blackness. "This is a storage room. Come on." They settled into a dark corner and heaved.

Nothing—and no one—came behind them. Blanca wrapped both arms around Mateo and held him tight as the war raged on.

———

Miles away, on a snowy field decorated with craters, a military truck emblazoned with Nazi emblems pulled up at the edge of the field and stopped. There, a group of German soldiers waited next to a body covered in a white sheet.

A bespectacled man in a suit emerged from the truck and approached the waiting soldiers.

"Dr. Heisenberg," greeted the commanding officer.

The bespectacled man, Heisenberg, observed the body beneath the sheet. "Let me see it."

Two soldiers moved and pulled back the cloth, revealing the cold and unmoving face of a dark-skinned girl with long hair. "These were the items we found on her, sir." They handed over a small box that contained a necklace, some clothes, and a small rectangular device with a blank, black screen.

"There are identification cards on the back," the officer informed him.

Heisenberg turned over the unfamiliar device and pulled out the ID card. His eyes ticked over the dates. "Do you know what this is?" he asked, holding up the small machine.

"No, sir."

The man replaced the items in the box, but he did not hand it back. Instead, he walked over to the body and studied it. "Well," Heisenberg said, eyes alight with interest. "We will have to find out." He took the box in his arms and turned away. "Put her in the truck."

The soldiers did as they were told, and then they left.

<center>~~~</center>

Bavaria, Germany
1942

In his childhood bedroom, he felt alien and out of place.

"Otto?"

He turned at the sound of his mother's voice. She'd left him alone for most of the day, stating with confidence that he needed to rest after his long train ride. He only had a few days at home, though, as his leave would be terribly short.

"Yes, Mother?"

Elisabeth Zimmler reached up and touched her son's face. It now rested a good five inches above her own.

"How are you, my son? Are you glad to be home?"

A trained smile took over his expression. "Of course."

Together, they sat on the edge of the narrow twin bed he'd outgrown years before. On a shelf behind them rested a row of schoolbooks and children's toys, all coated in a fine layer of dust. Banners from his secondary school still marked the walls. Above the bed was a poster for the *Flieger Korps* featuring a proud young German in an aviation uniform.

"Otto, I need to tell you. A girl from your class, Sophie, has been arrested." His mother frowned.

"Sophie?" Otto repeated, startled. "Why?"

"She and her brother have been distributing pamphlets telling people to resist the Nazi government," his mother explained quietly. "She was caught tossing them out of a window, and the Gestapo took her into custody that very day. Otto, she was not even allowed a defense. They have already found her guilty of treason."

Otto stood and paced. "It was foolish of her to do that."

"Well, I think Sophie and her friends are right, this is madness, what's happening—"

Otto rounded to face her. "Stop, stop talking like that! You will get yourself killed, Mother!"

"For what? Daring to ask questions?" Misery creased Elisabeth's weary features. "This war is a trap, Otto. I can feel it in my heart. We will be lost." She bowed her head, and Otto gathered her in his arms. "Tomorrow, they will execute that poor girl, and in doing so they will silence the voices of Germany."

She turned and left the room. Otto watched her go. The next morning, he left his childhood home and traveled to the city square. Despite the early hour, a crowd had gathered.

On a makeshift stage, surrounded by uniformed Gestapo men, was Sophie. A guillotine was positioned just behind her. The sun caught the glistening blade at an angle, creating a spectacular beam of light that fell over Sophie's rigid form and granted her an ethereal glow.

The determined look in her eyes, admirably free of fear, took his breath away. The executioner lowered her into the mechanism.

"An end in terror," Sophie called out passionately, "is preferable to terror without end!"

The blade rushed down and severed Sophie's head from her neck with a sudden, impersonal blow. Otto turned away with a grimace, as did many others. When he reopened his eyes, the crowd was dispersing.

"What a shame," someone muttered next to him. "If only she had kept her pretty mouth shut, she might have lived a long life."

Otto stayed behind after all the others had left, his eyes locked on a trail of blood as it wove its way across the wooden platform. When the executioner gave him a cold glare, he stepped away without a word and left.

CHAPTER 9

*Never shall I forget those moments
that murdered my God…and
turned my dreams to ashes.*
—Elie Wiesel

In the quiet of their hidden room, Blanca and the others waited in a tense huddle.

Otto found a candle and lit it with his last match. The small circle of light illuminated only a corner of the room, but it did serve as a reminder that they were not lost in a void of nothingness, and so in that way, it was helpful.

"I can't do this," Mateo sobbed quietly. "I can't—"

"Yes, yes you can." Otto held him close. "You did so well out there, Mateo. You fought with such bravery."

"No, I didn't! I was scared."

"We were all afraid," Otto murmured consolingly. "And yet you survived, and I am so proud of you."

Mateo lifted his head, face streaked with tears. "Really?"

"Yes, yes!" Otto pulled him into a hug, and Mateo whimpered. "You did so well. Do not be sad. You will make it through this. I know it."

Mateo's cries quieted, and Otto reached out to Blanca so she could join them in an embrace. They sank to the floor, grief-stricken and exhausted.

For a while, Blanca dozed with her cheek against Mateo's head and Otto's warmth at her side. Occasionally, she would open her eyes and scan the room with numb and devoid interest. After a while, she touched Otto's shoulder. "Stay here with Mateo," she whispered.

Otto was mostly asleep. "Where are you going?" he asked groggily.

"Just to check on Iain," she promised. He nodded and let her go. The tiny circle of light from the candle stayed next to him, and Blanca moved further into the shadows where Iain sat alone. "Hey there," she murmured. "You doing okay?"

Iain shifted so she could sit next to them. "I'm alright. How is Mateo doing?"

Blanca hesitated. "Not great."

Iain nodded. "Look, I know we've got enough to worry about as it is, but... I think something is really wrong."

Blanca's brows furrowed. "What do you mean?"

He held up the history book Blanca had been carrying in her bag. "I was reading Mateo's book earlier, trying to figure out our next move, and I read about this—this uprising, this attack on the Germans here in Warsaw." He leaned forward, expression grave. "You do realize everything that's going on right now is happening at the wrong time, right?"

Blanca sat up straighter. "What're you talking about?"

Iain tapped the book. "The Warsaw Uprising was in the *summer* of 1944, not January. Everything that's happening over our heads right now—it's starting six months too early." He bit his lip. "Something is wrong. Something has changed."

"That is *impossible*," Blanca protested vehemently. "We've only been here a few weeks. There is no damn way we could have affected a military operation that would have taken months to plan. We couldn't have done this."

Iain leaned back against the wall with a wince. "Perhaps not, but…"

"But what?"

Iain rubbed his jaw. "I've been thinking. Remember when we first landed in Poland? How many people were with us before the initial attack?"

"I don't know… Thirty or so?"

"Right," Iain said. "But how many people were in that building back in Texas, do you think? More than that. Far more."

"What're you getting at?"

Iain took in a deep breath. "I've been wondering ever since we got here… Why were there missing people when we landed? Priya's parents, for example. They were standing right next to her when the explosion happened, weren't they? So where were they when we arrived in Poland?" He waved a hand. "I had half a dozen men standing right next to me, and none of them appeared at the landing site, either."

Blanca leaned forward. "What're you saying, Iain?"

"I'm saying," he went on, "it's possible that not everyone who was affected by the explosion landed here in Poland. Instead, they might've been—"

"Scattered through space and time," Blanca finished, eyes wide.

Iain frowned. "Possibly, yes. And if that's true, we can't be sure of anything. There's no telling where or when they went, or if they're still alive." He pointed. "And I'll tell you something else. Those Soviets were not supposed to be there today. In our understanding of history, they held back their support of the Polish in the hopes that the two armies would destroy each other, but we led the Soviets into the city when you drew them into battle, and so they had to show up, whether they liked it or not." He sighed. "Who knows what might happen from here on out?"

Blanca fell back limply against a box. "So much for not screwing things up," she muttered. They fell quiet for a while. "What do you need to build the machine to get us back? Do you have any idea?"

"A lot," Iain admitted tiredly. "It's like I told you before. The Nazis are by far the most technologically advanced of all the societies in this era. Americans might be able to manage it, but even if I were able to introduce the necessary concepts to them, then what would we do? Leave that kind of technology behind?"

"Better them than the damn Nazis," she pointed out. "Just imagine what they'd do with the ability to manipulate time."

Iain smiled wryly. "They were working on it, actually. Or so say the rumors."

"Bullshit."

"It's not all that difficult to believe," he confessed. "The Nazis made incredible scientific leaps during their brief tenure. They were responsible for creating polyurethane, methadone, even the world's first digital computer, all in the 1940s. They also discovered a great deal about genetics, crossbreeding, human diseases, and much more."

"By torturing people," Blanca pointed out grimly. "They performed those experiments on unwilling prisoners."

Iain nodded. "Yes. Many of their discoveries came at the expense of the people around them. But the truth is, scientific advancements are often slowed—rather than helped—by moral and ethical constraints. The scientists of Nazi Germany didn't have those limits. Instead, they had an almost unlimited number of test subjects and *no rules*. Because of that, they were able to do things no one had ever done before."

He sighed.

"That's why so few of them faced justice during the Nuremburg Trials; the American government didn't want to execute them. They wanted to hire them."

Blanca scowled. "Figures."

"Aye. I don't know how far the Nazis got with their time-travel experiment, but I do know what it was called—*Die Glocke*."

"The hell does that mean?"

"The Bell," he said quietly, and Blanca felt a shudder move up her spine. "Anyway," continued Iain, "it all fell apart at the end of the war, as did most of their research." He made an exhausted noise, and Blanca patted his shoulder before getting up.

"Alright. Try to get some rest."

They shuffled back to where Otto and Mateo were sleeping, and Blanca stepped over Mateo so she could settle between them. Slipping down onto the floor next to Otto, she curled herself between them and soaked up the comfort of their nearness.

Shifting, Blanca peered behind her as Otto wound his arms around his torso and muttered something in dreamy German. She found his hands under the sleeping bag and closed her eyes, thinking back on the small house they'd left behind in the snowy woods. She wished they could go back there.

———⟨⟩———

Hours later, Otto drew a fingertip down the line of her jaw and woke her up. She turned to look at him, and he gestured for her to follow. The others were all asleep;

Mateo had tucked against Iain, who tossed and turned fitfully.

Reluctantly, Blanca rose and followed Otto out of the room and into the dark hallway. "Where are we going?" she asked anxiously.

"Just to the top floor. There is something I want you to see."

They climbed a flight of stairs and found themselves wrapped in broad daylight brighter and warmer than they'd seen in ages. As Blanca came to the top step behind Otto, he turned her gently and pointed.

"Look, *Schatz.*"

The blinding light faded and the room came into focus.

All around them, images cast in stained glass spread across the floor, pushed there by the sun's dazzling rays. Blanca walked, captivated, through a rainbow of holy images and glowing color. She passed pews lined with torn and shredded fabric, her fingers brushing over the leather-bound hymnals where they lay scattered along the aisles. Then she looked down the center aisle, and there, mounted on the wall, she saw a magnificent crucifix hanging above an altar. The curtains behind it—faded purple draped in gold tassels—still held an air of divine elegance despite the neglect they had suffered. Above them, a long balcony stretched the length of the chapel, and Blanca felt as if she could see waiting figures there, eyes turned up to the heavens as they sought reason, comfort, and guidance.

She lowered her eyes again to the altar, which had once been draped with a fine linen bearing a cross stitched into its center. The fabric was now crumpled on the floor, along with several goblets and vases.

Blanca approached, fingers clutched around her rosary. When she reached the front, she dropped down, one knee at a time, in front of the altar.

"I'm sorry," she whispered hoarsely, eyes turned up to the unmoving depiction of Jesus Christ. She held tight to her rosary. Outside, the world was quiet. Otto waited without speaking or touching her. In that moment, he was very far away.

Blanca was adrift, cast in a sea of bare and exposed agony.

"I'm sorry," she said again to the crucifix, clutching the miniature tight in her hand. "I wanted... I wanted to be strong." She pulled her clenched hands to her chest. Tears filled her eyes. "I tried...to be good. I promise...I swear, I did. I wanted... I wanted to be worthy, I wanted to be a child of God, but I'm... I'm not good enough, and I failed. I...I'm sorry."

She bent her shoulders forward. Images of Priya's face flashed through her mind.

"I didn't want this," she wept, dropping her head as she began to sob in earnest. "I didn't want to be this way, I promise, I...I tried, I'm sorry."

Jan dying with his family. Mateo's horrified cries.

"I wanted to be strong, I wanted to keep everyone safe—"

The face of every man she'd killed raced through her mind in a slideshow of heart-wrenching guilt.

"I wanted so much to be good, Heavenly Father, I really did." Blanca turned her face up to the divine image. "I'm so sorry, I...I'm so, so *sorry*." Words failed her, throwing her into heavy, deep sobs as the bubble of grief that had been building inside her chest burst under the weight of her misery. She curled over the altar, weak and childlike, babbling her apologies unceasingly.

"I wanted to be good," she whispered. "I wanted it so much. But I'm not."

She scarcely registered the hand at her shoulder or the sound of Otto kneeling next to her. He took her hands in his. "I do not know the Lord's Prayer," he admitted softly. "I have not said it in a very long time. So, you must say it for both of us."

"Do you believe it?" she asked in a small voice.

Otto paused. "I do not know," he said truthfully. "But you do. And what brings you comfort brings me comfort, also."

Blanca paused, lips parted as she fought for words. Then she closed her eyes, and Otto scooted a little closer. Together, they bowed their heads, and Blanca recited the Lord's Prayer as she had been taught to do so many years before.

When it was done, they opened their eyes and stood.

"Thank you," she whispered, eyes wide. Otto squeezed her fingers tenderly, and she pressed into his embrace, closing her eyes as his arms came up around her. They stayed that way for a few blissful moments, shrouded by the peace of the church. Eventually, she pulled away.

"We should go back inside. It's not safe out here."

She turned away, but Otto caught her hand. "Blanca, wait."

He shifted, looking uncharacteristically hesitant. Blanca stepped up to him again. Their hands remained joined, and Otto inhaled. "I wanted to—I wanted to ask," he started haltingly. "What if...you and Mateo do not return to America?"

Blanca's brows furrowed. "You mean, what if we get captured?"

"No, no." Otto stepped closer. "I mean… What if you choose to stay?"

Blanca's lips parted in surprise. "We can't stay here, Otto. There's a war going on."

"But that is just it," he pressed on eagerly. "The war will be over soon, and all those things you hate, all the fighting and the prisoners and the camps, all of that will be gone."

"When the Nazis win, you mean," Blanca guessed, closing her eyes briefly. "Otto, you know we can't live under Nazi rule."

Otto faltered. "Perhaps not in Germany," he conceded, before rushing on, "but here in Poland, it would be—more like a colony. The rules would not be nearly as strict. You and Mateo both—you would be safe." He curled her fingers in his. "Just think of it, Blanca. You two could stay here in Poland, and you could live in the city, and he could attend a university, and you could work or not work, it would not matter, you could do whatever you like. And you would never again have to worry about putting a roof over your head or food on the table, because I would—"

He cleared his throat.

"I would…take care of you," he finished softly.

Blanca stared. The full realization of what he was asking washed over her in a sudden wave.

Do not allow this conversation to continue, she thought.

"You would…stay here with us?"

Otto brushed his fingers over hers. "Well, I would have to return to Germany for a year to finish my service, but after that…" He met her gaze, eyes shining. "Yes, I could be back here. With you."

Blanca could scarcely look away from his hopeful expression. For a few seconds, she imagined, with agonizing clarity, what this promised life could be like.

"Otto…" she started weakly.

"Please, Blanca." He stood very close and pressed his forehead to hers. "Let me try."

Blanca's expression crumbled, and when he kissed her, she kissed him back because she knew it was very likely this was the last time he would ever let her. She held onto him, forgetting all about the war, the exhaustion, the near starvation. That impossible image—the one that showed her a future with someone who cared for her and only her—seized her mind with an unyielding grip.

How strange, thought Blanca, that she should only realize how miserable she was when threatened with happiness.

Otto's hold on her tightened, and the kiss deepened. Blanca tightened her hands in the material of his coat, but at the same moment, she pulled away.

"Otto," she whispered tearfully. "I have to tell you something."

Otto's features growing concerned. "What is it?" he asked very quietly.

"Look, um." She swallowed thickly and then, with a great deal of reluctance, met his gaze. "Otto, we can't stay here. No matter what."

"Why not?" he asked, voice strained.

"Because we aren't from here," she told him, and Otto opened his mouth to protest, but she waved a hand. "No, listen. I don't just mean we aren't from Poland. I mean… Otto, we are not from this *time period*."

His expression shifted to confusion. "Time…period?" he repeated, clearly doubting his English.

"Right. Even if we made it to the United States, no one would know who we were. There would be no record of us. We don't exist yet."

"Blanca, this does not make any sense."

"What year were you born?" she asked.

Otto seemed taken aback by the question. "1918."

Blanca stepped closer and pointed to herself. "I was born in 1997." At Otto's shocked look, she continued heatedly, "The year we came from was 2019. The reason you haven't heard of the war I fought in is because it hasn't happened yet."

Otto laughed a little. "Blanca, this is madness."

"No, I'm serious! Listen, Iain and some other scientists were working on some kind of—I don't know, surveillance evading technology, I think, and it exploded and caught the rest of us in some sort of black hole or something. We aren't supposed to be here. This isn't our time. It's our *grandparents'* time."

Otto folded his arms and stared at her in disbelief. "Do not be ridiculous."

"Wait, I can prove it to you." Blanca fished around in her pockets. "Look, this is my military ID. Look at it, Otto." She slapped it into his hand, and he raised a brow before shifting his gaze to the card in his hands. His eyes grew curious at the color photo, and he smoothed his thumb over the hard plastic.

"Read the dates," Blanca ordered. "This was issued in 2015. Don't you see?"

Otto looked over the card for what felt like a lifetime. Blanca waited, her heart pounding. At last, Otto looked back to her, and his eyes grew distant and cold; he was hurt.

"I see a card," he said finally, handing it back. "One that could easily be faked."

Blanca deflated. "Why would I lie about this?" she cried out.

"I do not know," Otto replied stiffly. "But the next time you wish to reject someone, you should probably save yourself some time and simply say 'no.'"

He turned and left Blanca standing in front of the altar.

"Otto, just—stop! Please, just—"

Otto stomped into the storage room, where the others continued to sleep. He stopped and surveyed the room stoically. Then, with an agitated shift, he crossed the floor and sat next to Mateo. The small light afforded by their candle reflected dimly in his gaze; he stared, occasionally shoving a dirty hand against the damp corners of his eyes.

We aren't from this time period.

Ridiculous. Otto chewed on his lip, glare fixated on the pitch-black ceiling. However, as he sat in the quiet, still darkness, doubt settled in his mind. Small moments resurfaced in his memory, things that had never made sense.

I was born in 1997.

Impossible.

Wasn't it?

Somewhat fearfully, he looked over at Mateo, who was still sleeping. Blanca's bag was next to him. After some internal debate, Otto opened the bag and tossed out the things he knew: the map, their coats, the med bag, extra ammo. Then his fingers brushed something else, and he pulled out a book.

American History: 1865–Present Day, it read on the front.

Otto opened it, eyes scanning the table of contents where each chapter was outlined. He read over the notes on the American Civil War, the Reconstruction, and then:

World War I, 1914–1918

Otto's brows furrowed as he looked at the dates. World War I? This was the Great War, the one his father had fought in. Otto kept reading, faster and faster, and as he did, his heart began to race. Fear coiled in his stomach, pushing up his throat and choking him.

World War II, 1933–1945

And below that, much further down, it read:

The Fall of Hitler

Trembling, Otto turned the pages furiously until he came to that chapter. The words blurred in front of his eyes. A black and white photo of war-torn Berlin made him curl forward, tears blotting the ink on the pages. His stomach turned, but he kept reading.

The Destruction of Nazi Germany
The Nuremburg Trials
The Berlin Wall

It was an hour before Blanca returned to the room and found him.

Near the room's entrance, pockets of sunlight slipped through gaps in the floorboards. It was in one of these illuminated spots that Blanca stopped, frozen, when she saw him. Otto was standing now. The book was clenched tightly in his hand.

"We lose the war?" he asked, voice cracking. Blanca said nothing. With a violent snap of his arm, Otto hurled the book into the wall. "AND BERLIN IS CONTROLLED BY THE *FUCKING* RUSSIANS?"

Mateo and Iain awoke suddenly, eyes wide, as Blanca held up her hands. "Otto, listen—"

"You knew this whole time?" Otto cried out furiously. "You knew that my country would lose *everything* again, that the Russians would take us over, and you did not tell me?"

"We couldn't tell you!" Blanca protested, gripping her hair. "I'm sorry, Otto!"

"*I have family in Berlin, Blanca!*"

"We were trying not to ruin everything!"

"Well, it is too late for that!" Otto shouted, eyes wild. "Because I will never be the same for having this knowledge. You have destroyed me."

Tears poured down Blanca's face. "I-I didn't know what else to do. We were just trying to get home—"

"Otto, it's not that bad, really!" Mateo looked fearfully between them. "Germany—it's okay, in our time. Blanca's known plenty of people stationed there, it's doing fine—"

"Stationed there?" repeated Otto, and Blanca sucked in a breath across the room. "There is an American military base in Germany?"

Blanca lifted her head reluctantly. "Yeah."

"More than one?"

She swallowed. "Yes."

"And how many German military bases are in America?"

There was a long pause.

"None."

Otto chuckled bitterly. "Then we are not 'okay,' Mateo. We are *occupied!*" He lashed out with an arm, sending a box flying into a wall and making the others flinch.

"Otto, please—"

"You," Otto spat venomously, pointing at her, "You betrayed me."

"I didn't—"

"You lied to me!" Otto roared. "I cannot do this. I cannot stay here, knowing this. I have to get back."

"What—no!" Mateo hurried forward. "You're leaving?"

"I am sorry, Mateo," Otto said stiffly, shifting his eyes away from the boy's pleading expression. "I need to return to Germany. I need to get my grandparents and other family out of Berlin before the goddamn Russians get there."

"Otto, you can't go!" Mateo begged. "After everything that happened with Priya, please don't leave!"

Blanca said nothing, holding her shoulders tight and her gaze low.

"I have to," Otto said firmly. "I need to get back to my squadron." With that, he shifted coldly away from Mateo, who stared in disbelief. Otto said nothing for a few seconds as he shoved his things into a bag. Then he turned, unprepared for what was coming.

Thwack!

Otto's head snapped to the side and he crashed to the floor. Mateo stood over him, fist still clenched from the hit he had delivered to Otto's jaw.

"Go then," Mateo growled between clenched teeth.

Otto watched, eyes wide, as Mateo turned and disappeared behind a door at the back of the room. Finally,

Otto pulled himself to a stand and spoke to Blanca without looking at her.

"I would like my identification tags back."

There was a long moment in which nothing happened. Then, moving as if underwater, Blanca reached for the chain around her neck and pulled it off. Tags clenched tightly in her hand, she walked over with slow, measured steps. Otto looked up when she came to stand in front of him. Her dark eyes had grown angry. When she moved, it was only to shove the tags at his chest, leaving him no choice but to reach up and take them. Blanca yanked her hand back before their fingers could touch.

"Maybe if you're lucky," she said lowly, "we'll fix all this, and you'll never even know we existed."

Otto's eyes flickered and his mouth opened as if he might speak, but Blanca did not give him the chance. Instead, she ducked past him and marched on, leaving the way Mateo had gone.

Iain lingered.

"We didn't expect all this to happen," he mumbled. After that, he followed the others out, and Otto was left alone.

Chest concave, Otto abandoned the darkness of the room and walked numbly up the stairs. Once he was at the surface, he trekked into the battered landscape and left the church behind. It wasn't until much later that he thought to look at the tags in his hand. He realized then that they were Blanca's, not his. She had given him the wrong ones.

———— ✦ ————

Blanca and the others waited a while longer before leaving the safety of the cathedral's basement. There was no real reason to linger, but none of them had the energy to move.

Blanca didn't know if she could face the sun. Any bit of light would turn her to cinders, she was sure of it.

Mateo appeared next to her, and without a word, he handed her the now-battered American History textbook. Blanca shoved it in her bag; they couldn't leave it behind.

"When we get home," she said to Mateo, "you might not even remember all this."

Mateo's dark eyes slid in her direction. "I hope not," he said coldly. "I hope all of this is nothing more than a freaking nightmare."

Blanca couldn't think of anything to say to that.

Together, they went through a series of doors and crept up the staircase again, moving on into the church sanctuary. Blanca refused to look at the altar when it came into view. The cathedral was still, and the only movement was the occasional rustle of paper as it tumbled by, caught in the wind. All was quiet. Their group felt shockingly small.

They crossed the sanctuary and headed in the direction of the arched double doors at the front. Mateo took notice of the church, and his gaze grew softer. He turned back to Blanca.

"Blanca, I—"

But Blanca never learned what he meant to say, because in that instant, Mateo's head jerked to the side and a spray of blood burst from the other side of his temple. His eyes grew round, his head lolled to the side, and for a haunting moment, he remained standing.

Then his knees buckled, the rifle fell from his hands, and he dropped to the floor of the church.

For three loud heartbeats, Blanca stayed where she was, immobilized.

"Mateo?" she whispered, stricken.

"EVERYBODY, GET DOWN!"

Iain tackled her to the ground just as another heavy shot blasted through the corner of a church pew, spraying the air with splintered wood. Blanca felt her head hit the ground hard, but she never lost sight of Mateo where he lay sprawled on the cathedral floor just a few feet away.

More shots rained down on them from above. The gunmen were in the balcony behind the altar.

Voices, shouts, cries. Returned gunfire. Someone was calling her name.

Blanca reached forward, fingers curling manically in the ripped carpet. Bullets fell all around her, and one hit her bag. She shoved it away carelessly. Another bullet hit her bicep, but she crawled on, body shaking, mouth open, until she reached Mateo.

"You're okay, Mattie," she whispered, smoothing a hand over his forehead. "I'm going to fix it."

He was still warm. His eyes were open. She thought she saw him looking at her, but it was a trick of the light. His gaze was empty.

"BLANCA, GET OUT OF THERE!"

"I'm going to fix it," she told Mateo, her voice strangely high pitched. "It's alright, I can do this. I'm going to be a doctor, remember? I can fix this."

But as Blanca curled Mateo in her arms, determined to shield him from humanity's end days, her little brother's head fell back with a sick, lifeless jerk, and the illusion was shattered.

Mateo was dead.

Fury filled her. This thing—this damn thing—was not her Mateo. How dare this empty shell stare up at her without the soul that had carried it? How dare this body house a spirit so loved, so cared for, only to throw it away? It was there! The vessel was there! And yet when she looked at this face, everything that had made Mateo what he was had vanished. This cursed, barren husk had once been her brother, and now it was *nothing*, empty and mocking and dark. Blanca shook it as hard as she could.

"Mateo! MATEO!" she screamed, spittle falling from her mouth, filthy hands gripping his face. "Mateo, wake up!"

A hundred unfamiliar doors flashed through her mind. "BLANCA, WATCH OUT!"

Running steps approached from the side. A Russian soldier appeared suddenly next to her. Blanca's eyes snapped open, and her mind splintered and went dark. The world around her became indistinct. There was no mercy here—not from the soldiers, not from God, and not from Blanca.

The blindness set in.

With a jerk, Blanca bolted upright and buried her knife in the shocked soldier's neck before viciously ripping it free, spraying the church pew next to her with blood and shredded bits of skin. The Russian soldiers were still firing from the balcony above, where they hid behind a pile of sandbags.

Blanca saw none of this. She registered only the movement of her hand as it slipped over a bottle the Russian soldier had been carrying; inside, volatile liquid sloshed back and forth. Small areas of the church were already on fire. Blanca stalked forward, trudging through a storm of bullets, and she dragged the bottle through one of the open flames so that the cloth tip caught fire. Her skin curled and charred under the heat, knuckles burning black, but she did not notice.

"BLANCA, NO!" Iain screamed from his spot.

Blanca walked jerkily forward, moving faster and faster, and then she pulled back and hurled the bottle at the balcony with all her might. The soldiers shouted and dove aside, but it was too late. The explosive cocktail hit home, shattering in a blaze and enveloping the nearby munitions.

The balcony exploded, bursting into a blood-filled cloud peppered with sand and metal. Fire spread quickly, growing wild and uncontrolled in a matter of seconds. The crucifix at the center of the cathedral's northernmost wall took on an incredible shine until the flames swallowed it. The hand-painted face, already streaked with tears, perspired until it melted away. Stained-glass windows convulsed under the heat and then shattered, spraying the ground with glimmering shards. Engraved stone faces contorted behind the blaze before vanishing entirely. The altar, heavy with fabric, ignited like a gas-soaked torch.

At the center of it all stood Blanca, surrounded by scalding heat and flames, screaming endlessly into the air. Ribbons of blood poured down her neck, and flesh dammed under her fingernails as she clawed at the tender skin of her throat. She bellowed at the ceiling, unflinching as the building crumbled and fell around her, large pieces of ceiling dropping from above and erupting as they hit the ground.

In a sudden flash, hands ripped her from her spot and dragged her away.

The heat pursued them as they made their mad dash to the door, and only Iain's persistent grip kept Blanca moving. They barreled forward into the open air, and smoke billowed out of the gaping entryway behind them.

"BLANCA, STOP SCREAMING!"

She jerked, eyes wide and frantic. "More soldiers are coming! Let's go!" Iain shouted, pulling her along with his one remaining hand. Even as they fled, Blanca's gaze stayed on the charred cathedral behind them as it collapsed into a fiery ruin.

⸎

Parwan, Afghanistan
2019

"Congratulations, Hernandez. You're heading home."

A few seconds passed in awkward stillness before Blanca reached out and accepted her paperwork.

"Thank you, Sir."

The uniformed man behind the desk shuffled his papers. "What're your plans once you return to the States?"

Blanca tried to smile. "My little brother is graduating high school."

The man nodded. "Good. Enjoy yourself."

Blanca took the paperwork and left. After several hours of waiting, she joined the other returning soldiers on their way out of the country. Like her, they were all antsy creatures in green fatigues, jiggling their legs and looking around anxiously.

The flight was just one of several Blanca would have to take to get back to Texas. She tried to sleep away the time, but whenever she dozed off, the plane would rattle ominously, and she would jerk awake, alarmed.

One flight, and then another. Shuffling, hauling, moving around. Time became irrelevant. Daylight and darkness meant nothing. Eventually, the military presence melted away and was replaced with a civilian setting.

That night, she spent ten hours in an airport in Istanbul, awkwardly slumped over a pair of hard-backed chairs. Her stomach turned at the sight of any food, and the nausea made her head pound.

At one point, a pair of women in hijabs passed her. They were minding their own business, but Blanca flinched all the same.

Finally, she boarded her flight out of Istanbul. This one would take her to Boston, and after that, she would arrive in Texas.

But at some point during the long flight, Blanca felt her relative calm fade away. Suddenly, all she could hear was the wind sucking away forcefully at the thresholds of the plane and the metallic grinding and shifting of the engines. The people around her seemed placid, stupidly so, and Blanca watched them with suspicion.

The plane finally landed, and the passengers headed down the terminal in an exhausted cluster. Three uniformed soldiers trailed behind her. When they emerged from the tunnel, a few waiting people cheered and clapped. Blanca balked, startled at the noise, and she immediately turned away from the attention.

An old man caught Blanca's arm. "Thank you for your service, young lady."

Blanca made a strange noise in the back of her throat. At last, she managed a stilted nod. She didn't respond because she didn't know what to say.

By the time she got away from the staring people at the terminal's entrance, Blanca was hurrying along in short, uncertain steps, and her vision had started to blur. The hypersensitivity that had manifested on the plane came back in full force, and Blanca stopped in the middle of the airport, frozen, unable to break away from the savage assault of sights and sounds. The busy civilian world encroached on her with vicious disregard.

"Ma'am?"

Blanca jolted. A security guard was watching her closely.

"Do you need some help finding your flight?" he asked.

"No," she managed hoarsely. "I've got it."

The security officer nodded, but he continued to watch her until she was out of sight. Blanca left and wandered. She found her terminal, but it was packed with people, so she camped out on some chairs next to a tall window. Nearby, a family with two small children stopped and waited. One of their little boys watched Blanca from a distance. She shifted away and hid her face behind her arm.

A few minutes later, she heard crying. The little boy was screaming, and his cries only seemed to grow louder by the second. The noise was a great, keening wail that pierced Blanca's rattled mind.

She leaned forward and put her hands over her ears. *Please, God. Make it stop.*

The cries continued, echoing endlessly in the dark corners of her mind. Why wasn't someone shutting that kid up? Did parents just let their children cry and shriek for no reason now? The hysterical screaming became even louder, and Blanca crashed very suddenly through her last threshold of tolerance.

"*SHUT THE HELL UP!*" she screamed, whirling to face the family and their sobbing child.

The family was gone. There was no crying child.

A few passing patrons paused, startled, and stared in Blanca's direction. She scanned their worried faces for a hazy moment before snatching up her bag and stumbling away. Sweating profusely, she raced into the nearest bathroom and burst into a lone stall, where she convulsed into sobs. There, Blanca gripped the edges of the toilet and vomited, all stomach lining and bile because she hadn't eaten in days.

Falling back against the cool, grimy tile, she slumped next to a wall and buried her face in her arms. The worn rosary dangled at her wrist, momentarily forgotten under the weight of her panic.

Suddenly, Blanca wanted nothing more than to be out of her uniform. She began clawing at the green army fatigues, fighting against every inch of fabric with stunning ferocity. *I want it off, get it off, I can't take it anymore!*

When the airport security finally arrived, Blanca was half-naked on the floor, one boot kicked out from under the stall and her bag of meager belongings strewn across the linoleum. They took her to their office for questioning and kept her there for hours.

By the time Blanca was released, the flight to Texas was long gone. Devastated, she collapsed into a chair and prepared a text to send to Mateo.

CHAPTER 10

*In the final choice, a soldier's pack is
not so heavy as a prisoner's chains.*
—General Dwight D. Eisenhower

Miles away, Otto sat under a blinding white light and
tried not to flinch. Upon his arrival, there'd been
no grand welcome, no joyful embrace. Instead, he'd spent
hours getting debriefed by his skeptical superiors. Perhaps
it was not the light that bothered him, but instead the
bare, naked visibility that came with it. He looked across
the table.

Where had he been?

He wasn't sure.

Who had been keeping him?

Some soldiers. He didn't know anything about them.

Where were they going?

He didn't know, and couldn't he return to his damn
squadron, already?

So far, both sides had been unsatisfied with the
exchange. And now, here he was again, looking down the
length of a cold austere table at an incredibly important
man he'd never thought to see in person.

Hermann Göring was the commanding leader of
the Luftwaffe, a man second in power only to the Führer

himself. Otto had never once warranted his attention, and yet here he was, intense gaze fixed squarely on Otto's face.

Otto kept very still. However, he grew frustrated when the other man did not speak.

"I have already been debriefed, sir."

Göring's beady eyes ticked over Otto's face. "Yes, I know," he said at last. The older man shuffled some papers and peered down at them. "You state you were held captive by foreign soldiers for nearly a month's time, and yet you cannot tell us anything beyond a few names. Why is that?"

"They did not reveal anything to me, sir."

"Did they speak around you at all?"

"Yes, sir."

"And you did not learn anything valuable from them?"

Otto shifted. "As I reported, I could not understand them."

Göring looked back at the files. "Our scouts believe they might be American."

Otto moved his hands in a noncommittal gesture. "Perhaps."

"Then why could you not understand them?" Göring asked. "According to your file, you are fluent in English."

"I am," Otto said. "But they weren't speaking English."

"Oh? Then what language was it?"

"I think it was Italian, or possibly Spanish."

Göring raked his eyes over Otto again. It was uncommon for Otto to recoil under the gaze of any man, but the instinct to do so now was almost unbearable.

"Italian... or Spanish," Göring repeated slowly. "Interesting."

Otto waited tensely.

"And what names did you hear?"

Otto fought to keep his hands from clenching. He had already *gone over this.*

"As I—"

Göring looked at him sharply, and Otto cleared his throat, carefully pressing the agitation from his tone. "There were two women and two men. I'm not sure of their names."

"You heard nothing else?"

"No, sir."

"And you haven't any idea where they are heading?"

"I was blindfolded," Otto informed him. "They rarely allowed me to see anything."

"Did they abuse you?"

Otto paused. "They handled me roughly sometimes, but nothing too severe."

"So," Göring said, quite abruptly so that Otto's heart spiked, "you spent a month with these foreign soldiers, learned none of their names, nothing about their plans or nationalities, and now you are here, having escaped their clutches by some impressive combination of skill and luck. Is that right?"

Otto hesitated. "Yes, sir."

"Why did they not kill you?" Göring asked, almost too kindly.

Otto motioned with his hands again, that same uncertain gesture. "Perhaps they hoped they could trade me for safe passage."

"Did you aid them at all while you were traveling together?"

"No, sir."

Göring leaned close. "Are you lying, Lieutenant?"

Otto cut his eyes a little at Göring. "No, sir. I did nothing to aid them. I have already sworn this."

Silence followed. A chill dropped down Otto's spine as Göring's features shifted and became calculating once more. "Interesting," he said again, looking back at the papers.

Otto waited, fingers twitching. "Sir, my squadron—"

"Your squadron has been disbanded and reassigned," Göring interrupted without looking at him. "Only two of your fellow pilots survived the last mission. Your captain is also dead."

Otto brought his hands back to his lap so Göring would not see how they clenched into fists. "When will I be reassigned, sir?" he asked through gritted teeth.

"Soon," Göring said casually. "But for now, you will remain here." He stood, and Otto quickly did the same.

"What? Why? I need to be out there flying, I need to—"

Göring held up a hand. "These...outlaws—the ones who held you captive—must be brought to justice. You may yet be able to provide information that will lead to their capture."

"I already told you," Otto said daringly, "I don't know anything else about them. I have no idea where they are. The last I saw, they were caught in a battle far south of Warsaw." He cleared his throat. "If they're going anywhere, it's east. Into Slovakia, I think."

Göring raised both brows, scribbled something on a sheet of paper, and then offered Otto a tight smile. "Thank you, Lieutenant. That is very helpful." There was nothing beyond the thin line of his lips to indicate any semblance of kindness. "You are dismissed."

"Sir, please, I want to fly again—"

"*Dismissed*, pilot."

Otto shut his mouth with a click. Göring stepped aside, and Otto left, only to be replaced by a bespectacled man in a suit. The newcomer watched Otto's retreating back and waited for him to vanish around a corner before speaking.

"We found another," Heisenberg said.

Göring looked over at him. "Did you? Where?"

"A chapel in Warsaw. We had to chase off the Russians to get to him."

"And did you learn anything?"

"Oh, yes." Heisenberg's voice had a quiet, strained excitement to it. "More than we could have ever hoped for."

———

They were sheltered just outside the city, trapped between feuding armies and the natural elements. A makeshift lean-to was their only source of comfort. Night crept closer, promising to chill them to the point of no return.

Blanca sat without speaking or moving. Iain hovered nearby, the fingers of his remaining hand locked around his rifle. Dizziness hit him, and he was forced to sit. The wind seemed to cut straight through their coats. Blanca continued to ignore him. It had been like this for days.

"Blanca, you've got to eat or you are going to die out here."

This, at last, attracted Blanca's attention. "What does it matter?" she croaked. "I couldn't protect him, Iain. He's gone." Iain reached out to her, but she shoved him away, eyes wild. "He... He's gone. I watched... I watched Mateo...die."

"But you're still here, Blanca! You've got to live!"

She gripped him, her expression frantic.

"No! I was put on this earth to *protect Mateo!*"

She hunched forward, fingers curled tightly in Iain's ragged shirt. Tears poured down her cheeks. "I was made… for him," she finished in a dazed whisper.

A furious resolve filled his expression, and he grabbed Blanca, pulling her roughly to face him. His hand moved to the back of her head, and he forced her to look at his face.

"No," Iain growled, eyes shining. "No. You. *Weren't*."

Blanca stared up at him, shocked.

"No one," Iain continued fiercely, "is put on this earth for anyone else. Your life is your own. Do you understand?" His gaze softened. "I'm sorry, Blanca. I know you miss him. I know you would have gladly given your life a thousand times over to save his. I know, I know! But the truth is, you were not made to protect him. You are your own person."

Blanca made a noise in the back of her throat like a gurgle. "I don't want to be my own person. I want to be dead."

"Then you are wasting everything Mateo ever gave you!" he exploded, jarring them both. "Every moment you two spent together, every second of joy and love and happiness, you are throwing all of that away by refusing to live your own life! You are going to grieve yourself to death and let everything Mateo ever gave you just vanish!"

Iain pointed to himself.

"I know because I've done it. My fiancée—a woman I loved since I was six years old—was killed in a car accident that I caused, and I spent the next three years of my life as a bloody heroin addict because of it! I missed my mother's death, I lost my home, I lost my job, and I—" He sucked in a deep breath, shaking violently. "I contracted HIV while living on the streets."

Iain curled his fingers at his side. "I ruined my family, my health, and my whole bloody life because I couldn't move on from my grief! And I'll never be able to get that back! I'll never be able to undo it! All because I couldn't understand that I was my own person—that I *could* live without her."

Iain made a motion as if to reach out to her again, but this time, he jerked back his hand and kept it at his side.

"Blanca, you're allowed to grieve. You should. You've got to, you've got to do that for yourself. But for the love of god, don't believe for a second that your life is meant to be nothing more than an accessory to his. You exist in your own right. You are enough on your own."

Blanca closed her eyes as Iain stepped closer.

"Mateo's death doesn't destroy what he gave you—all the love, all the memories, all the joy—those things can live on. But if you let yourself just—disappear, then all of those things will fade away, too." Iain hovered very near her. "Do you understand? You are *wasting* what he gave you if you refuse to live on after him."

"He was my best thing," Blanca whispered.

Iain blinked rapidly against his own tears. "You are your best thing, Blanca."

Blanca fell back heavily against the snow and pressed her hands over her face. Together, they curled up and wept.

———&———

The base was a hive of anxious activity. Planes went out and never returned. Platoons, likewise, were given their orders and never seen again. Those that remained behind fared little better. The military had always been well-fed before, but now, even they were seeing mass shortages.

The morale of Nazi Germany was eroding.

Otto ate dinner with the other pilots, none of whom he was personally acquainted with. Once that was done, he retreated to the showers and stepped into a stall, making sure to pull the curtains tight around him. He stripped off his clothes, tossed them on a bench, and stepped into the hot water with a miserable noise.

Blanca's tags dangled from his neck, swinging under the water's blast.

The shower did nothing but make him feel hot and overwhelmed, and when he got out a few minutes later, he felt worse than before. Dispirited, he got dressed and left, ready to head back to the barracks.

However, his walk was detoured abruptly when Göring rounded the corner flanked by two uniformed soldiers. "Lieutenant Zimmler," greeted Göring. They saluted. "We are in need of your assistance once more."

Without waiting for an answer—*It's eight in the evening, what sort of assistance could they need*, Otto wondered—Göring turned and went down another corridor, obviously expecting him to follow. He did, of course, stomach roiling unpleasantly. "May I ask how I can help, sir?"

Göring looked sidelong at him and said quite casually, "We have one one of the foreign soldiers who captured you."

Otto's expression went blank.

"Or so we believe, anyway," Göring continued. "We need you to identify the body."

Otto stopped outside the door to what he now realized was the morgue. "Of course, sir," he managed with difficulty.

Göring gestured to the door. "It is in there, on the table."

Otto hesitated, and then he turned and pushed open the door, which had been unlocked with a key. The morgue was a large open room, kept quite cold, and the ceiling lights were blinding. Otto was reminded of the area he'd been "debriefed" in. It had felt much more like an interrogation.

This, too, had a layered quality to it. Otto was not fooled; this was a test.

Unfortunately, he was not sure he could pass it. The body on the table—covered by a white sheet—arrested him, freezing him in his spot for a half-second too long. "Go on," Göring urged, standing a few feet behind him. "We need to know if you can tell us anything. Take a look at it."

Mechanically—and with every effort at forcing the tremors from his hand—Otto reached forward and pulled back the sheet.

His body briefly convulsed. He did not realize his expression was reflected in the steely wall of capsules in front of him.

"Do you recognize it?"

Otto delicately replaced the sheet. "Yes, sir."

"Do you know his name?"

"Not quite, sir. I—heard it, sometimes, but it was foreign. I could not say it."

Göring appeared at his side and looked down coolly at the corpse. "Pity."

"You did not find any identifying information on him?"

Göring looked directly at Otto. "No, I am afraid not. However, at least we know he was one of those who tormented you."

Otto met the other man's gaze. "Was he the only one you recovered?"

Göring smiled. "For now," he said. "Strange. You claimed you last saw the group heading east, but this body was discovered in a church in Warsaw. They must have changed their minds."

Otto said nothing.

"If you have nothing more useful to tell us, Lieutenant, you may return to your barracks."

Otto left immediately. As soon as he was alone, he slammed a fist into the nearest wall and let loose an animalistic noise of grief.

⊷⊶

In her mind's eye, she saw him as a little boy.

He'd been small for so long, Blanca had worried he'd never grow. He didn't get enough to eat, she knew that. She'd tried stealing, but she looked exactly like the type of kid who'd steal, so she rarely got away with it.

And then one day, it happened in a flash.

He was taller than her. His arms were thicker, and his hands were bigger. His voice changed, squeaking for just a month or two and then growing deep and rough. He grew up, suddenly and without mercy. But in her mind's eye, he was still that scrawny boy who never got enough to eat.

Blanca stood at the edge of the Vistula River. Soon, they would be at the coastal city of Danzig.

She unfurled her fingers and stared at the unmoving crucifix sitting in the center of her coiled rosary beads. The tiny etched face was static; it didn't react to her narrowed eyes or trembling grip.

With a slow tilt of her hand, Blanca let the totem of faith tumble from her palm and into the river. The raging water swallowed it up in an instant.

"Blanca?" Iain appeared. "It's time to go."

She nodded, picked up her gun, and followed. They walked until they could see the city lights of Danzig before stopping to make camp one last time. Iain took a seat and prodded ineffectually at the bandages covering his injured arm, which now ended at a bloody knub.

"Let me see it."

Iain looked up at her in surprise. "Blanca…I-I told you—"

"I remember." She took a seat in front of him and yanked his arm to her. Iain's expression creased with worry, but he didn't pull his arm back. "S'that why you didn't want me to treat you all this time?" she asked, carefully unwrapping his bandages. "Because you're positive?"

"Aye," he admitted shamefully. "It's why I was always so fanatical about washing my hands, too. I was afraid there would be blood."

Blanca wiped at her face with her shoulder, eyes on his injury. "Pretty shitty you didn't tell me before, considering you knew I'd probably have to fix you up at some point."

He hesitated. "I know."

"Be glad any medic with half a brain cell treats all blood like it's infected."

Iain nodded slowly.

"So, why didn't you say anything?"

Iain frowned. "You know why."

"Tell me."

Iain's expression grew frustrated. "No one wants to admit they have HIV, Blanca."

Blanca pointed a finger at him. "That—that shit right there, that's why this doesn't get fixed. You can't solve a problem if no one's willing to talk about it." She unrolled the last of their fresh bandages. "You would've told me if you'd had diabetes or—asthma or anything else—"

"That's not the same," he muttered.

"Because of the damn stigma, Iain." Blanca looked up at his face. "People don't want to admit they have HIV, so they don't get help, and things don't get better. The stigma turns into rumor and rumor turns into hate, and it just goes on and on and on, in an endless loop of bullshit."

Iain fell quiet, but his expression was brooding. After a few minutes, he said, "I wouldn't be so ashamed if people didn't act like it's damn leprosy. One bloke didn't even want to shake my hand after he found out."

Blanca shrugged. "People are trash. Keep your expectations low, and you'll find life a lot easier." She took their water canteen and used it to wash the blood away. Iain flinched in pain when she pulled off the last of the bandages, hurrying to get the wound sterilized. She didn't talk for a few minutes, and Iain, likewise, kept silent.

When the bandage was secure again, Blanca washed her hands thoroughly. Then she held up her palms. "No scratches, see? I'm good." Iain exhaled a little. Blanca settled her elbows on her knees and tilted her head at him. "You do know you can still be with someone, right?"

Anger clouded Iain's expression. It looked terribly out of place on his gentle features.

"I'm serious."

Iain shook his head and looked down at his one remaining hand. "Not going to risk infecting someone else with this."

Blanca sat back. "How do you think HIV is spread, Iain? Did you talk to your doctor about it?"

He paused. "Some."

"Some?" she repeated harshly.

Iain scowled. "I didn't think to ever worry about it again. I didn't want a relationship. Not after the accident, and certainly not after this. I didn't think it mattered."

"It does matter. What if you meet someone you really like?"

"Then I'll keep it to my damn self," he said flatly.

"You didn't answer my question. How do you think HIV is spread?"

He thought about it. "Well, from my experience, sharing dirty needles is one good way."

"Yeah, so don't do that."

Iain glared at her.

"How else?"

Iain shrugged. "Sex."

"Unprotected penetrative sex without medication," Blanca corrected sharply. "Oral sex has almost no chance of passing along HIV, and it can't be transmitted through saliva or tears. You do know that don't you?"

Iain's brows furrowed.

"You could kiss someone all day every day, and you wouldn't give them HIV. Your mouth would literally have to be bleeding *into* their mouth for there to be even the slightest chance."

Iain's lips parted in surprise, and Blanca, acting on a sudden, determined urge, gripped his shirt and pulled him over so she could press her lips against his. Iain sucked in a breath, freezing against the kiss. Blanca held the motion for just a few moments, and Iain relaxed into it just before she pulled away.

"Would I have done that," she asked quietly, "if I thought you were going to infect me?"

Iain shook his head jerkily.

"Exactly." Blanca let her head fall back against the tree behind her. "You told me I still have to live my life…that I owe it to Mateo if nothing else. But you think it's already too late for you. It's not."

Iain reclined next to her, and they looked up at the stars where they appeared between the jutting tree branches. "Are you still using?" Blanca asked.

"No, thank god."

"Good. Takes a lot of strength to get out of it." They fell quiet for a little while. "What was her name?"

Iain exhaled. "Adia."

"That's pretty." Blanca shifted uncomfortably. "Was she like you? Was she warm?"

Iain smiled sadly. "She was the sun in the sky."

He brought up the ruined end of his left arm. "We never got married. We planned to, but I kept putting it off because I wanted to buy her a nice ring. She'd always say she didn't need one, though, and then she would take a pen and draw a circle around my ring finger. She'd tell me, 'anything that ties me to you is beautiful to me.'" Iain chuckled tearfully. "But I was stubborn. I wanted to give her the world, so I held off, tried to save some money. And then one day, we were driving to the market, and I ... I pulled out in front of a truck by accident, and..."

He stopped and cleared his throat.

"After she died, I...I couldn't help but think how stupid I was. Why didn't I just..."

He sighed heavily.

"I'm sorry for all of this," Blanca said quietly. "We really are in hell, aren't we?"

Iain looked around. "I don't know. Seems a bit cold for hell, don't you think?" He nudged her with a little smile, and Blanca let out a huff like a laugh.

"Good point," she whispered.

Łódź, Poland
1943

Otto struck a match and let the flame hover over the end of his cigarette. Once it was lit, he tossed the match away and puffed mindlessly.

After a while, he straightened away from a brick wall and walked, having no real destination in mind. The base was crowded with people, but he didn't stop to talk to any of them. No one here had his interest or trust.

Eventually, his stroll took him to a nearby Polish village occupied by German soldiers. There, he spotted a group of off-duty soldiers wrestling a man onto a crude wooden platform. They secured his arms above his head against a post centered on the stage, and once that was done, they did the same to a terrified young woman. The couple was tied back-to-back.

Otto stepped forward. "What is going on here?"

One of soldiers sneered. "Read the sign," he said, pointing to the woman on the other side. Annoyed, Otto rounded the post to see her, and when he did, he realized her head was shaved, and she had been severely beaten.

The sign around her neck read in German: *I am a race-defiler*. Below that, it said: *I let myself go with a Pole*.

Otto's eyes flickered back to the Polish man imprisoned with her. He had received an even more brutal punishment than the woman, and his legs looked twisted and broken. Both the German woman and her Polish lover remained admirably silent, even as the men continued to taunt them.

"You bring dishonor on Germany!" one man shouted at the woman, who flinched and turned her face away. One of her eyes was swollen shut.

"Slut!"

"Whore!"

The beatings and taunting continued for hours.

Eventually, the soldiers grew bored and left. The area fell still. Otto climbed the stage and looked over the German woman critically. Her body was limp, and her eyes were closed. Otto then looked to the Polish man, who was almost certainly dead. To his surprise, the Polish man met his gaze squarely. Otto moved around the post to face him.

"Is your crime valid?" Otto asked without inflection. "Did you go to bed with a German woman?"

The question was in German, but the Pole clearly understood it. "Yes," he answered stoically.

"Did you know the law?" Otto asked curiously.

"Yes," the other man repeated.

"Then why did you do it? Why did you choose this death?"

"I didn't," said the man. "I chose this life."

Otto's brows furrowed. "And now, for all your foolishness, it must end."

"The end of something," said the man, "does not erase it. All things must come to conclusion. The only choice you can make is the path that leads you there."

Otto watched the man for a long time. Finally, he nodded in the direction of the woman. "She is gone. I am sorry."

The man lowered his head and said nothing. Otto felt a strange pain in his chest. His eyes shifted to the man's battered legs. He would never walk again.

"You are satisfied with your path, Pole?" Otto asked.

The man looked up again. "Yes."

"Good." Otto reached to the holster at his side and pulled out his pistol.

The Polish man smiled. His expression was one of utter relief.

Otto fired the shot, flinching against the sudden booming echo. The man sagged, now a limp mirror image of the woman behind him. Together, they cast a striking silhouette. Otto tucked the gun back into his belt and rounded the platform.

As he left, he took the sign off the woman's neck and tossed it to the ground.

CHAPTER 11

We were eighteen and had begun
to love life and the world...and
we had to shoot it to pieces.
—Erich Maria Remarque

I n the early hours of the morning, as the base personnel stirred from their beds and the night watch was relieved, Otto strode purposefully to a locked room on one of the lower floors. There, he lifted the key he'd stolen from a staff member and used it to unlock the door. The morgue was dark and quiet. He kept the lights off, instead using a flashlight to find the label he needed.

Quietly, he opened the capsule and looked at the body where it lay under the sheet. His stomach turned, but his touch to the exposed hand, which had fallen to the side, was gentle. He pulled over a rolling table and moved the stiff, cold body onto it. Once that was done, he turned and wheeled the body out of the room and down the hall. Only one person saw him, and they spared him barely a glance.

He reached the building's exit in record time, and once he was outside, he placed the body in the back of a waiting truck. The sun was only just peeking over the horizon when he drove away from the base, steering the truck down a dirt path and weaving his way deep into the woods. Despite the anxiety he'd felt that morning, the early morning light lulled him into a strange sense of ease.

After a few hours, he came to the spot he'd picked out, and he got out from the truck with a shovel. It took nearly two hours to dig a hole deep and wide enough, and he was soon drenched with sweat despite the cold air. Heaving in a deep breath, he reached up and pulled himself out of the hole, briefly rolling onto his back so he could stare up at the dusty pink sky. His eyes shifted to the truck, where the body waited.

With a sudden burst of resolve, he got up and gingerly pulled the body from the truck's canvas-covered bed. Bare feet, paler than they'd been in life, dangled past his forearm.

Otto shifted, readjusting the weight in his arms before hopping into the hole, which went higher than his shoulders. Without letting go of the body, he looked at the earthen walls with a sudden dissatisfaction.

"This is not good enough for you, Mateo." Otto looked down at the covered face. "I wish I could do better. I am sorry."

Reluctantly, he lowered the boy's body to the earth, his own knee deep in the dirt. He reached up, pulling back the sheet and instantly flinching when the familiar features, now ashen, came into view. He exhaled.

"But this, at least, is better than a laboratory," he murmured. "I hope you can rest easier here."

Otto bit his lip, unwilling to leave. Instead, he sat back in the small space by Mateo's ankles. He was dirty and tired, but he couldn't make himself leave the teen behind.

"I am so sorry, Mateo," he whispered shakily. "I am sorry I left, and you died thinking that I did not care. I am sorry I disappointed you like so many other people in your

life have done before. And—and most of all, I am sorry—"
Tears overwhelmed him, and his voice cracked. "Because
the first thing I felt when I saw you was relief." He curled
one arm around his head, eyes clenched shut.

"You were right, Mateo," he whispered. "You cannot
help who you love."

With that, he swiped at his tears, pulled himself out
of the grave, and grabbed the shovel. Fifteen minutes later,
Mateo was gone.

Otto tossed the shovel into the back of the truck, but
instead of driving away, he returned to the new grave and
stood at its edge so he could read from a wrinkled piece
of paper in his hand:

"There is a time for everything, and a season for every
activity under the heavens: A time to be born and a time
to die, a time to kill and a time to heal, a time to mourn
and a time to dance, a time to love and a time to hate."
Otto inhaled deeply, lowering the paper as he finished. "A
time for war and a time for peace. May God bless you and
keep you. *In nomine patris, et filii, et spiritus sancti.*" He
made the sign of the cross, as he'd seen Blanca do. "Amen."

He closed the paper and shifted uncertainly in his spot.

"I hope that was good enough for you," he called up
to the sky. "I know you have no reason to take my word for
anything, but Mateo was good. You should remember that.
He deserves good things." Otto lowered his head again,
giving one last look at the fresh pile of dirt.

"Goodbye, *Brüderlein*," he murmured. "Watch over
your sister."

Otto got back in the truck and left the unmarked
grave behind. His eyes watched it in the rearview mirror
until it was out of sight.

When Otto arrived back at the base, a line of uniformed men was waiting for him. Göring stood at the center. He was no longer smiling.

Otto parked the truck and watched the men through the windshield. After he was satisfied he'd made them wait, he got out of the truck and grabbed the shovel. Then he stopped in front of Göring and jabbed the spade tip into the earth.

"Can I help you, sir?" he asked.

"Where is it, Zimmler?" Göring approached him. "Where is the body from the morgue?"

Otto, who was still dirty and holding a shovel, shrugged. "I don't know, sir. Are you in the habit of losing dead bodies?"

Göring's glare deepened. "Arrest him," he said flatly, and the other men surged forward, grabbing at Otto's arms even as he jerked and tried to pull away.

"You can't do this to me," Otto snarled. "I'm a German citizen!"

Göring smiled thinly.

Without a word further, the men dragged Otto inside the building and shoved him into a brightly-lit room where he hit a table hard with his stomach. Before he could right himself, hands came at his back and slammed him against the wood, causing him to grunt.

Göring appeared on the other side of the table.

"Do you know, Zimmler..."

Otto's strained eyes looked up, even as he fought to breathe.

"...there are many who might wonder how a loyal German such as yourself could turn so treacherous."

Göring put his hands behind his back. "They might
assume money or a desire for power is to blame, but I
know better. There is only one thing that could corrupt a
man to the point of such villainy—only one possible source
of such terrible contempt."

Göring leaned close, and his voice dropped to a
whisper.

"A woman."

Otto clenched his jaw.

Göring nodded to the men, who yanked Otto up,
straining his back painfully as they locked his arms in
place. Göring stayed on the other side of the table and
leaned forward, placing his hands flat on the wood.

"Tell me where they are, Zimmler, and your disloyalty
will be forgiven."

"I don't know where they are," Otto growled.

"Stop lying!" the other man snapped. "You are
protecting them, and that gypsy woman most of all."

Otto shoved hard at the men holding him, and they
were forced to back off.

"Latin."

Göring narrowed his eyes. "What?"

"She isn't a gypsy," Otto hissed. "She is Latin. And
you have no reason to chase her or the other Americans.
They are no threat to you!"

"No threat?" Göring snarled. "You see *this* as no threat?"

He tossed down a heavy book, and Otto's eyes
widened.

"This text is threat enough!" Göring howled. "State
secrets! Classified information!" He yanked open the
very same American History book Otto had discovered
in Blanca's bag. "Detailed descriptions of our operations,

our planes, our bases! Sensitive information concerning the Führer himself!" Göring's face contorted into a look of disgust. "You recognize this book, don't you, Zimmler? You knew this existed?"

Otto swallowed hard. "You cannot believe that is real, Sir—"

"*How else am I to believe when the evidence sits right before me?*" Göring raged. He pointed at Otto vehemently. "And the futures foretold in this text... With all of this information at their fingertips, who is to say the Americans don't have the technology to see into the future?" He rounded the table and stood in front of Otto. "I need the Americans here, Zimmler. I need to know what they know. They must answer for this."

"They cannot help you!" Otto insisted heatedly.

"But you can," Göring said. "You can help your country, Zimmler, and yourself, by telling us where they are, where they are heading."

Otto fell silent.

"If you do," Göring went on, voice softer now, more alluring, "I swear to you, the woman will not be harmed."

Otto's eyes flickered up, and then he lowered them again.

"You and she will be able to live out the rest of your lives in peace," Göring promised. "And you will be hailed as a hero of Nazi Germany for your contributions. Isn't that what you want? To use this information to our advantage?" Göring grew eager. "If we can adapt this American technology for ourselves, we can have the world, Zimmler. We will truly be the empire we were destined to be. And you will have your part in it. The woman, too. She's yours. But only if you tell us where they are."

Otto shifted, eyes cast to the side.

The woman, too. She's yours.

Otto wondered what Blanca would say if she'd heard that. Something violent, he was sure.

"If you do not do this," Göring went on when Otto didn't respond, "if you do not aid your countrymen, Nazi Germany may collapse into ruin."

Would I be safe in Munich?

Otto held his arms tensely at his sides and closed his eyes.

I would be dead or a prisoner under Nazi rule.

Otto opened his eyes and narrowed them at Göring. "Then let it collapse," he snarled.

Göring's expression shifted into shock. "You are a traitor!" he shouted furiously.

"No!" Otto roared suddenly, slamming his hands on the table. "Hitler is the traitor for dragging Germany into a war it cannot win! Nazi Germany is not meant to endure! You should take my advice, Göring, and leave those Americans alone." He leaned very close. "Because you will never be able to contain that woman. And if you catch her, she will kill you."

Göring's expression twisted with rage, but before he could say anything further, a soldier appeared at the door. At the soldier's rushed whisper, Göring's fury melted away and was replaced with grim satisfaction.

"Well, Zimmler, it seems we will get to test your theory sooner rather than later," he said arrogantly. Before Otto could process this, Göring looked at the other soldiers. "Put him in a holding cell. We wouldn't want him to miss his friends when they arrive."

Otto's eyes widened, and panic seized him.

Göring disappeared from the room, and two men grabbed Otto and jerked his arms behind him. Otto fought wildly, but they managed to cuff him and haul him out of the room. As they dragged him down the corridor, Otto's frantic gaze spotted Göring assembling men and giving them quick directions.

No, Otto thought desperately. Göring was sending a whole platoon after them.

With a sudden jerk of his body, Otto slammed one of the men down a flight of stairs and fell with him, forcing the other soldier to come running after them. The first soldier landed at the bottom with a groan, and Otto immediately rolled over and kicked out, catching the man's chin forcefully with his boot.

The soldier let out a sharp cry, and a crack reverberated through the air. The other soldier slammed into Otto from behind, but Otto threw his weight forward and they fell again. He rolled his shoulders, bringing his cuffed hands forward, and slammed his joined fists into the other man's stomach. They grappled, crashing back into the wall and bouncing off the railing. Otto grabbed the man's uniform and hurled him down to the floor, following it swiftly with a knee to the soldier's gut. The soldier fought back, punching Otto in the jaw and rolling them over. He made a move for the radio, but Otto brought up both feet and kicked him off.

The man scrambled to get back up, but Otto was faster. He brought both hands down like a club on the other soldier's throat. The man gasped, eyes growing wide with pain before he rolled over. Blinking past the blood in his own eyes, Otto raised his hands again and beat the other man into unconsciousness.

Panting, Otto pulled himself up and grabbed the keys to his cuffs so he could cast them off. His gaze landed on a large mural bearing the swastika at its center, and rage filled him.

"*I did everything for you!*" he screamed.

But no more. He was done.

With one last heated glare at the emblem, he turned and rushed out.

⚬⚬⚬

As Blanca and Iain drew closer to Danzig, her heart began to race. Her skin prickled uncomfortably. Something wasn't right.

That was when they began to emerge. Dozens of German soldiers, armed and foreboding, poured out of the city of Danzig and formed a line. Trucks appeared, rolling forward with sadistic purpose. Blanca and the others came to a grinding halt. They stood now in front of nearly fifty armed men, none of whom looked surprised to see them.

"Shit," Blanca hissed, and they turned to flee. Shouts rang out, and bullets followed them, dogging their every step.

The soldiers advanced unhurriedly, and their shots always fell one step short of their targets. Blanca sped away, chest burning and arms pumping, but after several feet, she realized the soldiers weren't trying to kill them.

They were herding them.

"Over here!" she shouted, and they scrambled behind a line of natural rocks just outside the city. Bullets continued to rain over their heads, but the soldiers didn't advance further. Instead, they pinned them down and kept them there. They were waiting for something—for *someone*. Blanca's heart seized.

Exhaustion plagued her limbs. Each joint trembled and felt weak. She closed her eyes, sweat pouring down her face despite the chill. Strangely, she found herself wishing desperately for that little house in the woods.

"Oh, God," Iain groaned, eyes turned up. "They're sending planes!"

Blanca opened her eyes. In the distance, a small dot approached rapidly. The soldiers were closer now. The gunfire was near constant, and it deafened Blanca to the others. The sight of the plane struck her, though, and she stood up, moving away from the cover of the rocks.

"Just one?" she questioned, standing straighter.

"Blanca, stay down!" Iain ordered, but Blanca stumbled further out, eyes on the sky. The dot was closer now; she could see the outline of a lone plane. The sight of it rooted her to her spot.

"BLANCA!" Iain shouted again, and Blanca scrambled behind some cover just as a German fighter plane rushed over their heads with a deafening roar.

As soon as it crossed them, the plane fired mercilessly on the line of waiting soldiers and trucks. The shocked Germans shouted and ran, but there was nowhere for them to go.

Blanca twisted, mouth parted in disbelief as the plane turned sharply and swooped down on the dazed Germans again. Machine-gun fire blasted from its turrets, blistering the line of men until they were forced to scatter. Trucks burst into balls of flame, and the gunfire came to an abrupt stop. The Germans, unable to retaliate, fled or burned.

"Come on!" Iain pulled on Blanca's arm, and they raced across the open field.

The plane circled back, annihilating a truck as it tried to escape the massacre. Blanca turned, jogging backward as she looked up desperately. She couldn't see the cockpit of the plane no matter how much she strained.

Otto Zimmler could see her, though, on the field of snow below him as Iain dragged her along. He took his eyes off the sky just long enough to watch Blanca escape the dying Germans. There was nothing on earth he would not have given to be running with her to a land far, far away.

"Be safe," he whispered shakily.

When he lifted his eyes again, it was to see an entire squadron of German fighters heading right at him. Fear— an unfamiliar sensation—encased his heart. He would not escape this. He knew that.

A sudden memory came to him, unbidden. *The end of something does not erase it.*

Otto reached up and clutched the identification tags beneath his shirt, closing his eyes briefly as he remembered what it had felt like to hold her. This brought him the courage he needed, and he opened his glassy eyes to face the other German pilots as they raced in his direction.

His hand tightened on the control column, and with a last deep breath, he slipped a thumb over the gun button.

On the ground, Blanca and Iain found a truck left unscathed, and Iain hopped into the driver's seat while Blanca dove in the back. As they sped off, Blanca hurried to the truck's edge and looked out.

In the sky, a furious battle was taking place.

Otto's plane unleashed a barrage of gunfire before twisting straight into the group of enemy fighters, splitting it apart. Blanca's expression filled with horror as the other fighters converged on his position. He managed to shoot down two, but he was far outnumbered. No matter he tried to evade, there were always more planes just behind him.

Finally, an attack hit the plane's tail, and it ignited in a ball of flame before breaking apart. Blanca gripped the back of the truck as she watched it spin wildly in the air, descending further and further until it disappeared from sight. She could feel the crash from their spot. Flame and smoke jumped into the air beyond the tree line. Otto's plane was gone.

Blanca fell back, unable to breathe. "*Nooooo!*" she wailed into her hands.

The truck sped on.

<hr>

In her vision, she was stretched out on a warm bed with clean sheets.

When she rose, it was to find her mother sitting at a large kitchen table filled with breakfast foods. The windows were open; a light breeze stirred the curtains. The only sounds were the chirps of birds outside and the laughter of her family.

Blanca gazed over her mother's face, and her heart filled with pride. Her mother's hair was loose and soft, not pulled back in the stringy bun she'd worn day in and day out, scrubbing people's floors or cooking in a hot kitchen. For one beautiful moment, she was happy and safe.

"*Al mal tiempo, buena cara.*"

Blanca smiled.

"*Sí, Mamá.*"

The light from the bright day suddenly became blinding, overtaking Blanca's senses before fading again. The wonderful vision dissolved. The cold returned.

They were outside.

The truck had run out of fuel. They were stranded and starving. Hours after the truck stopped for good, the German soldiers found them. There was no fight.

"Pity," Göring said in English. "Zimmler tried so hard to protect you."

He stooped in front of Blanca's dirty, tear-stained face. Despite her weakness, she gritted her teeth and growled at him.

"Was your life worth his sacrifice?" Göring wondered.

Blanca dropped her head. She had no answer.

⸺⸺

Texas, USA
2019

The summer weather was brilliant.

Blanca drove down the sunny streets with the windows rolled down. There was an upbeat pop tune playing on the radio. It transitioned into a mellow ballad before being replaced by a long-winded commercial about community theater productions.

She stopped at a gas station to fill up. Someone waved at her, thinking she was someone else. She waved back anyway.

Next, she drove to the grocery store and walked the aisles, picking up things they needed back at the apartment. An old woman asked for help getting a can of cranberry sauce. Blanca grabbed it for her, and the woman patted her shoulder with an appreciative smile. Blanca made sure she knew it was no problem.

There was a two-for-one sale on Mateo's favorite brand of chips. Blanca picked up four. Teenage boys ate a lot.

At the register, Blanca nodded and smiled as the cashier greeted her.

"Do you have any coupons?"

Blanca fished one out of her purse and gave it to her. The girl scanned it and tossed it into a pile. Blanca thanked her, and when the groceries were loaded up in her cart, she took them out herself ("No thank you, I've got it") and put them in the used car she'd bought the month before.

At home, Blanca unloaded the groceries and put them away, careful to place the canned food and boxes facing out so their labels were visible. She put the chips Mateo liked on the counter so he would see them.

Once that was done, Blanca closed the cabinets and looked at them for a long time before going to her bedroom and closing the door behind her. There, she pulled a handgun from the bedside table, put it to her temple, and pulled the trigger.

The gun jerked.

Silence.

Blanca lowered the gun and scanned it with wide, shining eyes. The barrel was open. The gun had jammed.

In the living room, a door opened and shut.

"Blanca? Blanca, it's time to go!"

Numbly, Blanca cocked her head in the direction of the closed bedroom door.

"Blanca?" Mateo's voice came again. "Where are you? Come on, we're going to be late!"

Exhaling, Blanca put the gun back in the bedside table and closed it. "Yeah, I'm here," she managed at last, standing up and clearing her throat. She changed her shirt because the other one was damp with sweat, then left the room.

"Hey there, kid," she greeted, smiling. "You ready for orientation or what?"

CHAPTER 12

Arbeit macht frei.
[Work sets you free]
—Gate of Auschwitz-Birkenau Concentration Camp

One.
Four.
Nine.
Six.
Eight.
One.
Prisoner Number 149681.

———∞∞∞———

One.
Two.
Three.
Three months.

———∞∞∞———

One.
Two.
Three.
Four.

Five.

Six.

Seven.

Eight.

Nine.

Ten.

Eleven.

Block 11.

KLASSIFIZIERTE INFORMATION

Sicherheitsdienst des Reichsführers
- SS - Geheime Staatspolizei

VERBATIM TRANSCRIPTION

Auschwitz - Birkenau, Province of Upper Silesia
Regierungsbezirk Kattowitz, Landkreis Bielitz

Participants:
Reichsführer Heinrich Himmler—[HH]
Reichsstatthalter Hermann Göring - [HG]
SS-Hauptsturmführer Wilhelm Boger—[WB]

Detainee:
Blanca Hernandez—[BH]

[Start transcription 1]
HH: Today's date is January 12th, 1944. My name is Heinrich Himmler. With me are Hermann Göring and Wilhelm Boger. This interview will be conducted in English.
HH: State your name.
BH: Fuck you.
[End transcription 1]

[Start transcription 2]
HH: Today's date is January 28th, 1944. My name is Heinrich Himmler. With me are Hermann Göring and Wilhelm Boger. This interview will be conducted in English.
HH: I trust you are more compliant today?
BH: Where is Iain?
HH: He is detained here as well.
[papers shuffling]
HH: Miss Hernandez, do you know why you are being kept here?
BH: No.
HH: It is because you and your companions have broken our laws, caused problems for German military forces, and brought harm to innocent civilians.
BH: We just want to go home.
HH: And where is home, Miss Hernandez?
BH: The United States.
HH: Right. Because you are "lost."
BH: Yeah.
HH: So your possession of a book detailing Nazi procedures and personnel—as well as bold predictions of a failed future Germany—means nothing, then?
BH: It's just a book. It doesn't mean anything.

HH: Your movements here seem to suggest otherwise. Your personal information, too, seems at odds with your claims of innocence. What year were you born?

BH: 1918.

HH: Do not lie. We already have your information.

BH: The fuck you ask me for then?

HH: If you tell us the truth, we will allow you to see your friend.

[No response]

HH: We have your date of birth listed in the year 1997. How is this possible?

BH: Magic.

HH: Herr Boger, please take her away.

[End transcription 2]

[Start transcription 3]

HH: Today's date is February 9th, 1944. My name is Heinrich Himmler. With me are Hermann Göring and Wilhelm Boger. This interview will be conducted in English.

HH: Miss Hernandez, you look tired.

BH: I'm—I'm fine.

HH: Did you enjoy your time with Herr Boger? He can be quite harsh, I know.

[No response]

HH: Are you having trouble sitting back in your chair?

BH: No.

HH: How many times did he flog you?

[No response]

HH: You do need not receive any more whippings. You only need to tell us the truth.

BH: I don't know the answers you want!

HH: What device brought you here?

BH: A machine, I don't know!

HH: Tell us more about the machine.

BH: I can't, I don't know how it worked! It was just—

HH: Herr Boger, please—

[muffled noises]

[crying]

HH: Now, Miss Hernandez, please—

BH: I—I can't—

HH: Are you right-handed or left-handed, Miss Hernandez?

[No response]

HH: I believe she is right-handed, which means she does not need full use of her left.

BH: I don't know what to tell you! It was a machine at a university, it blew up, we landed here!

HH: From where? What year did you travel from?

BH: 2019! Jesus, we came from…2019.

HH: 2019?

BH: Yes.

HH: Are the predictions made in this textbook true from your perspective?

[No response]

HH: Who can tell us more about the machine?

[No response]

HH: Herr Boger, take her away -

[crying]

[a woman screaming]

[End transcription 3]

[Start transcription 4]

HH: Today's date is February 15th, 1944. My name is Heinrich Himmler. With me are Hermann Göring and

Wilhelm Boger. This interview will be conducted in English.

HH: Miss Hernandez, this device is one of Boger's own invention. Would you like to learn how it is used?

BH: No.

HH: They call it the Boger Swing. To use it, we would strip you naked, lay you over the bar in the air, tie your wrists to your ankles, and let you hang under your own weight while suspended from the ceiling. It is a very effective way to obtain information. Would you like that?

BH: No.

HH: Can you offer us anything in return?

BH: What do you want?

HH: Tell us how the machine works.

BH: I don't know how the machine works, I was there by accident—

HH: Who can tell us?

[No response]

HH: Tell us who can explain the device! Now!

[muffled noises]

[a woman screaming]

HH: Take her to Mengele. She is not the one we want.

[End transcription 4]

KLASSIFIZIERTE INFORMATION

Sicherheitsdienst des Reichsführers
- SS - Geheime Staatspolizei

VERBATIM TRANSCRIPTION

Auschwitz - Birkenau, Province of Upper Silesia
Regierungsbezirk Kattowitz, Landkreis Bielitz

Participants:
Reichsführer Heinrich Himmler—[HH]
Reichsstatthalter Hermann Göring - [HG]
SS-Hauptsturmführer Wilhelm Boger—[WB]

Detainee:
Iain Claflin - [IC]

[Start transcription]
HH: Today's date is February 17th, 1944. My name is
Heinrich Himmler. With me are Hermann Göring and
Wilhelm Boger. This interview will be conducted in English.
HH: State your name.
IC: Iain Claflin.
HH: Nationality?
IC: Irish.
HH: Not American, then?
IC: Obviously.

HH: That attitude will not serve you well here. Are you associated with the military?
IC: No.
HH: What role do you serve amongst your group?
IC: None. I came here by accident like the rest of them.
HH: What is your occupation?
IC: I'm a doctoral candidate. A student.
HH: In what field?
IC: Physics.
HH: Interesting. And what was your part in obtaining the information in this book?
IC: None. I don't know where that came from.
HH: Life will be much simpler for you if you tell us the truth.
IC: That book is fake. It's a lie.
HH: Then why does it have accurate information about secret military operations?
IC: I don't—I don't know.
HH: Mr. Claflin, what is your date of birth, including the year?
IC: April 5th, 1987.
HH: And the year from which you came?
[No response]
HH: You appear to be a smart man—much more so than your companion. It would be wise for you to answer.
IC: Will you let us go if I do?
HH: That depends on the information you give us.
IC: You can't keep us here indefinitely.
HH: Why not?
[No response]
HH: Is it because you know something we do not? Perhaps something to come?
[No response]

HH: Do you know what this book tells us about our camp here?

IC: No.

HH: It says the Soviet Army will triumph over us…next year. Is that true?

IC: I don't know.

HH: I will ask you again. How did you gain this information? And how did you arrive in Poland when and where you did?

IC: Look, it was—a fluke.

HH: What kind of "fluke," Mr. Claflin?

IC: A malfunction. It was an accident. One we can't redo.

HH: Was it a device? The thing that brought you here?

IC: Something like that. But I don't know how it worked.

HH: Yes, you do. You are an educated man. I believe you know more about the device that brought you all here than any of your comrades. As such, I am willing to make you an offer. You will be spared the treatment of a prisoner if you aid us in our endeavors.

IC: And what endeavors would that be?

HH: Aims similar to the one you were working on, I expect.

IC: I was working with a university interested in experimental physics. We were examining electromagnetism and gravity. We weren't trying to do anything like what you're thinking.

HH: And what are we thinking, Mr. Claflin?

IC: That the knowledge I have can be useful to you in terms of time travel. It isn't possible. And even if it were, I can't replicate it. I'm useless to you.

HH: That is unfortunate. Herr Boger, please bring her in.

IC: What—'her'? [a door opening] No, no! Blanca— Please, please, don't hurt her—

[a woman's screams]

IC: Stop! Stop this now, for—for God's sake—

HH: Stay calm, Mr. Claflin.

[screaming]

IC: Please, please—just stop it—let her go, God—

HH: Are you sure you cannot be of use to us, Mr. Claflin?

IC: I—I don't—I don't know—

[muffled noises]

IC: Blanca! Stop, stop—bloody hell, please stop!

HH: Do you think she would be more helpful if we left her with the soldiers for a few days? I am sure they have ways of getting her to open up—

IC: This is bloody madness! How can you do this to someone? No—stop!

HH: Do you comply or not?

IC: Alright, alright! Just—stop—leave her alone, god— Blanca, I'm so sorry—

HH: I think he has seen enough. Take her away.

[crying]

[door closing]

[end transcription]

—⚬⚬⚬—

Blanca opened her eyes.

The sockets were swollen and sore. She kept her half-lidded gaze on the wall for hours, curling and uncurling her hands on the grimy concrete beneath her. Tiny pieces of loose gravel cut into the tips of her fingers.

Faintly, she tried to remember how to straighten her spine.

After a while, Blanca inhaled. It was a ghastly noise, a broken thing that rasped and shuddered. It was not a sound that should have come from a person, but it was all she could manage. Slowly, she twisted her head in the direction of the bars at the front of her cell. Her good hand reached out, but there was no one.

She inhaled deeply and let out a violent noise of grief. Blanca was alone. In her cell, she threw her head against the wall and screamed.

Göring, Heisenberg, and Himmler advanced at the head of a troop of high-ranking officers. When they reached the end of a corridor, they nodded to the pair of soldiers guarding a small room. Inside the room was a cot, a bucket, and a man with one hand.

The soldiers opened the door, and Göring looked down at the man sitting in front of him. Iain had his elbows on his knees, and his face was low. The jumpsuit he'd been given to wear hung loosely from his body.

"Up," Göring ordered.

Apathetically, Iain lifted his head.

When the soldiers advanced, he stood without a word and allowed himself to be herded down the hallway as he had many times before. However, instead of heading into the massive laboratory, he was taken up to a control room lined with glass walls. It overlooked a large, open chamber with a bell-shaped device in the center. Around it, men in protective gear moved around the platform, checking gauges and monitoring devices.

In front of Iain was a switchboard he had worked with many times before. This was what controlled *Die Glocke*—The Bell.

It was not a true bell; instead, the contraption resembled its namesake only in shape, having a large spinning center and a flat metal foundation meant to keep it under control. The Nazis had been further along than Iain had expected upon his arrival. They didn't yet have the innovation to complete the device, but their theories were sound. Now, though, they had everything they needed.

Iain had made sure of that. The device was ready.

Behind him, important men in uniform gathered in anticipation. Heisenberg could barely contain himself; this was the moment of actualization. The efforts of the war would not be in vain, for—if the success of this experiment proved true—it could always be redone.

The possibilities, Heisenberg told the waiting generals, were endless. The very essence of time was now in their hands. Iain listened to the rapid German without much understanding. His eyes remained obediently on the control panel.

Mengele and Göring waited near his elbow. Göring had personally brutalized Iain for each mistake while working on their project. Bruises in shades of deep purple and black dotted Iain's arms and legs.

The exchanges and introductions behind him were done. Heisenberg nudged him roughly.

"Begin," he grunted at Iain.

Iain's eyes flickered in the man's direction, and he gave a faint nod, reaching forward and moving his practiced hand over the keyboard switches and dials. He nodded to another scientist on the opposite end, who activated his own series of levers. Someone handed Iain a key, and he placed it in the slot, turning it so that the control panel lit up in a flurry of lights and colors.

In the center of the room below them, The Bell began to spin. A purple glow infused the air around it, and the crew on the ground stepped back. Iain continued to work, eyes on the pressure gauge, and he elevated the power when it was ready.

"Behold!" Heisenberg cried out in a manic fervor. "The greatest victory of Nazi Germany!"

Iain clicked a red dial, and then his fingers fluttered over one last switch. At the boast behind him, his apathy melted away and reformed as a steel blade. His eyes narrowed deeply, and he hit the final switch.

A split second lingered in stillness, and then pandemonium consumed them. The right wall exploded violently, shattering the glass and sending the men running for their lives. Iain jumped, rolling on his side and ducking under the control panel. He let out a cry of pain when the heat surged up next to him, scorching the air along his arm and ribs. The other men in the room were engulfed in a matter of seconds, swallowed up by explosions that triggered in rapid succession like a row of falling dominoes.

Inside the room below, an electric pulse erupted from The Bell, and the subsequent shockwave stopped every beating heart within reach.

The building fell in on itself. More blasts triggered, causing the ground to collapse into a series of deadly sinkholes. One after the other, explosions rocked the camp and tore away the brick foundations. The crematorium trembled, and the great tower that had carried so many human remains into the smoky sky tumbled over and shattered on the earth. Fences were jarred and broken. Guarding SS officers were forced to run for their lives.

The camp was on fire. The detonations would not stop.

And then, at last, one surge of energy came racing to the block where Blanca was kept, and the wall separating her from the outside world shattered in a fiery cloud of heat and rubble. Blanca jerked, still lying twisted on the floor, and then her head turned up and she saw the grim, gray sky. Wheezing, she rolled over.

Prisoners were fleeing, and the guards couldn't contain them. The roaring wind pushed the fire and spread it over the landscape, blistering everything it touched. Sirens wailed, but it made little difference. A surge of people rushed past the gates, fleeing onto the railroad tracks that had brought them there, and the SS guards could do nothing but scramble for their own lives.

Gunshots rang out; some of the prisoners had picked up fallen guns and were attacking. The camp was in full chaos.

Blanca dug her fingers into the rubble and pushed herself up to her hands and knees, swollen eyes looking around. The smoke engulfed her, and she hacked, blood pouring from her mouth as she fought to stand. Heaving, she stumbled across the broken remains of Block 11. A nurse who'd taken Blanca's things on the day of her arrival pushed past a pile of rock, and Blanca staggered in her direction, teeth bared. When she caught the woman, she fought her to the ground and slipped a scalpel from her uniform.

"*WHERE IS MY PICTURE?*" Blanca screamed in a rage, stabbing the woman in the neck with the scalpel until they were both coated in blood.

The woman died quickly, and Blanca dropped the scalpel, crawling further until she found the overturned filing cabinets. A brick wall plunged into the earth next to her, and Blanca shielded her face from the flames and smoke as a nearby building succumbed to a blast from below.

Fumbling through the filing cabinet, Blanca found a box with her name on it. When she reached inside, she found her knife, Otto's identification tags, and the picture of her family. With a heave, Blanca shoved all the items into the pocket of her jumpsuit and stumbled forward. She made it only three steps before collapsing into the dirt, too weak to move on.

Then she looked up and spotted Göring, face burnt nearly beyond recognition.

He was on his hands and knees, trying to escape the turmoil. Resolve flooded her veins, and Blanca dug her bleeding fingers deep in the soil. With a feral snarl, she dragged her torso across the earth like a wounded animal until Göring was within reach.

Göring looked up and saw her; recognition passed over his mutilated features, and his panic increased tenfold. He tried to squirm away, but Blanca reached out with a grimy, blood-stained hand and grasped the front of his once-pristine uniform.

He tried to speak, but she never gave him the chance.

With the last of her strength, Blanca unsheathed the blade of her knife and jammed it into Göring's neck. Göring gurgled, blood spilling from his lips. Then his head dropped back, and Blanca released her knife, letting it drop with him.

Heaving, she fell onto her back next to his corpse.

People raced all around her, and the destruction raged on. Black smoke floated overhead, and Blanca reached up, letting it twist around her fingers. She closed her eyes, willing and ready to accept that eternal nothingness. Peace filled her.

She was going to be with her family.

Despite her best efforts, Blanca awoke. The light around her was soft.

A foggy, distant part of her mind registered the relative dimness of the room for a while before her body reacted. Her eyelids fluttered and took their time opening fully. Perhaps as long as a half hour went by before she turned her head. A pillow rustled next to her cheek. Clean, cool sheets lay over her. Somewhere in the room, a fan turned in whispered rotation.

Something in Blanca's mind snapped, and she shot forward with a scream.

"Whoa—Whoa, wait!"

The voice was very close to her side, making Blanca shriek and scramble across the bed. It was then she realized she was hooked up to an IV drip. She yanked at the needles, making hysterical noises. "Get away from me!" she screamed, only vaguely registering the woman who approached her.

"Please, stop! No, don't—Oh, for goodness sake. Blanca, please!" the woman protested, holding up her hands, wrinkled expression creased with concern.

Blanca turned swiftly, her watery eyes wild. "Don't say my name!" she snarled, fighting her way to the corner of the bed where she tucked in against a wall and curled up tightly. Tears poured down her face. Her vision quivered and then cleared. The old woman in front of her stopped, eyebrows furrowed.

"Please, Blanca..." the unfamiliar woman said gently. Her words were in English, Blanca realized with a start, but still heavily accented. Blanca recoiled when she stepped closer.

The elderly woman stopped, dropping her hands and then politely clasping them in front of her.

"I am sorry. I did not mean to frighten you." She watched as Blanca's eyes flickered over her white lab coat. She glanced down at it, and after a pause, she pulled it off, revealing a normal a blue cotton shirt and trousers beneath it. She gave Blanca an apologetic smile as she dropped the coat to a normal dining chair that sat off to the side.

"I do not blame you for being apprehensive of doctors," she admitted sympathetically. "I do not like them much myself." The woman chuckled and then chose another chair, this one with wheels. She took a seat a few feet away from Blanca's bed.

"Forgive me. My name is Klara Chociemski. You may call me Klara."

Blanca managed to choke out a few words. "Is this— camp?"

Every syllable was a struggle. Something in her neck itched and ached. She scratched at it absently, eyes darting to the high ceiling.

"No," the stranger said softly. "This is not the camp."

Blanca eyed her warily, fingers still scratching. When she felt moisture, she pulled them away and saw blood. The woman in the chair looked concerned but said nothing. Blanca forced her hand to drop, but her body still twitched. Everything on her felt wrong.

"Where?" she croaked.

"You are in my home," Klara explained as she gestured to the room, and for the first time, Blanca's nervous eyes noticed the arched doorways and dark wooden floors. She appeared to be in a dining room, largely empty of the traditional furniture and instead decorated with various cabinets and medical instruments. "Which also happens to double as my place of work, given that the Nazis destroyed my clinic two years ago," Klara continued. Her wrinkled face scrunched up in displeasure. The expression made her look decades younger than before.

Blanca's brows furrowed, but she couldn't think of what to say, so she let her eyes leave the woman and scan the room again. She had been sleeping in a soft twin bed, covered in white sheets and a blue quilt. She reached up a trembling hand—something in her fingers didn't seem to be working quite right—and then she touched her hair. It had been shaved upon her arrival in the camp, but it had grown out some, perhaps an inch or two.

Her silent contemplation led the woman, Klara, to speak again. "If you will, please drink this." She extended a small bottle of amber liquid to her. The label had unfamiliar cartoons on it.

Blanca eyed the bottle, instantly suspicious. Klara made a face. "It's apple juice. It will make you feel better." When Blanca still refused to take it, she set the bottle on a table next to the bed and reclaimed her seat.

"You speak very good English," Blanca whispered.

"I was educated in the United States many years ago," Klara explained, pulling out another juice bottle and drinking from it herself. "All the way from secondary to medical school, in fact. I returned to my homeland to open my clinic." She grimaced. "Perhaps not my best decision."

"How did I get here?" Blanca asked finally, and Klara hesitated.

"Iain brought you here."

Blanca's head jerked up. "Iain—he's here?"

Klara's twinkling eyes grew sad. "I am afraid Iain was gravely ill upon your arrival. He passed away within a few days, and I buried him here on my property. I will be glad to show you where he rests when you are well enough."

Blanca deflated. "I didn't even see him die," she murmured.

Klara watched her. "It does seem cruel, doesn't it? For such a valiant and caring young man to see such an unfitting end?"

Blanca narrowed her eyes.

"I'm not mocking you," Klara promised softly. "On the contrary, I am quite sincere. The truth is, Iain deserved far better. He had earned recognition and comfort. I only knew him for a few days, but I am confident he was a very good person."

Blanca stared at her shaking hands, jaw tight.

"Unfortunately," Klara went on sadly, "for every name we remember, for every leader we memorialize, for every effigy we erect in someone's honor, there are hundreds of thousands more who die alone, without anyone to see or mourn them, without even the respect or honor of someone noticing that this breath is their last."

Klara sighed.

"War remembers statistics and forgets that each of those numbers represents a person's *entire life*, from the day they entered this world and changed a family forever, to their first steps, their first loves, their tragedies, and their triumphs, all of which culminate in that exact moment," she snapped her fingers, "of death."

Blanca lifted her head slowly, and the two women met gazes.

"That's an awful lot of responsibility for just a number, don't you think?"

"Yes," Blanca agreed.

Klara settled in her chair again, this time close to the bed as she leaned forward. "Always remember that behind every face is a story, and every expression, a journey. A life is not a static thing, meant to be counted only once. It is an ongoing, thriving, cumulative masterpiece of knowledge, tragedy, joy, and love. And the loss of any one life—no matter how seemingly insignificant—means there is one less beautiful tapestry of experience existing in our confusing, tumultuous world. One less perspective from which we might learn to be true humans, with all the empathy and magnificence that makes our species so terribly unique."

Klara put her hand over Blanca's. "Never forget these stories, Blanca. Never forsake them, and never silence them. Always be ready to sit at the feet of your fellow human beings and *listen*. If you do that, you will always be wiser tomorrow than you were today."

Together, they clasped hands and bowed their heads. After a while, Klara gently urged Blanca to a stand.

"Come. I have one more item to give you, and then I will show you to a bedroom where you can rest." She reached behind her and pulled out an envelope. It bore Blanca's name in shaky writing on the front. "Iain left you this."

Blanca reached out unsteadily and accepted the envelope without opening it. Klara squeezed her hand, and then she showed her to a bedroom with a wrought-iron bed covered in a yellow quilt. "I've left some water and treats for you. I have milk in the kitchen if you'd prefer it, and I'll be glad to cook for you whenever you are hungry."

Blanca looked up at Klara and nodded jerkily. "Thank you."

Klara bowed her head and disappeared. Blanca looked down at the envelope in her hands. After taking a shaky seat on the bed, she pulled it open. Inside was a letter and a key. The key tumbled into Blanca's palm, and she studied it before turning her eyes to the letter.

Dear Blanca,

I'm sorry if this letter is difficult to read. It's very hard to write.

I wish I could see you wake up, but I don't think that's going to happen. Klara has done everything she can for me, but I'm too sick. Please don't hold it against her. She is a good person, and you can trust her. I'm sorry you had to suffer for so long. I tried to make it happen as quickly as I could. Either way, you're free of them now.

The key enclosed with this letter is very important. It goes to the chamber where The Bell is kept. I made sure to destroy as much of the camp as possible while keeping that room intact. So long as no one has shown up since we left, everything in the chamber should be as I left it.

With this key, you can unlock that room and activate The Bell. The system is already set. If everything goes as planned, it will take you back to the day of the initial time jump. I'm not sure if you will arrive in your previous body or in something totally new. I don't even know if you'll remember everything or just forget. All I can tell you is, I truly believe the machine works.

Blanca, I want you to think very carefully about what lies ahead of you.

I know you want Mateo and Priya restored to you. I know you want to undo all of this, to try and regain some vestige of control. I have spent many, many years thinking about what I would do with the ability to turn back time. There were so many mistakes I wanted to correct, so many things I wanted to undo.

But the truth is, even though I know I'm dying, and I'll probably never talk to you again, I can't help but feel happy. I'm glad that in all this madness, I was able to know you. I had forgotten what it felt like to take comfort in other people. I'm tired of regret. I refuse to die wishing things had been different. Instead, I'll just say this: I am happy to have met you—and Mateo, Priya, and yes, even Otto, too.

And so, although I can't even begin to imagine what you've been through, I want to ask you to remember what I said to you before. Please, please remember that your life is important on its own. You are your own greatest achievement, your own peace, your own center, your own deity, and your own spirit. It is a wonderful thing to love as deeply as you do, Blanca, but doing the right thing for the wrong reasons is the worst sort of deception, because it is the lie we tell ourselves. Do not lie to yourself, Blanca. You exist in your own right.

Live your life. It is yours and yours alone.

Love always,
Iain

Blanca turned her trembling gaze to the key in her palm while her other hand pulled the letter close to her chest. She closed her eyes, imagining. Then she took a deep breath and nodded. Her fingers closed around the key.

The day dawned in shades of orange and pink. Spring had settled nicely over the area, blanketing the grass with dew in the mornings and stirring gusts of wind in the afternoons. Blanca let her hand drift out of the open window as the truck moved along at a leisurely pace. The air pushed and pulled at her fingers as it rushed by, and she let her hand float along the current like she'd done when she was a little girl.

The truck slowed and then stopped. Blanca looked sidelong at the driver's seat, where Klara was waiting. She gave Blanca an encouraging smile, and Blanca nodded before pushing open the door and getting out.

Now alone, Blanca trekked across the charred rubble that remained. The sign that had stood so dominantly over the camp's entrance—*ARBEIT MACHT FREI*—was in pieces on the ground. Blanca stepped over it, letting the warped metal shift under her feet.

The ground was littered with bodies. Some were burnt beyond recognition. Others were in a grisly state of decay, rotting and putrid. Blanca moved past them without lingering. Parts of the camp continued to smolder. No one had come to repair it. The Soviets were too close; there was no point.

At last, Blanca reached one of the few remaining buildings. It was a small gray brick structure with a single unimpressive door. Beyond the nondescript front, however, was a grand metal staircase leading to a laboratory, and this was the room that housed the device Iain had called *Die Glocke*—The Bell.

Blanca stood a few feet away, eyes locked on the door. In her hand, she held the key Iain had left her. A deep breath filled her chest.

Then, with a snap of her hands, she struck a match and dropped it to the ground in front of her. The fire caught instantly and gripped the line of fuel she'd placed there. In seconds, it had traveled to the building and climbed the walls to the roof.

Blanca turned away and let the box of matches fall from her fingers. The building trembled ominously. The walls began to crumble. Heat pulsed behind her retreating back.

As she reached the broken sign, the building erupted into flame and consumed the contents inside.

Klara was waiting at the truck. When Blanca reached her, they embraced, and Blanca closed her eyes with a deep inhale. After a few moments, Klara pulled back, touched her face with a smile, and then gestured.

"Shall we?"

Blanca nodded, and they climbed into the truck. Once they were ready, Klara drove them both away.

───── ⊗∞⊗ ─────

In the summer of 1945, Blanca and Klara moved to San Francisco, California, to escape Poland's forcible induction into the Soviet Union. There, Klara opened a new clinic, and Blanca enrolled at a university.

Thanks to the turmoil of the war—and a few forged documents—Blanca was able to graduate from medical school in record time. At her graduation ceremony, Klara cheered louder than anyone else there.

During those years, Blanca and Klara lived together in a beautiful townhouse overlooking the city, and a diverse community sprang up around them. Blanca often left the sanctuary of her home to travel to areas of need, giving medical attention to those who couldn't afford it and delighting young girls who'd never seen a doctor like her before. To see her, they said, was to know they could do it themselves. Blanca always took special time with those children, and when the nights were long and filled with terrors from days past, Blanca would think on their faces and fight to recover her strength.

"The sun will always rise," Klara would tell her, "so long as you are there to see it."

So Blanca would push ahead, even on her worst days, ready to see the light of day once more. As Klara promised, the dawn's early rays always appeared, softening the darkness bit by bit until the shadows were cast out and the wonderful chaos of life resumed.

But Blanca never forgot, not even for a moment. She dreamt of them all: Iain, Priya, Otto, and of course, Mateo. Each night, she gathered them together in her mind's eye and fell asleep to the cadence of their conversations. She would tell them everything: what she'd seen, who she'd talked to, how she'd managed. She would tell them not to worry about her and that she was eating just fine. She would explain how she was helping build a new children's home nearby and that it was the finest she'd ever seen. She would tell them—laughing, smiling in her half-sleep— how she'd tried to cook a meal for Klara and nearly burned the stove beyond repair.

And then after a while, Blanca would drift off to sleep, fully enveloped in their warmth and well wishes. Their memories acted as a protective barrier against that intrusive darkness that had followed her nearly all her life, and in that way, they stayed with her.

One day a few years after the war, as Blanca strolled down the sidewalk on a spectacular, sunny morning, she spotted a family crossing the street in front of her. As she watched, the parents and their two children hurried up a set of steps and into an elegant white building with ornate wooden doors. Blanca's eyes flickered over the building's tall steeple and stained-glass windows, and she realized she was looking at a chapel. The family was going to church.

Blanca paused, her expression growing thoughtful. Then she tilted her head up, lips lifted in a smile, and went on her way.

———✎———

Tell me, what is it you plan to do with
your one wild and precious life?
—Mary Oliver

———✎———

THE END

Epilogue:

Kraków, Poland
1944

In the distance, a lone truck approached.

When it stopped, the driver climbed out and moved over the forgotten ruins with determined purpose. There was no one there to greet him. The Germans had fled months before, and the Russians had given it a once-over before declaring it useless.

The camp had, after all, been inexplicably leveled.

During the winter months, a shimmery layer of translucent powder had disguised the worst of the devastation, giving the blackened corpses and charred walls a shining, pristine quality. Now, though, the frosty weather had peeled back to reveal a tarnished square of salted earth. There would be no rebuilding here, no growth. The ground was sour.

As the driver crossed the ruins, he paused occasionally to look through a weathered box or dirt-caked file. When this did not reveal anything interesting, he continued on past a toppled brick chimney and into the camp's neglected center.

After a few minutes of searching, he found a lone steel safe, which was turned on its side and busted on one end.

The door sat slightly ajar, and bits of stone and concrete bunched around it, as if garrisoning the contents against curious onlookers. Kneeling down, the driver pulled away the rubble and peered inside.

There he discovered a pile of burnt folders, an empty box, and a book. The cover of the book read, in faded letters:

American History: 1865—Present.

ACKNOWLEDGEMENTS

Publishing *EPOCH* is the culmination of a lifelong goal, and I could not have done it without the help of my incredible family, friends, and publishing team.

First, I'd like to thank my fantastic parents, Brian and Janet Livingston, who always enthusiastically nurtured my love of reading and writing. They provided me with every resource I needed to grow in skill and imagination, and I could not be more grateful for their support. This book is, without a doubt, their achievement as well. To my parents, I love you both.

I'd also like to thank my publishing team, including my wonderful agent Linda Langton at Langtons International Agency. She gave me a chance when no one else would, and I will never be able to fully express my gratitude. Her patient guidance saw me this far, and I am excited to see what the future holds. Thank you, Linda, Lindsay, and Central Park South Publishing for seeing me all the way through to my dream.

Last, this book would not have been possible without the raw, honest, and often emotional feedback I received from real-life military veterans, including Rhett Roberts, SGT US Army, and James E. Nealey, SPC US Army. I cannot thank them both enough for sharing their thoughts and experiences, particularly in relation to combat. I sincerely hope this book does justice to their stories.

I'd also like to include a special note to Isaiah Beltman, a friend and confidant who constantly helped me evaluate ideas, establish plot points, and search for publishers. He never gave up on me or my book, and I will forever be grateful.